A LIFETIME'S JOURNEY
OLD MAN OF THE TYNE

Written and illustrated by
Barry John Cram

Regards Barry.

Xmas 2011

This edition printed in 2011

© Copyright 2011 Barry John Cram

ISBN: 978-1-907188-64-0

Author: Barry John Cram

Contents

Introduction

This story contains the adventures of a wealthy Geordie shipowner and his family, who, unbeknown to them, are about to set off from Newcastle Upon Tyne, on an extraordinary journey of a lifetime - especially the shipowner's grandson, Geordie Rigger, a very astute lad, who has the greatest journey of all.

Mysterious and unexplainable events occur, which bring out the most in the characters. A deep camaraderie is shown by all on board – a spirit of familiarity and trust found only between friends in such close proximity.

What makes a Geordie? For anyone who would like to find out, and get familiar with the well-known Geordie friendship, compassion and psyche, then this is the book for you; a warm and passionate story, filled with happiness, sadness, humour, love and romance – a great read for all ages.

CHAPTER I

THE DISCOVERY

This story begins in the wide Pacific Ocean, on board a luxury American cruise ship, the S.S. Albatross, on its return voyage from Australia.

"Look, look!" the English passenger cried to his American friend.

"Gosh, darn it! What is it now?" The American replied, slowly fanning his white Stetson across his fat, round face.

"Put your eye to the lens. Look man, look!" he ordered, as his monocle dropped from his thinly set face. "Tell me, what do you see?"

"Nothin', darn it! Nothin' but the wide blue sea!"

"To the left a bit old boy," said the Englishman, as he manoeuvred the ship's telescope.

"I can't see a darn... wait a minute... oh boy... it... it can't be!"

"Exactly, old chap;" the Englishman replaced his monocle with an air of majesty; "an inhabited island, dear boy; I distinctly saw a person on the beach."

"But that's not possible; the ship's brochure specifically states that there ain't no inhabited islands on this part of the route!"

"Bosun!" cried the Englishman.

"G'day Sir, what's your bid?"

"Be so kind bosun, as to look through this telescope and tell us if you see anything of interest."

The Bosun scanned the calm, wide ocean, and then breathed out a sigh of disbelief.

"Fair dinkum I do Sir; I'd better report this to the cap'n."

Holding his hat in one hand, while scratching his bemused head with the other, off he rushed towards the bridge - the last place he had seen the captain.

The captain put his binoculars to his eyes. "Impossible, Bosun! I've bin in this game long enough to know that there ain't no inhabited islands in these parts." He searched the horizon through the bridge window. "I'm sorry, Bosun, the heat's probably playing tricks on you; there ain't nothing out there."

"But Cap'n, I'm not the only one; those two cobbers down there saw just as much as I did; we definitely saw something out there... out there... on the beach."

"Don't waste my time, Bosun." The captain thumped his binoculars down onto the table.

The Bosun gently grabbed the elbow of the captain's jacket. "But Cap'n Wiseman, we can't sail on if there's a chance of someone being stranded out there."

The captain abruptly pushed away the pleading arm.

"Look, I've told you once too many, I'm the captain here... don't ever forget it! It was probably a monkey or a goat. Now get out of here!" He yelled, punching his desk and busting a knuckle.

"Please Cap'n, have one more look!"

"You're dismissed Bosun; one more word and I'll have you for insubordination!" The captain took a large, clean handkerchief from his pocket and began to wrap it around his bloodied hand.

Just as the Bosun was about to leave the bridge, he noticed an inquisitive crowd had gathered about the telescope, chattering much louder than the holidaymakers elsewhere.

"Look Cap'n'"

"What have you stirred up here, Bosun?"

"I'm sorry, Sir, but... "

"I'll deal with you later."

The captain left the bridge and pushed his way through the excited huddle to the telescope.

"It's a person, Captain!" a few excited passengers chorused.

"I suppose you started all this?" The captain gazed into the Englishman's naked eyes.

"That is right," he replied, as he regained his fallen monocle.

"I saw it next," the American crowed, looking around for contenders to the fact, while mopping his red damp face with a large white handkerchief.

The captain wasted no time.

"Make room, make room; don't crowd me." He surveyed the panorama. The telescope turned slowly to the left, and then veered abruptly to the right, stopping dead still. "My Goodness... the son-of-a-gun was right!"

He looked up at the bridge. The bosun was standing there, holding the rail - looking back with vexed anticipation. "Bosun, get me HQ on the phone, and call the medical officer to the bridge, immediately!"

"Aye-aye, Cap'n!"

Fifteen minutes later, back on the bridge, the captain put down the receiver with his freshly bandaged hand.

"Lower the anchor! Man that lifeboat! We're going ashore!"

The inflatable lifeboat purred softly and smoothly through the calm summer water, towards the approaching beautiful, green island. The snow-capped mountain and the smell of lush vegetation awaited invitingly, like an oasis in the wilderness. The captain tapped the chart on his knee with his index finger. "That there island was only GPS recorded and charted two years ago."

The reinstated Bosun looked towards the island, and nodded. "Yep, Cap'n, I imagine it would've been quite difficult to locate."

"Landing now Sir!" interrupted the helmsman.

The lifeboat met the warm, golden sand and became smoothly beached. Standing on the sand, the captain and his crew of four looked around in childlike wonder. A sudden change came upon them - a feeling of euphoria being remarked by all.

"Is this Eden?" said the ship's elder security officer, whilst replacing his handgun.

"Boy, oh boy, I ain't never seen so many wonderful trees and coloured plants in one place in all my life!" said his cheerful younger partner, closing his eyes, tilting back his head and inflating his powerful chest with a freshness he wasn't used to. "This must be heaven."

It was indeed a most wonderfully, picturesque scene; but there was another, more sagaciously beneficial, yet to unfold.

"I am overcome with a deep feeling of love... God is in this place; I feel his holy presence as never before," said the captain, raising his eyes to the heavens. Everyone instinctively knelt in earnest accordance, while crossing themselves.

"Amen," whispered the third officer.

"Amen," followed the rest.

Two minutes later, they were walking through a myriad of brightly coloured festoons, while the cushioned carpet of neatly cut grass below caressed their welcomed feet.

Being slightly ahead of the others, the bosun stopped and pointed. "Through here, Cap'n... there's an opening." They all passed through the entrance of an arched hedgerow, which was easily wide enough to take three men abreast and twice that height.

"What kind of god-ridden place is this?" said the younger security officer, looking about him; realising his blasphemy, he lowered his eyes and squirmed inwardly, as the others looked on remonstratively.

"Captain Wiseman, Sir!" the captain's executive officer sounded over the radio.

The captain took his radio from his belt. "Yes, Chief Officer?"

"Thank Goodness you're there, Captain; the passengers are getting agitated and blasé, Sir; and there's a madman with a monocle, gathered a band of passengers together; and they're talking about launching the lifeboats. He's got them all frantic, Captain... telling them that you have been captured by cannibals, and that if they don't attempt to save you, the ship could be stranded in the Pacific Ocean, forever!"

"Put me over the ship's PA system, Officer."

"Right away, Sir!"

May I have your attention? This is your captain speaking. The crew and I are safe and well, and have become occupied with new developments on the island - we'll rejoin you onboard later. Until then, continue enjoying your cruise as before. Tête-à-tête, Officer."

"Thank you Sir, that seems to have done the trick; the monocled man has motioned everyone away from the lifeboats; but what's happening out there, Sir?"

"We've come to a small bamboo built village: two impressive bungalows in the centre, and five bungalows - not so large - at the rear, shaded beneath a copse of trees; species old and new, and coloured flowers of every description all about. The last time I saw anything like this was in an English rose garden in Derbyshire, England - but that's an understatement.

THE DISCOVERY

I'm most impressed by the hedgerow we are now standing beneath - it must be all of eighteen feet high, fences in the whole village and has at the very least a diameter of 240 feet. A pristine lawn covers the whole centre. It's a magical place, Officer; we'll look for life here, and be back before dark - over and out!"

"Over and out, Cap'n!"

The captain thought he had seen it all, but he wasn't ready for what was about to be revealed to him.

The bosun stopped in his tracks. "Strewth! Who's that?"

A beautiful, benevolent looking old white man, with immaculate shoulder-length white hair, and a clean and wise, but sunburnt face, casually walked out from a bungalow and onto the lawn directly ahead. None of the crew moved. The old man seemed oblivious to their presence. He looked like he had stepped out of a museum; his tattered clothes were from a different era.

"Cap'n, I think we've found the ancient mariner, Methuselah or even Jesus Christ himself," whispered the bosun, with a bemused expression. The old man started doing some kind of rhythmical yoga.

The captain spoke quietly, "He looks a very fit man; see how he can easily hold those uncomfortable looking positions, and then, releasing his hold, he does it again, adding a few seconds more. I've seen this type of ancient yoga before, in the Orient, where they say breath is the essence of life. It's used by the Indian and Tibetan philosophers. Now what is it called?"

"Is it Tantric Yoga, Cap'n?"

"No, Bosun; never mind."

After watching for almost twenty minutes, the captain beckoned the crew and approached the old man. The old man stood calmly and looked at the crew that now surrounded him. His charisma was magnetic; his aura was illuminating.

The younger security officer's eyes widened. "Cap'n, his eyes are so... so... "

The captain nodded. "I know." He then spoke to the old man. "I am Captain Wiseman, of the SS *Albatross*; I've brought a search-party with me, to see if you need assistance."

"He doesn't look as if he needs assistance to me, Cap'n; he looks the most relaxed and contented man on earth," said the bosun.

The old man stepped directly in front of the captain, smiled, then placed his hand gently on the captain's bandaged knuckle and then removed it just as softly.

"The pain's gone! I don't believe it! It's gone!" The captain almost tore off his bandage and then stared at his hand in utter disbelief. His skin was totally unscarred or broken. "Look Bosun! I'm healed! Now I remember what it was, 'Hatha yoga'; you're a healer, old man!"

The captain lent forward and hugged the old man. "Thank you, old man!" He turned to his crew. "Down on your knees;" he did likewise; "a miracle has happened here."

The old man placed his hands on the heads of every man in turn, absolving them from all harmful guilt, and healing them of all physical defects.

"Wrongful thoughts create illnesses... No one is pressured into thinking wrongful thoughts," said the captain.

"Amen," said the crew, as they stood up.

"Hey man, my knee don't hurt no more." The elder security officer straightened his leg. "I feel great!"

"My backache's stopped nagging me." The younger security officer put his hands on his waist and twisted his torso - smiling - his elbows swinging akimbo. "My, I wish I could bottle this stuff and take it home with me - I'd be rich!"

"How about you, bosun, do you feel fine?" "Yes Cap'n, it's unbelievable... it still won't sink in! You see, I had terminal cancer, and I just know that it's gone. The awful unbearable pain has ceased - I kept it secret, because I was afraid I'd lose everything."

THE DISCOVERY

The captain put his hand on the bosun's shoulder, gave him a slow intentional two-eyed blink and then nodded. "An ailment gone is easily forgotten."

"Strewth, Cap'n, I've kept myself fit all these years, and I've never been crook in my life, except for a little toothache that has just now cleared up - thanks to the old cobber. Makes me wish I had more wrong with me - I feel downright cheated. To tell you straight, Cap'n, I don't know how, but I feel as happy as a possum in a gum tree."

The captain and crew basked in the ecstasy of their favourable condition, swapping tales of other newly vanished ailments.

Later, the captain realised he had a job to do.

"Old man, you have completely restored our integrity and physical well-being; our debt to you is immeasurable. We would like to know your reason for being here; where did you come from?"

"I don't think he understands English, Cap'n," said the bosun.

The crew asked the same questions, in as many languages as they knew between them.

"That's nine languages, Cap'n; he must know one of them. Either that or he's deaf or mute... or both!"

"Give me the radio, bosun." The bosun handed it to the captain.

As the old man turned away, the captain switched on the radio. A high-pitched note squealed into the airwaves. The old man turned sharply and looked directly at the captain. The captain kept the radio hidden behind his back and switched it off. "Well, he's not deaf, Bosun." He handed back the radio. "Where are you from old man?" The captain pointed out to sea. The sign language seemed to impress the old man. He too pointed out to sea, then led the captain and crew to one of the small bamboo bungalows in the centre of the village, and took them inside.

The old security officer looked around. "You're mime sure has stirred him now, Cap'n."

The sparsely furnished room they entered had four windows. There were a number of portraits hanging on the walls. There was a coconut mat on the centre of the floor; a wicker chair; a fine armchair, covered with clean white antimacassars; a wooden table with an old bible upon it and a beautifully carved old sea chest, to which the old man motioned the captain. The old man lifted open the defiant lid - the hinges cracked apart like arthritic knees. He leant the open lid against the adjacent wall.

The captain's eyes were everywhere. "This room's incredible; it seems as if we've stepped into a time warp."

The younger security officer walked outside alone to survey the back of the building, and was almost immediately heard to scream out in terror. He soon ran into the room waving his gun at the old man.

"Murder! Murder! He's gonna kill us, Cap'n!"

"Put that away, Officer, before 'you' kill someone."

"It's him who's gonna kill someone, Cap'n... us!"

"Don't be crazy, Officer, this quiet old man wouldn't harm anyone; pull yourself together."

"Come and see for yourself, if you don't believe me." The security officer beckoned, and they all followed quickly to the back of the building. The sight that met them was poignant indeed.

"There must be at least fifty graves here." The captain sighed. Each one had an old wooden cross. If there had been any names on them at any time, they were well gone now.

"What does it all mean, Cap'n?" said the younger security officer - his eye's darting from grave to grave.

"We'll get to the bottom of this, I assure you. There's probably a simple explanation. Are you okay?"

"Yes, Cap'n, I suppose you're right - I'm probably over exaggerating."

Back inside the bungalow, the captain recaptured the feeling of peace, which had ever so slightly disappeared. He knew mime was the only way to communicate with the old man, so he pointed from the window to the graves outside.

"Who are they?"

The old man turned his attention back to the open chest, pulled out a very heavy leather-bound book, and gave it to the captain.

"What's this?" The captain made himself comfortable in a wicker chair by the light of the window. "A ship's log-book dated 1806." He gently brushed some dust from the worn cover with his hand and peered more closely at the faded writing beneath. "The property of Captain John Rigger - this is getting more interesting by the minute. Everything seems old here; it's almost like seeing two hundred years into the past. It would be interesting to see two hundred years into the future." He grimaced slightly as he looked at the old, old man, whom he guessed had very little time left on earth. He composed himself and gently opened the book cover, exposing aged yellow pages - then looked at all present. They looked back intently. "I suppose, gentlemen, the only way for us to get to the bottom of this, is for me to read out this log-book. So here goes..."

CHAPTER II

THE JOURNEY BEGINS

In the year of our lord,
the third day of August, one thousand, eight hundred and thirty-two -
whosoever reads this book, pray for our souls.

My name is Captain John Rigger, Master Mariner, and once proud owner of the fated cargo-ship *The Turtle*, which sank in the year one thousand eight hundred and eight, leaving us stranded here on this mysterious island. I feel I must write an account of the events leading up to that fateful day - four and twenty years past - before I meet with Davy Jones' locker.

It all began on a scorching July day, in the year one thousand, eight hundred and six, aboard my ship, *The Turtle*, whilst berthed on the River Tyne, at the quiet fishing village of Dents Hole, Newcastle, Northumberland, England...

"Come on, man, James, get them animals on board," I said to my son.

"May I bring my tortoise on board, Granddad?" said Geordie, as he squashed passed the penned animals on the gangplank, with his tortoise held firmly in one arm and his schoolbooks tied in a bundle under the other. Matter of fact, I'm really Geordie's great uncle, or grand uncle.

"Yes, of course you can - as long as it doesn't eat too many rats." I laughed.

Geordie smiled at me in his sweet innocent way and then went off to find his bunk.

The ship was buzzing with activity as we readied ourselves for the long journey ahead. The crew of 44 are a merry lot; it's like one big happy family, for excluding the botanist and the doctor, we are all related in some way. Seven of them are my sons - big, strong lads they are.

"Here's my mam," shouted my son Dave, from up in the riggings.

An open-topped, two-wheeled gig, drawn by a single black horse, was cantering towards us, carrying my wife; or, as I sometimes call her - 'Wor Lass'.

"Hello John!" she shouted up from under her parasol as the gig pulled up at the jetty. "I was afraid I might have missed you." She came aboard, and stood beside me. "John," she said, pressing her hand in mine and breathing out a sigh, "I'd rather come along to keep a check on the lads - especially Geordie - than stay in that big lonely house at Ovingham."

"Why-aye, man, pet!" I gave her a big hug. "There's room aboard for a little lassie like you."

As I released her, Sophia let her hands slide softly down my arms until her hands were back in mine.

"Thank you John, you're such a loving and understanding husband. Am I at liberty to dismiss the servants, and lock up the estate?"

When I gave my consent, Sophia called down the orders to Edward in the gig, and off he went. I first met Sophia - a schoolteacher - at a garden-party at my elder brother's home in Heather village, Leicestershire. Her father - the local clergyman - introduced us. I fell in love with her instantly, and she hasn't changed a bit in 40 odd years. My son James walked towards me.

"That's all the animals on board, Dad."

"Your mother and I are going to my cabin, son; tell me when Henry and the doctor get here."

Henry - a good friend of the family - is a naturalised Englishman, from Denmark. My son Richard invited him on the journey, privately, to paint, and to collect botanical specimens of interest. The doctor - an alcoholic and a Scot - has a sad, but handsome looking face. He wears a black top hat, a long black cloak, and has a wooden leg that has an untimely habit of falling off.

Down in my cabin - which is commodious, with a raised roof surrounded with window lights - Sophia sat on my bunk as I sat on a wicker chair beside her.

"Is the cargo on board, John?"

"Yes, pet, the keelmen loaded the coal this morning at Felling Shore."

"That's good; where is it going to, dear?"

"The coal's for London. Then from there, we'll be taking household furniture to Australia. And on the return journey, we're expecting to bring back spices, sugar, opium and ivory."

"It sounds so exciting; I hope Geordie enjoys it, especially as it's his maiden voyage. And I do hope the lads won't tease him with stories of devils and sea monsters."

"It's alright, pet, I had a stiff word with them this morning, before Geordie came aboard. Anyway, I don't think there'll be much swearing with you about, dear."

We heard quick footsteps coming towards us, and turned as Geordie popped his head into the open cabin doorway, still holding his tortoise.

"Eeh! Hello Grandma! Do you like my tortoise?"

"It's well nice, Geordie."

"Granddad, my Uncle Dave said to tell you that the two men are coming."

"Alright, sonna; you sit here and talk with your grandma."

As I left the cabin, I heard Geordie telling his grandma, how proud he was to be going on a sea journey, now that he was 'all grown up' at last. A minute later, I was on the deck, making my two guests welcome.

"Welcome aboard, Henry, mate." I shook the botanist cordially by the hand and then waved two of my sons over. "Thomas! James! Bring their luggage aboard!" My heart sank as I turned to greet the doctor. He was three sheets to the wind, hobbling drunkenly up the gangplank with his cane beneath his arm. I knew he drank, but I had only just spoken to him an hour or so earlier, and he was sober then. He was all I could find at such short notice.

"Hullooo again, Captain Rigger, shh... Sir; Doctor... ugh... Doctor, Pess... Peas... Pearse; at your service!"

He slurred as he stood up to his great height, with his chest pushed proudly forward, endeavouring to preserve his self-respect. All of a sudden, his big, lumbering, wooden left leg came from beneath him, crashing obliquely in front of his right leg.

"Ha-ha! Look!" shouted my son Peter, to anyone who hadn't noticed - which wasn't many. "His drunken leg's fell off!" He screamed, as he curled up on the deck with tears streaming down his face. The doctor started to hop about drunkenly, with the most bewildered expression upon his face that I have ever seen. "He's going, Dad, he's gonna fall," continued Peter, his face in convulsions; his eyes barely slits now, and his black ferret-like teeth forced out between an ever expanding grin.

"Don't mock the afflicted, Peter," said I, suppressing a laugh.

"Where's my log... leg?" said the doctor, as he hopped and tripped forward over his very large wooden stump. He gave out an awful low-pitched moan, and then landed on the deck like an oversized string puppet. His top hat flew onto a bewildered chicken, and his medical bag burst open, scattering soiled, surgical instruments tinkling in all directions. His cane was - unbelievably - still under his arm!

"Oh no, I think it's bro... broken." There was a pause, as the doctor's hand felt its way beneath his cloak towards his chest; he moaned loudly.

My son Richard turned to me. "I think he's broken a rib, Dad."

The doctor pulled his hand from under his coat. It was stained blood red. "Och, no, it's bust."

We all gasped at the courage of the man; there was blood all over his chest. "I wonder if the other one's broken," he said.

Richard put his limp hand onto his neck, and gasped. "How could he bust so many ribs?"

Thomas looked on pessimistically, "He's gonna die - I know he is."

The doctor smiled to himself, "Oh, thank goodness that side's not broken too."

James grimaced, "This man's not human, Dad; he's not bothered about dying."

"I know son - I'd call for a doctor, but he's the only one at close call!"

Peter stood, posing theatrically, pointing with outstretched finger on outstretched arm. "Physician, heal thyself!"

"That's enough sarcasm, Peter - can't you see the man's on his last legs," said I. Well, that only set Peter off laughing again, didn't it?

Somehow, the doctor sat jolt upright, oozing more blood from his chest. "It's broken, but I don't care - I'm going to take it out anyway."

My son Richard had had enough, "O', by the torment of Harpies or Tantalus... he's mad. I'm not going to watch!"

The doctor reached into his bloodstained clothes, as we watched in anticipation. Then, my son Richard - ten years a sailor - fainted limply with shock. The doctor, still drunkenly unaware of his audience, knitted his brows and felt about beneath his coat.

"Ah, now I have you - it's no so bad after all," said he; "only the top has gone."

There was absolute silence from the crew, as the doctor withdrew his arm from his clothing, pulling out an intact bottle of thick red rum, which he placed to his waiting lips - the cork being absent. There was a pause as the crew and I swapped bemused glances. Then, in unity, there was one huge outburst of rip-roaring laughter.

"Put him to bed, lads." I stood wiping tears from my face. Two of the lads took the contented and smiling doctor and his bottles of rum to his bed.

A minute later, Sophia and Geordie came up on deck to see what all the commotion was. They laughed as they looked around the deck. Some men were lying about, curled up with laughter. The mirth was infectious. A two-legged top hat bumped into my legs and fell over, exposing a relieved chicken.

My wife put her hand to her mouth and laughed. "What's happened, John?"

"I'll tell you later, pet." I held my aching stomach. "You couldn't have

18

brought Geordie up on deck at a more appropriate moment."

My son Peter shouted down to the doctor through the hatch. "Ha-ha! Someone's going to have a head like a bucket of wet sand when they wake up - and it's not gonna be me!"

I once again began to regain my sense of authority. "Right-o, lads, the show's over, back about your business." They went back merrily to their particular duties.

My son Dave was up the riggings as quick as a monkey. I haven't seen anybody as fast. He climbed down just as quickly, minutes later.

"That's the last of the ropes checked, Dad." He reassured me.

"Right, son, tell the lads we'll be leaving in ten minutes."

"Aye-aye, Cap'n." he replied, with a cheeky grin - cocking his head to one side.

My son William, the first mate, and eldest son on board, called over. "Dad, here's our John's ship coming in."

John, my eldest son, lives with his lovely wife and bairns, at the small fishing village of Dents Hole, on the river Tyne, Newcastle - most of which he owns - willed to him by his paternal grandfather. Dents Hole is a natural deep body of water, even at low tide.

Like myself, John is a master mariner. He divides his time between farming his land at Three-mile-bridge, Gosforth, and his fisheries here on the Tyne. He berthed *The Sophia* to the fore of us. I went ashore to meet him; he was the first down the gangway.

"Hello, Fatha', what's that on your face... have you lost your razor or something?" He hugged me.

"That's me maritime look, son." I stood posing. "It gives me an air of authority, along with my bandy legs, don't you think? Anyway, it saves me toilette time. Did you catch much?"

"Yeah, we made quite a catch. I thought we would've missed you."

"You nearly did, son - we're about to weigh anchor."

John gasped, staggered a little and then steadied himself.

"What's wrong son?"

"Nothing Fatha', you know I always feel dizzy when I hit terra firma. How's Geordie? Is he still as keen as mustard?"

"Why-aye, man! He's telling everybody on board what a great adventure he's going to have... even your mother."

"My Ma'? What's she doing on board? She's leaving it a bit late, isn't she?"

"Oh, I forgot to tell you, son, she's coming with us."

"Come on, Fatha', you're leading me up the Northwest Passage... aren't you?"

"No, son; honestly. You go and speak with her while I go and say hello to the lads."

John left me as I boarded *The Sophia*. "Hello lads; did you have a good bit fishing?"

Joe stood proudly in front of me and held his arms out as if he was holding a huge invisible barrel,

"The nets were fit to burst. They were so heavy that we thought we had caught a school of whales!"

"Ha-ha! That's what I like to hear, lads. Well, it's nice to see you all again, but we're casting off now."

"Uncle John, can we see the lads before you leave?" said Fenwick, son of my younger brother Martin.

"Come on then - be brief." They all followed me en route to *The Turtle*, as a heavy breeze flapped the topsail - though strangely enough, not a breath of air rippled the surface of the river.

John was standing on the main deck, laughing, surrounded by the lads - all listening intently to Peter.

"You should have seen the doctor's face, John," said Peter, hopping back and forth on one leg. The lads laughed as Peter yelled out comically and fell flat on the deck.

I headed towards the steps leading below deck. "Right lads, you have until I come back on deck to say your farewells. John, what did your mother say?"

"Oh, I'm sorry Fatha', I was carried away; where is she?"

"Come on, she's probably down in my cabin."

John followed me into the cabin room. "Mother, you can't be serious." John swallowed hard, and shook his head. "Do you realise what you're getting yourself into?"

"Uncle John, have you seen my tortoise?"

"Oh-aye, Geordie, it's smashing," said John, dryly.

I took Geordie by the hand, "Come on, Geordie, we'll find some lettuce leaves for your tortoise."

Geordie is the grandchild of my dear departed sister Mary. My wife and I became his guardians when his dear widowed mother died of consumption. He's a very innocent, genteel and intelligent ten-year-old boy. "This is the galley, Geordie; we'll find some lettuce in here for... what's its name, Geordie?"

THE JOURNEY BEGINS

"My Uncle Andrew told me it's a giant 'Charles Island' tortoise, from the East Pacific. He told me it's a boy, and that they live for over three hundred years - so I've named him 'Charles Methuselah'. I read in the bible that Methuselah lived for nine hundred and sixty-nine years, Granddad. I hope I live that long."

"You're a bright lad, Geordie, and you make your grandmother and I proud; here's some lettuce for Charlie."

"Thank you, Granddad; me and Charles Methuselah are going to be friends forever and ever."

"Amen. Right-o, sonna, you stay here and feed Charlie, while I go a message. I'll not be too long."

"Okay, Granddad; will I give Charlie 'all' these leaves?"

"Yeah, you want him to grow up big and strong, don't you?"

"Yeah, just like me, Granddad." Geordie stood straight, and proudly pushed out his chest.

"Yeah, just like you, Geordie." I left the galley with a smile.

"Well, if that's how you feel, Mother, after all I've said to dissuade you..." John spoke softly, surrendering the argument, just as I entered the cabin, "... then you're a very determined woman indeed, and I just wish you the safest weather possible," he added, as he hugged her tenderly.

"Hey son, less of the woman if you don't mind," I joked, trying to relax the atmosphere even further. "Your mother's a lady."

"Hey, Mother, I've always treated you like a lady; haven't I?" John tried to flatter his mother, smiling cheekily down at her.

"You won't get round me that easily, John," she replied, sportingly. "I have no favourites amongst my sons or daughters; you all treat me like a lady."

"Oh, is that right?" John narrowed his gaze as he folded his arms. "What about our Peter, then?" The humour dropped from Sophia's face.

"That's different, John - you know it is."

"How's that then, Mother?"

"He's never been the same since he fell off the dock and nearly drowned twenty five years ago."

"There's no need to treat him differently, Mother, just 'cause he's lost his anchor. I know he's daft 'n' that, but I still love him all the same. I wouldn't let anyone harm him, 'cause I'd be the first one to deck them."

"That's enough, John; you can see your mother's getting upset."

"I'm sorry Mother, I didn't mean to hurt your feelings;" John, unfolded his arms and quickly wrapped them around his mother; "I love you more than

21

life itself."

I gave out a small sigh of relief. "Come on then, we had better be moving; I'll go and fetch Geordie."

Later, up on deck, the air was enthusiastically filled with warm, emotional, farewell banter. I felt ill at ease to end this parting pleasantry. John must have sensed my awkwardness.

"Right-o, lads," he shouted, "it's time to shove off; let's get the fish ashore!"

I grasped John's forearm and looked him in the eyes. "Thanks son; you'll take care of everything while we're away, and look after the family - won't you?"

"Aye, Fatha' - you look after Geordie and my mother. I must say, Fatha', the lads were quite embarrassed and unnerved by Mother's presence on board. I told them that a female aboard might sink their hearts, but not necessarily the ship."

"Your mother couldn't bring anyone bad luck, son. They're only vexed, 'cause they're constrained by a ladies presence."

"Aye, you're probably right, Fatha'." John led his crew down the gangway, towards the shore.

The gangway in, and the ropes free, I spat on a coin and threw it overboard - an old sailor custom. Now we could push off. Friends and family on shore waved and bade us farewell, as the river began to swirl, and a slight breeze moved us gently from the dock and allowed us to drift slowly down stream.

When the dock finally disappeared out of sight, Geordie looked up at me.

"Will we be at sea soon, Granddad?"

"You can tell Charles Methuselah it won't be long now, Geordie."

Sophia stroked Geordie's hair; "Do you want to come below, Geordie? It's a bit hot for Charlie, out here."

"Oh, yes, Grandma, I wouldn't want Charlie to get overheated."

"Okay then, we'll find him some water and cool lettuce leaves."

The ship headed carefully round the formidable weather-beaten crag of Bill Point, towards Felling Shore. A few miles down river, the ships on both sides of the river lay together so snugly - bow to stern and some three abreast - that I ordered all available hands to seize their pikes and guide us through with stabbing caution. We made it through the congestion without collision. As we neared the Haining Wood, my son Robert and his sailmaker mates rowed a large boat out to us.

My son Peter looked overboard at the oncoming boat and waved his arms about in a jocular manner, "Hey, move that rickety old haystack out of the way!"

"Ha-ha! Look who's talking;" retorted Robert; "it's a scarecrow!" Peter did indeed look like a scarecrow; his dry, straw-like hair was bleached yellow by the sun; this, he now covered with a wide brimmed hat. His trouser legs and uncuffed shirtsleeves were half-mast. He completed the picture, by wearing a string belt.

"I'm a scarecrow! I'm a scarecrow!" Peter danced wildly around the deck, seeking attention, which he graciously received.

Robert shimmied up the Jacob's ladder that had been rolled down to him, lifted his legs over the starboard side and deftly climbed down onto the deck.

"Hello, Dad, I've brought you a few more sails than you might have expected."

I looked over the starboard side with pride, into the over-brimming boat below. "A few more? It looks like you've brought enough canvas to equip an armada!"

"Well, it is an exceptionally long voyage, Dad. You can't take too many sails - no canvas, no journey."

"You're right son, thanks very much. It must have taken an age to make them up; there must be a full replacement for the ship, at least."

"Never mind, Dad, you're worth it."

Sophia and Geordie came on deck, both happily surprised to see Robert. Geordie smiled up at him with wide eyes.

"Hello Uncle Robert, I'm going to Australia, now, you know."

"Yeah, I know, Geordie; it's wonderful, isn't it? By the way, where's Charlie? Are you looking after him?"

Geordie pointed below deck. "Yeah, Uncle Robert, he's in the galley, eating lettuce."

"Oh, that's good." Robert hugged Geordie, and then walked towards his mother, embracing his arms fully around her.

"Are you finally taking that well deserved holiday, Mother?"

"Yes, son, your father tells me the air is invigorating at sea."

"Yes, Mam, my dad should know, being that he's a fresh-air enthusiast."

I nodded to Dave and James, a signal to bring the sails aboard.

The gang set about their task as Robert made his fleeting salutations. The heavy, abundant canvases were winched aboard with deft momentum.

It wasn't long before Robert was afar in his boat, waving goodbye to us as we stood on the forecastle.

"I must tell you, Geordie, sonna, once at sea, there are many things you must not do that are considered very unlucky. Never point at another ship or anything you need. And avoid mentioning how many vessels are sailing together. Many words are forbidden on board, because they are deemed unlucky, so we use substitutes, like the white stuff - not the stuff you put in tea. The handled thing you cut with, or, the thing you have scrambled for breakfast.

THE JOURNEY BEGINS

Geordie spoke cautiously, "Is my 'pet' that eats 'lettuce', unlucky, Granddad?"

"No, Geordie," I laughed reassuringly. "You're allowed to mention tortoise. However, there are certain animals that are never mentioned or allowed on board, like the sly one with the bushy tail, or the one that meows. But the worst is the 'pink curly tailed snorter'; it is believed they can sense the wind; and if they can, they will - leading to our stormy end."

"Eeh, Granddad, how will I remember all those names?"

"By the time you come back home, bonny lad, you'll know a lot more than just the names; you're so omnivorous.

As we rounded the heavily wooded Hill of Hebburn, a beautiful, timeless sight bestowed us: Hebburn fishing village - an ancient Hamlet nestled on the shore of the Cockcrow Sands. Just beyond the shore, on open pasture, where the roses bloomed and the berries ripened, lay the fisher-peoples' dwellings: three green upturned barges, with a single black funnel protruding atop each one.

An old fisherman sat cosily on a sturdy wooden chair, under the window of one of the dwellings, weaving a bobbin of string through a broken fishing net sprawled across his knee; his wife stood at the doorway throwing grain to a few well-fed hens. Their sons were out fishing at sea. Their grandchildren, playing in the orchard behind the village, noticed our ship, and with great joy ran down beside the coble boats and creels on the golden sandy shore. They began to smile and wave at us - we smiled and waved back.

Geordie, still smiling, looked up at me as we sailed by and said, "Wasn't that nice Granddad?"

"Geordie, Sonna", I replied, "as you know, Hebburn people are the most charming folk you're every likely to meet."

All was well as we passed the Ballast Hill: a fairly recent landmark, built from almost twenty years of discharged ships' ballast. This is predated by the nearby Halfway Tree - or Mid Oak - a giant and ancient maritime landmark, situated high on the Hebburn Fell 'halfway' between Newcastle and the open sea at South Shields.

We followed - but steered clear of - the Cockcrow Sands, which stretched almost the full length of Hebburn Shore; at places, pushing well into the river. A little further up the hill, lay a more active scene - the Hebburn Colliery; a dirty place by contrast to the fishing village and farming community that surrounded it.

I watched, as some Rolleymen led empty coal tubs pulled by pit ponies, back up to the pit, while others led full wagons away from the pit, along the tracks down to the awaiting river keelmen at the Black Staith. These keelmen, constantly ferried the black heaps in their keelboats from the Tyne's bank to the hungry colliers waiting mid-river; and the colliers in turn shipped it to several dozen ports - mainly London and the rest of England.

As I watched, I drew the last piece of shag tobacco from my waistcoat pocket, rubbed it in the palm of my left hand and proceeded to fill and light my pipe. I puffed away for a minute or two with a meditative air, turned to Geordie, pursed my lips and then motioned my eyes towards the pit's wooden headgear.

"You see that place over yonder - just beyond the Cockcrow sands?"

"Hebburn Colliery, Granddad, the coal mining village? Yes, I know it well."

"Yeah, Geordie, I know you do, sonna; but I must inform you that some of our Rigger relations that you've never met work there, on the south side of the river. They're not close relations, but they're family all the same… so never forget it."

"I won't, Granddad. Have you ever met them or spoken to them?"

"Alas. No, Geordie. I can't give a reason why, but I do give generously to the miners' widows' welfare." These poor mining families endure the most despicable hardships imaginable.

Geordie looked up at me anxiously and raised his brow. "Granddad, are you crying?"

"No, sonna," I masked my emotions with my handkerchief, "it's this heat; plus I was up very late preparing for today's journey. You run along and play with your tortoise; I'll shout for you when we reach Tynemouth."

"Thank you, Granddad." Geordie skipped away to the cooler innards of the ship.

Even though the sun glowed in a clear blue sky, my mind was clouded with reflections of the fatal pit explosion that occurred at the mine only ten months past.

Since it opened in 1792, the pit, owned by Mr Wade, has been plagued by dreadful bad luck, especially to it's denizen workers. Through neglect, greed and ignorance of the most elementary safety precautions, the mine is in a state of almost constant flood.

It was on the sixth of October, last year, when the ground heaved to a massive explosion down in the lower main seam.

The pit has three shafts: 'A', 'B' and 'C'. 'A', situated at the top of the staiths, serves for the drawing of coals and for man riding. 'B', just in view on Black Lane, near the Shields Road, is used for pumping out water, and 'C', which is near the Halfway Tree, is used for the upcast of ventilation by means of a large fire blazing at the bottom of the shaft. The expansion of the hot air and gases makes it lighter than normal atmospheric air, so it quickly rises up the pit shaft causing a vacuum. The shaft would be previously partitioned off by means of heavy sackcloth known as brattish, forming a flu for the rising gases. The vacuum created by the rising heat, causes cold atmospheric air to descend, thereby ventilating the pit with a crude method of gravity-air exchange. Unfortunately, the rate of air exchanged could be quite insufficient to sweep out the noxious gases in quantities capable of keeping clear all of the pockets of methane and carbon monoxide, ensuring the safety of the miners who would be toiling in multi-dangerous conditions, such as were prevailing and tolerated with impunity.

The villagers live 'on bank' - that is anywhere above the pit head and around their little homes: white cottages, seemingly washed over in a coat of lime, in the ongoing war against ticks, fleas, bugs, smallpox or many of the other scourges of the times, which the people endure as best they can in the will to live. A hardy race of mining families, subdued by hunger and want - they are relics of the feudal system. Though still deferential to their betters, fingering their forelocks in esteemed reverence to the very people whom they knew cared nothing about them: the rich, who exploited them and unashamedly called themselves magnanimous against disease, unless the same circumstances were liable to come back to themselves. These were the people; they had wives and children on bank that waited for the pit hooter to sound 'loose!' Pronounced 'lowse': meaning another twelve hour shift safely over for the men and lads working in the bowels of the earth. The feeling in the air seemed to say 'what is wrong today?' Some felt impending peril, but most went about their usual activities; they were quite used to the muck and stench of excreta and urine emanating from open lavatories, known as 'netties' or 'bogs', which they resembled. Such human waste is often covered with ashes from their fires; the midden men; conscripted by the authorities in the course of time, to move this unhealthy effluent; come on their collections by lamplight; through the night, as the pong is really stupendous - to be tipped in some reasonable remote field; where the residual fluids would seep away northwards to the nearby river; and eastward down into the bogs and marshes in the lowlands of Jarrow.

The pit hooter, or, as it was known then, the pit buzzer, started blowing long before lowse, 'something's wrong at the pit! I wonder what?' People may have thought. The low rumble of the explosion could not very well be heard on bank; it could not be heard up at the Old Hall; it could not even be heard in the cottages by the river, but the buzzer kept on blowing in its urgency: 'An accident in the pit! An explosion! My God, I hope the bairns are all right! Is it a big one? What seam is it in?'

Sunday was the day before payday. Pay was once every fortnight. Crowds collected; it was a massive explosion; the explosion was in the dreaded lower main seam. People clutching at metaphoric straws had little consolation that at least some of their kin might escape from higher seams. The constant fight in the pit against flooding - which was often a possible source of cutting off air-supplies, therefore allowing gas to accumulate - was a hazard among the many, which were taken for granted in the struggle for coal and life itself.

Explosion is sudden; death is sudden; the sudden loss of kin is shocking. The appalling strain of shock to the community on bank took its many forms - some tears of panic and hysteria, but, mostly evident was the subdued and solemn quietude of despair.

I remember the feeling of loss was stupendous. While underground, there was a spontaneous, unceasing drive at rescue work, until the very last body was recovered. The exertions of the rescuers were continued without interruption, and it is inevitable that they too became casualties. Through the rush and extra energy exerted in the voluntary efforts to attempt to save life, the poisonous proliferation of gases following an explosion are enough to endanger the lives of rescuers very seriously. Blackdamp, as it is known, is extremely poisonous, and kills very quickly; so also does it much more quickly snuff out a candle or the life of a small canary bird.

About seven o'clock on Sunday night, the mutilated remains of Thomas Telford, a youth, were brought to the surface - and at about nine o'clock, the bodies of two other men were brought up, but in such a dreadful mutilated state, that recognition was impossible. Sixteen of the bodies of the sufferers were found the following day, again, all sadly mutilated by the explosion. Indeed, as before, many were so much disfigured that it was impossible to identify them. The bodies were placed in decent coffins, which were waiting to receive them when brought to the surface. One body thought to be that of my relative George Gibson, found on Monday, was, on Tuesday discovered to be that of Thomas Davidson - Cousin George having been found on Sunday afternoon. Davidson, who had been conveyed to my cousin George's home, was, accordingly removed to his own couch. Cousin George was placed upon the now vacant couch. In several instances, the surviving friends and families had to mourn over a heap of mutilated remains, without having the melancholy satisfaction of knowing with certainty that they were with their own kindred.

By Wednesday morning, hope of finding any survivors was fading, when John Barthold was dug out of the debris of the mine in a shocking state of mutilation.

The excitement prevailing on Thursday was greater than at any previous period since the explosion. Alas, the unceasing drive at rescue work, and the attempt to recover every last body, was unfruitful. Seven bodies were never found, though the twenty eight recovered were conveyed to the grave in the Jarrow churchyard in carts belonging to the colliery - their obsequies being witnessed by upwards of three thousand spectators, many of whom had come from a considerable distance.

Some of the surviving relatives joined the melancholy processions, and as usual in the colliery districts in the north of England, the Old Hundredth Psalm was sung on the way to the burial ground.

The scene was exceedingly solemn, and many tears of sympathy were shed on that melancholy occasion. Twenty five widows and eighty one children were left unprovided for.

My sombre reflections were cut short, as Sophia walked suddenly towards me laughing nervously with wide eyes; the fingers of her left hand distended over her chest.

"Eeh, John, Geordie's just given me such a fright. I was daydreaming about sea monsters, while sitting on a chair in your cabin, when, with eyes closed, I heard a most unusual noise: a slurping, devilish kind of sound, coming towards me. I opened my sleepy eyes, apprehensively, to behold an ugly beast staring closely into them. I leapt off the chair in panic. 'It's alright, Grandma, it's only me and Charlie'. Geordie said to me. Geordie had been holding Charlie not one inch from my nose, while it chewed nonchalantly on a large piece of wet lettuce. As I cried out, the tortoise looked at me in wide-eyed surprise, and dropped the lettuce from its gaping mouth in disbelief. 'Oh! Geordie, you made me jump,' said I, with one hand on my chest, catching my breath. Realising how farcical the situation must have looked, Geordie and I both giggled."

My wife's entertaining anecdote brought me out of the doldrums. "Thank you, pet - I needed that."

CHAPTER III

GEORDIE'S MAIDEN VOYAGE

Later, I summoned Geordie, as the ship headed for the open sea at Tynemouth. "What do you think of that then, Geordie?" I gently nudged him as we stood side-by-side, looking out to sea.

"It's wonderful, Granddad; I've never seen anything like it."

"There are more amazing sights yet to see, Geordie."

"Ooh, I can't wait, Granddad."

"There's reasonable hope of an offshore wind," I whispered.

"Granddad, why are you whistling?"

"If we whistle gently, Geordie, a wind might begin to blow; it's called sympathetic magic. However, to whistle out at sea is unlucky, as it might call up a gale. There's one exception though, the cook can whistle anytime he pleases, because then we know he isn't eating the rations."

Geordie chuckled to himself.

The sails unfurled as we caught the summer-sea-breeze and headed south.

"It's magnificent, Granddad. The wind-filled sails look tremendously beautiful; how do they not pull the main mast over?"

"Don't worry, Geordie, nothing will pull the main mast over; there's a silver coin holding that up," I reassured him.

The riggers were hard at their work, so I joined them in a sea shanty, singing the verse softly, as they roared out the chorus. The shanty is a rhyming work-song, the beat corresponding with the tempo of the physical task at hand - different undertakings requiring different shanties.

"Granddad, everyone sounds so happy, singing along."

"Yes, Geordie, it's an enjoyable uplifting song," said I, during a chorus. The word's vulgar connotations were alien to Geordie's ears. His innocence of corruption is overwhelming. He's a righteous lad, who has no fear.

"That was beautiful, Granddad. Ooh! Look at all the sea gulls; they're floating about like feathers from a burst pillow."

The scene was wonderful. The ship cut calmly through the water, while the full, white sails were contrasted against a bright blue sky, dotted here and there with flecks of life.

"Look, Granddad, there's a seal; I think it came to hear the singing."

"You're probably right, Geordie. Seals are said to go ashore at night, shed their skin, and assume human form, where they would sing and dance - resuming their animal form before sunrise. If a man took a seal-maiden's abandoned skin, cap, or belt, she would stay with him until it was recaptured

- often bearing him children."

"Granddad, are any of my aunties seals?" He asked, with the tilt of his head.

"No, sonna; I don't think so."

"I wonder if they taught sailors how to swim?" Geordie looked dreamily out to sea, with his head on his folded arms, which rested on the starboard of the ship.

"Most sailors don't learn to swim, Geordie. William was allowed to, because he was born with a lucky caul on his head - that's a membrane covering some babies' heads at birth. Some people sell these to sailors for large amounts of money - though William still has his."

"That's fascinating, Granddad. Does anyone else have one?"

"No, Geordie. Oh, wait a minute, let me see... yes... your Uncle Fenwick has one," I said, in retrospect, tapping the stem of my empty clay pipe against my bearded chin. "Now where did I put my other tobacco pouch?"

"Here it is, dear, you left it in your cabin," said Sophia. "I thought you'd need it sooner or later."

"Thank you, pet."

"John, dear, this heat's overpowering; I think I'll go straight back down below to keep cool."

"Alright, pet, I'll see you later."

"You see this tobacco pouch, Geordie? It was made from the webbed foot of an albatross." I pressed some tobacco into the pipe-bowl, with my thumb.

"Granddad, I thought the albatross was unlucky?"

"Ha! It must be, sonna, as they keep losing their webbed feet to sailors. But seriously, Geordie, they are related to the storm-petrel, which, as its name suggests, is the harbinger of storms."

Our conversation was interrupted by a commotion coming from the quarterdeck; Geordie and I went there to investigate.

A few of the lads were taking advantage of their present respite, by challenging each other to bouts of strength. Others watched amused, while sitting, bending together fancy knots, or shaping bone or wood into beautiful carvings. Alf Bennet - one of the joiners - took a hammer and six-inch nail to the centre of the platform, then proceeded to drive the nail almost five inches home, into the deck.

"Right, Davy!" he said to my son. "If you think you're so strong, see if you can pull 'that' out with your teeth!" He laughed heartily, in mocking defiance.

Peter scuttled up to the nail, on all fours. "I'll do it! I'll do it!"

GEORDIE'S MAIDEN VOYAGE

My son Thomas, known to the crew as 'Doubting Thomas' shook his head pessimistically from side to side, as he took in a sharp intake of breath, through his puckered lips. "Don't try it, Peter; you'll never do it! You'll smash your teeth! You'll be in agony!"

Peter didn't have many teeth to start with - the irregular ones he did have, looked like feeble black charcoal tacks.

"Hey-man, watch this!" he commanded, as he bit into the metal with the ferocity of a wild dog, whose motive was to demonstrate its leader-like prowess. At first, there was an alarming crunching noise, followed, by a sharp angry crack. We all winced in pained agreement. "Aagh... me teeth!" Peter cried, as a few blood-covered teeth fell to the deck. "You knew my teeth would smash, our Tom! Why didn't you stop me? I'm going to tell my mam!"

"Wasn't that silly, Granddad?"

"Yes, sonna; but never mind, he'll be back soon, as cheerful as ever, once he's had a drink of grog to abate the ache inside his mouth."

Bennet laughed at Peter's misfortune. "Come on then Davy, have a go, or has your brother's pitiful exhibition made you faint-hearted?"

My son David didn't answer - he just dropped down onto all fours, gave the bloodied metal a quick clean with his handkerchief and then grasped it in his strong white teeth. As he pulled at the nail his face reddening with exertion - it gave a bit. He tensed his jaw muscles; his blood vessels looked fit to bust; small beads of sweat rolled over his eyelids.

Thomas shook his head, "You'll never do it 'our kid'; you may as well give up now; you saw what happened to our Peter!"

Peter came on deck, smiling. It looked as though he had a mouthful of wet liquorice.

"Come on 'our kid', you can do it!" he slurped. David paused to position his arms in the form of a press-up, and tilted his head to one side, giving one last colossal grip with his vice-like teeth. The nail moved slightly. The crew looked on with hope.

"Come on, Dave! You're stronger than anyone! Peter bellowed." David growled with determined rage. The nail moved steadily upwards; up, up it came, inch by inch, as David's face betrayed his feeling of apprehension. His face was turning a bluey-red, but still he continued. "Just one more inch, Dave - Go! Go! Go!"

The crew stood up now, in support. The last inch groaned defiantly in the hard sun-baked board. David didn't relent, his growling and snorting more loud and aggressive now.

A LIFETIME'S JOURNEY

"Stop, Dave! You'll kill yourself, man!" shouted Thomas. This unsupportive pessimism seemed to bring a new angry strength to David's veins - for, he glared up at Thomas, and with one extra hard spasm, withdrew the nail from the deck. The lads cheered.

Peter was dancing wildly. "I knew you could do it 'our kid' - I knew you could do it!"

Without a word, David placed the nail between his two hands, equally, then walked up to Bennet, and bent it severely, right before his eyes.

"Straighten 'that' if you can, Alf!"

"That's ridiculous; it's easy to bend, but impossible to straighten."

"Give it to me, man!" David snorted. He grabbed the nail from Bennet, and then gave the angled nail a sharp burst of directed strength, straightening it in one.

"It's as good as new," said Peter, proudly holding up the trophy for all to see.

Bennet shook David by the hand, "You're as hard as nails, Davy, and a good man to work with too; I can't argue with that."

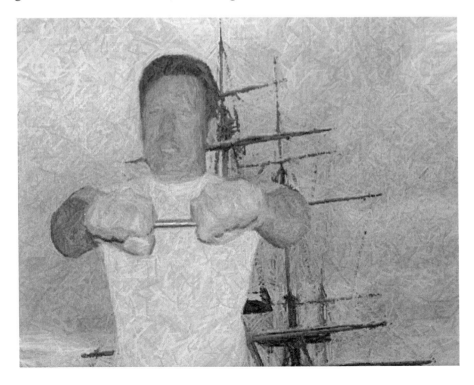

David then swaggered menacingly up to his brother Thomas, as Geordie walked away to the forecastle.

"Thanks Tom, I couldn't have done it without you, you pessimistic agitator."

"But you could have broken your teeth, twisted your arm, or even burst the blood vessels in your head! Then you'd have been in Davy's grip!"

"So what?" said David. "By the way, what's that on the water?" He continued, sarcastically, whilst winking to James. "It looks like a piece of flotsam."

"What... where?" Thomas turned with eyes blazing. He looked at what he thought was the aftermath of a disaster at sea. He feared some sort of mysterious, contagious disaster would strike them too. "Fetch Dad! Is that a storm-petrel?" He added, placing his hands on either side of his head. "Does the sky look a bit darker? I reckon there's a storm coming. We've only been out at sea a little while and we're all going to die! That's it... I just know it!"

"Oh, shut up, you pessimistic doom-dweller! I'm only gulling you man. It's a seal... look!"

"Oh, aye!" Thomas peered timidly over the portside. "It is... I think!"

"You know what your problem is... eh? You love the bad weather, don't you, you barmy blockhead? You're a sad man. Go and whittle yourself another lucky charm!" David walked away from Thomas shaking his head.

Thomas is a prophet of doom. He gives out depressing judgement with such sympathetic compassion, that a person finds oneself chagrined with their induced, insincere agreement, leaving one with a bemused fondness for the man. His middle name is Peter, so he's sometimes known as Pessimistic Pete.

The sun still blazed in the cloudless sky, while the sea breeze spirited us gracefully along. The atmosphere was tranquil as the crew returned to their light-hearted work.

Henry, the botanist, gaily and softly brushed bright yellow pollen, from the 'M' collar of his flamboyant tailcoat. "May I put some of these flowers on the forecastle, Captain?"

"Oh, yes of course! Feel free to place them anywhere on deck." He had boxes of magnificent coloured plants, the blooms very pleasing to the eye. In less than one hour, the ship was bedecked with a delightful progression of pulchritude. Gay flowers adorned skylight window boxes. The breeze fresh fragrance was deliciously alluring; the delectable efflorescence, invigorating. This serene milieu was cut short by the alarming cries of a madman.

A LIFETIME'S JOURNEY

"Help! Help!" the doctor cried, as he scrambled hopelessly up the steps, leading towards the deck, with a look of horror on his face that was frightful to look upon. I immediately asked one of the lads to find Geordie, and take him below.

"What is it, man? Calm yourself. We're all here to help you," said I.

"Aaaarch! It's the rat from hell!" He pointed convulsively at the hatch. "A bigger rat I never did see."

The crew listened gleefully - they loved rat hunts.

"I awoke fully-clothed, lying on my straw mattress, with my wooden leg attached to my person, and a half bottle of rum by my side. I took a swig to shift the wretched queasiness from my brain - taking care not to swallow any broken glass. Then, as I looked up at the hanging cot-bed above, a huge brown rat dived from it onto my bed below, sinking its monstrous teeth into my wooden leg. I instinctively picked up my empty chamber pot and smashed it across the poor beasties head. The brute gave out a huge squeal as it tumbled through the air, landing on the floor with a dull thud.

"I dived out of bed with the alacrity of a man possessed. In a moment, I had emptied the contents from my heavy sea chest, placing it upturned over the stunned creature. As I looked down at my pierced wooden leg, there protruding from it were two vicious white teeth. I removed them with my surgical tooth extractors, and then lay down panting on my bed. The thought of the ship's fever that might have been, horrified me. While I rested, the sea chest came to life. I looked in disbelief, as the 'scourge of ships' almost lifted the cumbersome chest far enough off the floor to escape. Leaping from the bed, my wooden leg fell off, hindering me in my endeavour to secure my captive troublemaker. Its head violently thrust from under the chest. Shuffling along on my side, I stretched out my arms and pulled at a chest of drawers, toppling it headlong onto the sea chest, pressing it evenly onto the floor, trapping the rat's nose. It wriggled desperately - until, eventually, it retrieved its inquisitive, ensnared snout and became deadly silent.

"I replaced my leg and stared in utter horror, as yet again, the beast within strove furiously to break out. I picked up my heavy travelling bag from the floor, for the purpose of adding extra weight to the now quiet sea chest. As I did so, the chest lifted from the floor, as the rat once again came to life. It pushed its nose underneath a gap it had made, then wriggled and writhed, beserkly, until, in a flash... it escaped! As I stood there, it came at me menacingly, so I kicked it violently across the cabin floor, and then made my escape, closing the door behind me."

The lads looked at each other, gleefully, reading each other's thoughts.

"Rat hunt!" they shouted, as they rushed below deck, towards the doctor's cabin.

"If the rat's there, Doctor, the lads'll find it," I declared, as a magnificent cloud of smoke billowed proudly from my clay pipe.

Twenty minutes later, the lads came cheerfully up on deck, carrying their live prey - a prize catch indeed. It was roped motionless to the middle of a long plank, carried by two of the crew upon their shoulders. What a size. In all my years as a sailor, I have never seen so big a rat. It resembled a beaver in certain designs, excepting that it had a long thin tail, and now, no incisor teeth.

My son James placed a long pair of tongs firmly, but gently, around the rat's thickset neck, and then nodded to Thomas.

"Open the slip-knot, the rat's secured now."

Thomas looked nervous, "Are you sure? What if it gets loose? It'll get me first. Let someone else do it!"

"I'll do it! I'll do it!" Peter jumped forward with childlike enthusiasm.

James shook his head at Thomas and then turned to Peter, "Oh, go on then."

Peter opened the slipknot as the two crewmembers lowered the plank, leaving the rat dangling heavily from the tongs.

The plank was then appropriately thrown into the sea.

James hung the intruder over the side of the ship - a frequent ritual on board *The Turtle*.

The crew watched with interest. "Go on, James, let it go!" cried the lads as they hung over the side of the ship, waiting for the next scene.

"Here goes." James opened the tongs, dropping the rat into the sea. It landed with a hefty splash. Unharmed, it swam towards the nearby plank.

Peter was excited; "It's going to make it! Yes, its front legs are on the plank now."

"Ooh - it'll never make it to shore;" Thomas shook his head; "it'll get tired, and drown."

"There you are 'our Tom', it's lying on the plank, now; it's definitely going to make it to shore; I'll bet you a pouch full of baccy."

"But Peter, you don't even smoke tobacco!"

"I know that, but I don't need any baccy to bet 'you' with."

"Why not then?"

"Because I'm definitely going to win yours!" retorted Peter.

"You cheeky tar pot! I'm not betting with you now - not even if you tied the ship's anchor around the rat's neck; it would probably still make it to shore, 'cause you've more luck than me. You're a slippery eel!" Thomas threw his hand up. "That's it... the bet's off!"

Peter stuck out his tongue and crossed his eyes. "Killjoy!"

We watched, as the rat paddled the plank towards land.

Later, with the aid of my telescope, I espied the creature meeting with dry land, as all the other rats had on previous occasions. I informed the betting crew of the rat's survival, to the joy of some, and the chagrin of others.

"Right-o, lads, you all deserve a drink of ale." I felt a merry time approaching.

The doctor licked his dry lips. "I wouldn't mind one, please. The rat's gone, but it's left its mark on me."

"Dave! Alf! Bring a cask of ale up on deck!"

Twenty minutes later, with Sophia and Geordie sitting beside me, and most of the crew sitting around, we had a merry singsong. William, Andrew and a few other teetotallers were at their positions.

GEORDIE'S MAIDEN VOYAGE

The botanist spoke kindly to my son Richard. "Please give us a tune on the virginal."

Richard played the precious family heirloom beautifully. We took turns to sing delightful worded sea-shanties and old village pub songs. The animals blissfully joined in the singing with their untimely cacophonies. Henry, the botanist, has a singularly sweet voice for a man.

Sophia smiled at me contentedly - the tea in her china cup reflecting the sunlight into her bright eyes. "Now I know why you like going to sea, dear."

"Granddad, I don't want to get back home in a hurry; a sailor's life is a wonderful life," said Geordie, as he offered Charlie a drink of his ale.

"Aye, on board 'this' ship it is, sonna." I winked at him as I puffed on my pipe.

On most ships, a sailor's life is a miserable, expendable existence. Men tend to disappear, like effervescent spume as it hits the shore, dissolving, never to be seen again, as others despairingly follow in their wake. Some are treated like slaves, often beaten to death for the most trivial of reasons. These captains rule with omnipotence; they seem outside the law's reach, rarely being prosecuted. If Geordie thinks my ship is a representation of general life at sea, so be it.

I refilled Geordie's cup. "We spoil most the ones we love best."

"That's enough, John," said Sophia; "we don't want Geordie's head filled with confusion."

"Alright, pet, I think two cups are enough for today; he'll work it off in this heat anyway."

"Meat nourished on fodder and salt spray, *dint harf* taste delicious," said Ralph, our portly Norfolk cook, as he rapped his ladle furiously against the ship's bell.

"Even though it's mouth-watering, salt beef's the coarsest part of the animal," said Peter, glumly. "I can't eat that, Ralph; the few teeth I do have left won't stand any more hassle."

"It's alright, Peter, I've mashed some potatoes especially for you; it was your mother's idea. I've also made you a delicious chocolate cake."

"Mmm... thank you Ralph, you're the best mate a crewman can have."

I crossed my knife and fork on my plate and pushed it to one side. "That meal was wonderful Ralph; you're a real connoisseur."

"Thank you, John." Ralph nodded, then quaffed off the remainder of his beer mug.

I was now on deck, seated in a wicker-chair, with a cigar in one hand and a two pint stein in the other, the sun blazing down on me. Sophia had gone below deck. I put down my stein to stretch my tired arms, ash falling to the deck. "This is the life, Geordie, eh? It's great to be able to relax. Your Uncle William will be taking command of *The Turtle*, next journey, sonna."

"Do you mean you're not going to be the captain anymore, Granddad?" Geordie's, face was downcast, like a child's when it has just learned the truth about Saint Nicholas.

"Oh, don't worry yourself, Geordie; I'll still be coming along now and again." I patted his shoulder, reassuringly. "You see, Geordie, I'm getting too old and stiff to do this job; it's too demanding for an old man of seventy. I know they say 'You're as young as you feel', but I feel seventy!" I laughed.

"But Methuselah lived for 969 years, Granddad!" pleaded Geordie, kneeling on one knee in front of me.

"I know, Geordie, but did he have a debilitating profession, like captain of a cargo-ship? I think not," I laughed, clasping his hands in mine. "Anyway, sonna, I'm going to retire and place the whole cargo business in William's hands. Heaven knows, he deserves it."

"At least we'll see you every now and then, Granddad." Geordie sat on my lap, cuddling into me.

Peter walked towards us with a bemused expression upon his face. "Dad?"

"Aye, what is it son?" I licked the froth from my moustache.

"Well, you know when we have white dandruff on our collars?"

"Yes," I smiled with precocious intuition.

"Well, do black people have black dandruff and brown people have brown dandruff?"

A few of the lads laughed out.

"You've been drinking too much, man, Peter." Thomas laughed. "You're talking crapulously."

"No, I'm not! Well then, dad?"

"I'm sorry, Peter, but I must tell you that no matter what the colour of the skin, once it dies, it shrivels up and turns white."

"There you see - I knew it was the drink talking." Thomas pulled a snidey face. "Anyone knows all dandruff's white," he added, boastfully.

Peter looked Thomas in the eye. "It's not fair, you've been to Africa."

"Ha-ha! Do you think that I went all the way to Africa to find that out, man?" Thomas shook his head condescendingly. "You're as daft as a brush!"

Peter walked away, smiling, seemingly unaware of his present dispute, distracted by a beautifully coloured parrot that had landed on the lifeboat

nearby; the sheep penned inside, were unperturbed by its presence.

"Come on my pretty." Peter held his hand out to the bird. Amazingly, the bird hopped onto Peter's arm. Peter caressed it lightly. "It's tame!"

"I belong to Peter! Sammy wants a biscuit!" shrilled the bird.

"It knows my name! It wants a biscuit from me!" Peter's eyes bulged with surprise. "Thomas! Come and look at this! This bird's me best mate, and I've only just met it! It knows everything about me, man! It must have been watching me for ages!"

It wasn't long, before Peter's hullabaloo, attracted the lads' attention.

"What's this then, Peter? Have you made yourself a new mate?" said Alf Bennet.

"Aye, listen to this... come on my pretty... come on," coaxed Peter.

"I belong to Peter! Sammy wants a biscuit!" the bird replied.

Alf smiled and then gave out a whistle of surprise. "Hey, that's some bird you have there, lad; it's very intelligent, isn't it?"

The lads looked at the bird, then at each other, nodding approvingly as numerous hands made their way down to stroke it.

"What's this, then?" I pressed through the exited throng.

"Dad, can I keep this bird?" Pleaded Peter, his head tilted to one side like a begging dog. "It can't half talk."

"Well, it looks healthy enough. Let me have a look at it."

It was a beautiful macaw - one of the largest members of the parrot family, and just over two feet in length. It had a brilliant plumage of glossy blue above, and deep yellow below, and had white bare patches on its cheeks, lined with rows of small feathers. On examining the parrot further, I found a silver snap-on identity ring, wrapped around its left leg. It read:

NAME: SAMMY.
OWNER: PETER HOPS.
ADDRESS: WHITE SWAN PUB. LIDDELL ST. NORTH SHIELDS.

I know Peter Hops - the landlord of the 'White Swan Public House' on the North Shields quayside - very well, and have drank at his pub for many years; it's the haunt of many a sailor. However, the last I knew he kept a very talkative mynah bird, not a parrot.

It seems apt that Peter is the only one of my sons that cannot read, for it would break his heart if he knew the truth.

I gently removed the ring, and slipped it, unseen, into my waistcoat pocket.

GEORDIE'S MAIDEN VOYAGE

"You can keep the old bird until we get back home; and then, if we find it belongs to anyone you can hand it back. Is that fair enough, Peter?"

"Aye, Dad! That's great! I'm going to get Sammy a biscuit, and then show him to my mam."

Peter's wide-eyed, beaming face showed so much expressive joy and delight, that it almost looked as though someone had just thrown a bucketful of ice-cold water into it.

"By the way... Sammy's a macaw parrot!" I shouted to Peter, as he danced merrily out of sight, heading below deck with Sammy in his arms.

Geordie went below for a biscuit and a nap, taking his pet tortoise with him - the fresh sea air having made him tired and peckish.

I decided to go for a stroll around the deck. Everything was clean and shipshape. The ship was basically running itself. Some of the lads were standing on the topmasts, just for the sheer pleasure of it. The botanist was sitting on a barrel with a canvas on his knee and a paintbrush in his hand, making a fine portrait of my son William.

"That's a very good likeness, Henry."

"Oh, thank you, Mr Rigger." He set the painting down to dry.

As I watched, he picked up a clean white canvas that was stretched upon a wooden frame. Upon this, he quickly pencil-sketched a portrait of my son Andrew, who was standing on the quarterdeck. He then mixed some coloured paints, and, a few brush strokes later, the portrait came to life.

"You have amazing dexterity, Henry." I took my pipe from my mouth.

"Thank you, again, Mr Rigger; it's wonderful what you can learn from nature." I nodded my agreement.

William and Andrew were now both on the quarterdeck, deep in conversation.

"The doctor should be sober at all times," said William to Andrew, as I stepped up to join them. I turned to look at the doctor, who was sprawled out in a stupor on the deck.

"I agree son."

"But, Dad, what can we do about it?" They asked.

"I'll tell you what, lads. William, I promised I would give you full ownership of *The Turtle*, next journey. Well, I've changed my mind... you can take command now... the ship's yours. Andrew, you're now first mate."

It took a while to sink in, but we eventually swapped hats, with the idea to regain our own snugly fitting ones later, when the cap badges had been transferred. I was now second mate.

William frowned. "But Dad, you've put a lot of money into this venture!"

"Look, I know exactly what I'm doing. I've made more than enough money from cargoing to eventually have you all running your own businesses. That's why - with the exception of Peter - we had you all educated. Cargo money set your brothers John and Robert up in business; and now it's your turn William... I think you're ready. And soon, Andrew, it'll be your turn to run your own business. Your mother and I have a wonderful mansion at Ovingham village, and more than enough money to retire on."

William put his hand on my shoulder. "Thank you very much, Dad; but why didn't you retire years ago?"

"I needed to show you the ropes, son. This is a family business; I want you all to do well, and keep your mother and I proud; because when we're gone, you hold our future in your veins. So, William, your first priority as captain, is to sort out the doctor."

Andrew looked at me somewhat confused. "Hey, Dad, what are the lads going to call you if our William's the captain now?"

"They can call me John, Uncle John, Granddad, Dad, or anything else, as long as they don't swear," I laughed. Andrew and William smiled.

William took command. "Dave, Alf, put the doctor to bed."

"Aye-aye, Captain! They replied. William looked bemused.

"It's the ears up in the riggings, William." I quickly turned my eyes upwards. "News spreads as quickly as ships fever. Besides, your new hat's a bit of a giveaway."

"Thanks for the advice, Dad," said he, altering his cap while scanning the riggings.

Meanwhile, the doctor was carried off to bed. A few lads came up to see if William really was the new captain. They went away happy and content.

"Dave!" I shouted, as he came back on deck.

"Aye, Father? What is it?"

"William wants to give you something." I handed my new second mate's hat to William, and then William handed it to Dave.

"You're my second mate, now, well done."

"Second Mate? Wait till the lads hear this, eh?" David was thrilled. Thank you, William. He swaggered off with his new hat perched proudly atop of his large, strong head.

Andrew was standing with his telescope to his eye, looking out to sea.

"We've passed the Dogger Bank, Dad."

"Thank goodness for that, son - I'm so relieved."

The Dogger Bank is a fishing ground in the North Sea, about seventy miles from Yorkshire. I have some painful memories of that awful place. It is so deadly to ships and men, during the violent northerly, or north-westerly gales, that it has been named '*The Cemetery*'. When I was younger, about four and twenty years of age, I was a fisherman, trying to find my sea legs aboard my Uncle George's ship, '*The Pelican*'. He had six craft out on that fateful journey. It was a bitter, cold, March night, when a sudden ferocious storm appeared. We didn't have time to take in the sails; in a moment they were ripped to shreds. The masts were kissing each other. We felt insignificant, like small model ships in a shaken bottle of fizzy spume, ready to burst with the inestimable pressure of the sea. One craft was completely reeled over, coming upright with all hands gone. *The Pelican* was the only vessel to reach port. The smaller fishing craft were dashed to pieces.

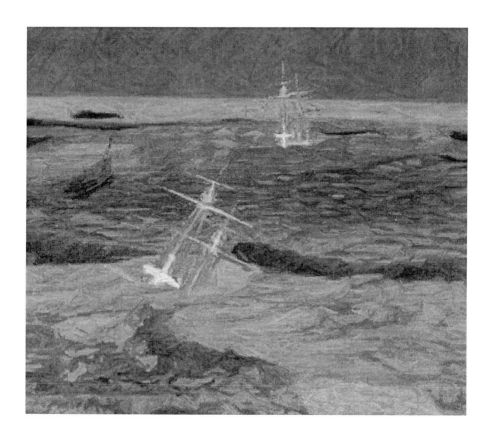

A LIFETIME'S JOURNEY

The next day, my uncle's great friend of many years, was found washed up dead on the beach by the locals. My uncle made his way to the beach, walked up to his dead mate, shook him by the hand, and said, 'goodbye old friend'. Only a few fishermen survived; many never braved the sea again, their spirits subdued.

"Aye, it seems just like yesterday." I looked dreamily out to sea.

"Never mind, Father;" Andrew comforted me; "Six weeks after London, we'll be sitting in the Canary Islands."

Andrew was accurate to the day. In six short weeks, we landed on the exquisite Spanish island of Tenerife, the largest of the volcanic Canary Islands. I've travelled the world over, and can say without doubt that Tenerife has one of the most favourable atmospheric conditions in the world - clear skies abound.

We rested there a few days, to replenish our water and other resources in overabundance, as caution for any eventuality. Not once has scurvy shown its unsightly face aboard my ship, in all my years as captain - it was kept at bay with a copious profusion of fruits and vegetables. The stocks restored, and everyone happy and content, we headed south. We were well south of the Canaries before we sighted Africa. Then we headed 800 miles southwest, towards the Cape Verde Islands to avoid the doldrums and awkward currents of the Gulf of Guinea, as well as the bad weather area off Southwest Africa. We were now nearer to Brazil than Africa.

Ninety four days later, we arrived at the beautiful St. Helena Bay, in the South Atlantic, one hundred and twenty miles north of the Cape of Good Hope. It was here that Henry collected over 40 different species of plant, which I have never seen anywhere else. We stayed only long enough to renew our supplies.

CHAPTER IV

THE AFRICAN EXPERIENCE

A week after rounding the Cape of Good Hope, we reached Mossel Bay, on the southern coast of Africa, a banana plantation and fishing village. It was there, that we overhauled the entire ship. The people there were all similarly dressed, wearing only brown leather loincloths, with tasselled bands around their arms and legs. We did a little trading with them, exchanging pots and pans for their luscious fruits and vegetables.

"There you are, Geordie, there's a banana for you." I couldn't hide a whimsical smile as I handed him the large green fruit.

"I've never seen anything like it Granddad; how do I eat it?" Geordie looked mystified.

"I'll show you, sonna." I proceeded to peel the banana, revealing the white palatable interior. "There you go, Geordie; but watch you don't eat the green skin."

"Mmm... it's delicious, Granddad." Geordie munched on his newfangled fruit. "Can we take some home to Newcastle with us?"

"I'm sorry, Geordie, but they would perish, long before then."

A LIFETIME'S JOURNEY

An hour later, Sophia walked towards me, on the motionless, almost deserted deck. She was wearing a white, short-waisted, trained gown, with long tight sleeves and buffon. She also wore a pink bonnet upon her head, tied under the chin with a pink lace ribbon, and a parasol in her hand to match.

"John, are we going ashore, dear?"

"Of course, pet. Just give me a few minutes to dress."

A short while later, I was on deck, feeling like a dandy, wearing my silk hat, leather boots, pantaloons and tailcoat.

"You look first rate, John."

"Thank you, pet, but what about our Geordie, here?" I motioned him over to us.

"Ooh, you do look attractive, Geordie," said Sophia, whilst straightening his collar. He was wearing a brown three-piece-suit, especially bought for the occasion. His new shoes were also brown, and his white silk shirt was frilled at the neck and cuffs.

The three of us linked arms and headed for shore. The weather was glorious. The air was filled with an appetising, fruity aroma. The brown, friendly natives seemed to be everywhere, some bringing fresh water, some faggots for the ships stoves and others helping in any way they possibly could.

We met William on the beach. "How's everything getting along, son?"

"Well, Father, we'll have plenty fresh meat for a while," said he, pointing to an ox he had just bought and tethered to a rock; "the young native wouldn't take no for an answer!"

"Ha! They'll sell you almost anything if they know you have enough pots and pans to trade - to the natives they're a very valuable asset indeed. Just make sure Ralph doesn't start trading the galley pots by mistake; though the ones we brought expressly should be enough."

Andrew was calling down orders to a gang of natives floating in the water. They dived below the water line, checking the sheets of copper plating that covered the ship's hull, protecting it from the wood boring worms of the tropic seas.

"It good! It good!" shouted an excited native as he reappeared on the surface. "You give pot-pan, now?" He added, gesticulating with his hands, his happy face beaming with anticipation. More natives resurfaced asking for their rewards.

"Thank you," said Andrew, as he threw them each their desired compensation, which they caught with amazing dexterity - almost like dolphins.

"William! We've finished mending the sails!" shouted David, from up above, as he began briskly descending the riggings.

"Thanks Dave. Was there much damage?"

"Not really. There was a tear in the foresail, where a few ropes had opened - and an upright cable bracing the main sail had snapped; but apart from that, the riggings are ship-shape."

"Aye, Dave, our Robert knows how to make a dependable hard-wearing canvas." William re-boarded the ship.

James was exhausted. He wiped the glistening perspiration from his face with his forearm, his shirt collar clinging to his reddened neck. "William, that's all the provisions on board, now."

"Hey, James, get a hat on, lad. The sun's unbearable, man - you'll get the fever."

"Hey, it's not my fault, man." James remonstrated. "It's our Peter. He came up behind me, slipped my hat off my head and then ran off, shouting, 'I'll bring it back later, our kid.'"

Just then, Peter strolled carelessly on deck. He held two hats in his arms, both over-brimming with an assortment of nuts. He emptied these into a large pan, which was lying beside him on the deck; then walked up to James nonchalantly. "There's your hat, our James." He tossed it swiftly through the air.

James looked at Peter, quizzically, shaking his head in disbelief. He then turned to William.

"What's he doing, now?"

"Don't ask me." William shrugged his shoulders.

"Hey! Don't let anyone touch these nuts, mind, they're for my Sammy." Peter was very protective towards his parrot. "Come on, my pretty, come on," he called, as he held out a brown nut, enticingly, in his leathery sunburnt hand. Almost immediately, there was a bright flurry of colour, as the parrot swooshed magnificently into view; its tail feathers fanned out so neatly, slowing its descent.

"This is what you want, isn't it, my little beauty?" Peter waved a nut as the resplendent bird settled on his arm.

Sammy delicately picked the nut from Peter's fingers with its skilful bill, then, began rotating it with the aid of its gentle tongue and claw. When it had found the exact position it wanted, it cracked the hard nut open sharply with its strong beak, and cleverly extracted the seed with its tongue.

James watched in astonished admiration. "Dear me! I bet you our Dave couldn't even do that with his teeth!"

"Oh, yes he can!" argued Peter; "and two at a time... 'cause I asked him to! Hey, man, our Dave could mash anything with his gnashers. He's so strong, I bet he could pick you two up with one hand and hoy you both overboard... if I asked him to!" he added, glaring at them. "Don't forget, no one else could head-but that six-inch nail into the mast."

Before James or William had a chance to answer, Peter dashed away below deck, singing a merry ditty, with the parrot still on his arm.

"Oh, well, I don't think he 'knows' what a compliment is," James laughed.

Without warning, Peter came back up on deck. William and James braced themselves for a barrage of inimical words.

Peter held out a handful of nuts to William and James. "Do you want one?"

William winked tactfully to James. "Why-aye, man, we love nuts, don't we James?"

"Oh-aye, we love them." James winked back. "I bet you our Dave could crack four of these between his toes, man."

Peter stared. "Don't talk daft." He then skipped off towards the gangplank, and left the ship.

On shore, he met Richard and Henry, who were huddled together over an easel, fingering the canvas upon it, knowledgeably.

"Yes, you're right, Richard," Henry nodded, as Peter approached. "It is the best angle from which to portray the scene."

"Hello Richard. Hello Henry."

"Hello Peter," they replied, gaily.

"I'm going back to the village to see my mam; are you coming along?"

"We'll be there presently," Henry smiled. Peter waved goodbye over his shoulder, then followed the well-trodden, sun-baked footpath to the small, quiet village; the foliage becoming denser as he neared his destination.

Five minutes later, he arrived at a clearing in the wood, which contained about forty mud huts. At the head of the village lay a great fallen tree. Into this was carved a most beautiful throne, which would befit any king or queen of Europe. On this royal seat presided a most prestigious looking man - Chief Bantu. He wore a loincloth, and his fit, muscular upper body was vividly painted. He wore gold bands upon his arms and sparkling jewellery about his ears. There were white animal teeth laced upon his neck and braced upon his wrists. His head was crowned with an interesting richness of plumage.

My wife and I sat upon wicker chairs, whilst most of the natives and some of the crew, sat upon the dry, dusty earth, listening intently to the Chief's words of wisdom. I was quite surprised at how well his understanding of the English language had improved since my last visit. His wisdom was immense.

"I will speak with the boy, now," said he, in his deep friendly voice, pointing to Geordie, who was standing beside me, charged with interest. Geordie made his way over to the Chief, and knelt down courteously at his feet. "You have a look of wisdom upon your face. I will enlighten you in the many ways of our ancient rituals; but first we must exchange gifts." The chief took the majestic chain of teeth from his neck, and placed it reverently upon Geordie's.

"Thank you, I'm honoured." Geordie then showed his appreciation. He reached deep into his jacket pocket and withdrew a large magnifying lens, which was seated in a band of ivory; attached to this, was an ebony handle. "This is for you, great Chief. It can make small things large." He, demonstrated, placing the lens to his magnified eye. The Chief laughed out in surprise. "It can also make fire." Geordie announced, as he placed his handkerchief onto the parched earth, igniting it instantly with the aid of the lens. The natives stirred with excitement - eyes wide with wonderment.

Geordie placed the lens in Chief Bantu's eager, outstretched hand. The Chief held the incredible novelty up towards the heavens, and then spoke out several mystical sounding words. The natives lay face down in the dust. The Witch Doctor seemed to appear from nowhere, bringing forth an aged, wooden bowl, containing a thick yellow liquid.

Geordie's head was gently lowered, then there was a 'laying on of hands'. The Chief anointed Geordie's forehead - an ancient symbolic ritual.

"Never enmity between our blood," the Chief spoke. "Let wisdom prevail."

Earlier that morning, I had presented Chief Bantu with the various gifts he had requested from England: more looking glasses and pans. These looking glasses were mere paltry amusements in comparison to Geordie's magnifying gift. To the Chief, the invaluable curiosity was a spectacle to behold indeed.

The Chief thanked Geordie. "You have given us the means of instant fire. Never before, have we known a jewel to have so much potential energy."

Geordie pointed to the sky. "The sun is the source of its illuminating power, and God is the creator of the sun."

The Chief nodded.

Geordie excelled himself, his diplomacy fully grown.

A LIFETIME'S JOURNEY

A moment later, Richard and Henry appeared from the heavily shaded wood, out into the dazzling sunshine, and started towards us.

"Hello Father. Hello Mother," whispered Richard; "Henry's painted a beautiful portrait of the Chief - I think he'll be very pleased with it," he said, setting down the paintings.

"Oh, Henry, that one's well nice," whispered Sophia, pointing to a portrait of the Witch Doctor, in all his finery. "The large silver earrings are nice, but the bone through the nose looks very painful."

"It's Geordie's moment of glory," I whispered. "And I'd be truly thankful, Henry, if you would leave the presentation of your beautiful coloured pictures, until tonight."

"Oh, yes of course. I'm very sorry for seeming so inconsiderate. I wouldn't for a moment detract from Geordie's honour."

"The feeling's mutual... I'm sorry too, Father," said Richard.

"Not at all, lads; you couldn't possibly have known. Now find a place to sit, and then listen to what Chief Bantu has to say."

"How come you have so much knowledge for a little man?" Chief Bantu asked Geordie.

"I was taught by many wise people, known as 'teachers', in a place called 'school'. Many people, past and present, have written lifetimes of knowledge into books. These 'teachers' show us how best to understand and extract this knowledge. My grandmother is a retired teacher, whose knowledge has been an invaluable asset to my education."

"You are very erudite. You have experienced many feelings and careers from books. In reading lies knowledge, in knowledge lies wisdom. It would please me very much if you would bring me books of knowledge on your return voyage. I cannot read English yet, but I will learn."

"Of course, Chief Bantu, I'd be happy to oblige."

The Chief clapped his hands, and the sound of tom-toms filled the air. The natives before us joyously arose en masse and began dancing vigorously to the beat. An appetising feast was then brought forward, wonderfully displayed upon a long, makeshift table.

"What a skilful array of seafood, meat, fruit and vegetables," gasped Sophia.

"Guests are always welcomed this way, dear."

The Chief beckoned us towards the table. Henry set to work immediately, emulating on canvas the delicious looking food in front of him. Soon, hands began to make their way towards their selected choices. By this time, the dancing natives had moved away from us, so as to keep down the dust.

David collected some seafood from the exquisitely decorated seaweed, and put it into his upturned hat. "Hey, it's incredibly exotic, isn't it?"

Andrew shyly handed David his hat. "Hey, 'our kid', get some for me. Andrew then turned to me as he picked a piece of fruit from his hat and popped it into his mouth. "Father, me and Dave are going on watch, now, and William and James will be here shortly; will you save some food for them?"

"Why-aye, lads, there'll be plenty for them." When they arrived, there was more than enough.

"How's the doctor, William?"

"Ah, he's not bad, Father." William bit into a small piece of beef. "He's as drunk as ever, but pacified."

"Well, as long as he's no trouble, we can relax."

In the evening, Henry presented a very delighted Chief Bantu with his portrait, and the Chief promised to exhibit the picture with pride.

That night, we celebrated our alliance, for the morrow we would part.

"We've had a wonderful time, Chief Bantu; the meal was excellent. Thank you very much; we will retire now and see you in the morning."

"You are very welcome, Captain Rigger. We will join you on board your ship on the return journey, as you agreed. A few of my sons will see you safely to your ship."

"Thank you, Chief Bantu - goodnight."

"Goodnight, everyone... goodnight," said the Chief.

It was almost midnight as we reached the ship and said goodnight to the natives; we watched them until they disappeared through the moonlit trees.

We climbed the gangplank.

"Are you happy, Geordie?"

"Yes, Granddad, Chief Bantu's a great man."

"Yes, Geordie, he's a man of great integrity. You made your grandmother and I proud, tonight - the way you presented yourself in his presence."

"Good morning! So you found your way home, eh?"

"Oh! David! You gave me such a fright!" gasped Sophia.

"Where's Andrew, son; why's he not on shift?"

"Oh, I told him to go to bed hours ago, so he would be fresh for the next watch. It's no good both of us being tired, is it?"

"Good thinking, David," I yawned. "It seems that everyone else is too tired to keep watch, now. Never mind - bring me a palliasse up on deck to rest my weary bones upon, and I'll keep watch."

Geordie suppressed a yawn. "I'll keep watch with you, Granddad."

"Thank you for the offer, sonna, but you had better get a good night's sleep. The Chief wants to see you in the morning; and he doesn't want you yawning all over him, does he?

"No, Granddad - I had better go to bed," Geordie yawned through a smile.

Sophia kissed me gently on the cheek. "Goodnight, dear."

"Goodnight, pet. Goodnight, Geordie, sonna."

"Goodnight, Granddad."

"Dave, son, you had better get yourself off to bed."

"But Father, you said there must always be two of us on watch at any particular time."

"There's a very good reason for that, son. You see, it takes years of practice at sea to distinguish between one noise and another on board any ship. It is only then, when you become familiar with all of the possible creaks and groans that you can then clearly discern between actuality and false alarm - I don't usually make false alarms."

"Ha! Make false alarms!"

"What's up with you son - you been moon struck?"

"Oh, I'm sorry, Father... no. I was just thinking of the only time our Peter ever stayed on watch. Remember when he woke everyone up that time - running about the deck at four o' clock in the morning like a madman, screaming, 'we're being attacked! We're being attacked!' Remember it?"

"Yes," I laughed, "and all because Thomas fell asleep. You see, David, if you haven't had the experience, then you could easily start seeing things when on watch alone. That's why I used to put two lads on watch when I was the captain."

"Oh, I see. I'm quite familiar with all the noises in the homes of my kin, but, on my return visits, new noises reveal themselves. And it's the same on board, Father. While on watch I hear unfamiliar noises, and start to imagine the most fearful things. Then, our William would say, 'oh, it's only the anchor rope being stretched taut'; or, 'oh, it's only a rat'; and then I'd be at ease."

"Exactly, son. It's not only experience that matters, but also the use made of it. If you didn't have someone with William's resolution and discernment, there might have been a false alarm. That's the main reason I made him captain." I filled my clay pipe with pungent shag tobacco, in readiness for a double watch. "Right, son, get yourself off to bed."

"Right-o, Father," David yawned as he stretched out his arms.

"Goodnight, Son."

"Good morning you mean, Father?" David grinned as he headed

exhaustedly to bed.

"Aye; good morning, Son."

I took a glowing ember from my tinderbox and pressed it carefully against my pipe bowl, and puffed until I drew smoke.

The bright moonlight cast my lone bearded profile onto the deck, as a plume of smoke billowed from my pipe. The air was cool and still; the ship creaked softly, quietly, rhythmically.

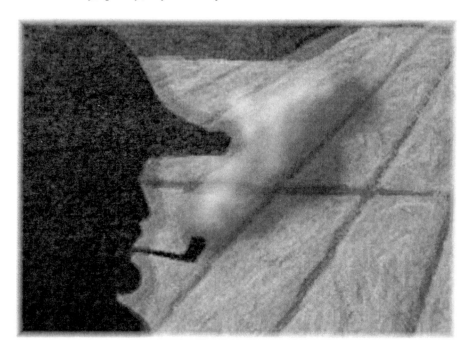

The air was quickly warmed as the moonlight changed to dawn sunlight, bringing solace to the downcast atmosphere. Before long, the natives began to stir upon the shore. A few of them placed fishing nets into their shallow boats and headed out to sea. They cast their nets way out on the horizon; their little bodies silhouetted by the sun. I watched for an hour or two, my eyelids growing tired. I took the cold pipe from my mouth and placed it gently on the deck. Sitting up, on the soft palliasse, I stretched out my arms, and yawned. My whole tired body shuddered violently as I did so.

"Good morning, Father," Andrew smiled, as he walked sprightly towards me carrying two teacups.

"Ah, Andrew, you've caught me having a sly yawn." My body gently relaxed.

"Here, Father, get that down you." He handed me a hot cup of tea. "David mentioned that you were on watch."

"Thanks Andrew. You're up early, aren't you?" I sipped my tea.

"Yeah, I just couldn't lie in bed any longer, father. I went to bed at about nine o' clock last night. It's only five o' clock now - why don't you go and have a few hours sleep?"

"I think I'll just do that. Oh, Andrew, I'm as stiff as a board." I held up my out-stretched arm. "Give me a hand up will you?"

"No problem, Father." Andrew firmly gripped my arm and gently pulled me to my feet.

"Oh, that's better." I took a few doddering steps. "I'm getting some feeling back in my legs. I'm off to bed; I'll see you in about two hours."

"Alright, Dad, see you then."

Two hours later, the whole ship was awake. It was another glorious day. I was freshened up and ready to face the world.

William was on deck to meet me. "How are you faring, son?"

"Great, Father! Everything's ship-shape, as usual! We're ready to leave, anytime you give the word."

"That's good, William; you're doing an excellent job."

Richard caught my attention and motioned far in land. "Dad, the Chief's coming."

The crew lined the side of the ship facing the shore.

"I'll go ashore to greet him. Tell your mother and Geordie to follow me."

David smiled, whimsically. "Father, I think you should wipe your neck first."

"What do you mean, son?"

"Your neck's covered in soapsuds, man. I think you're getting a bit sloppy in your old age." David shook his head.

I clapped my hand to my neck and met with a clammy mass of lather. I was discommoded by the confusion in my hand.

"Oh, dear; I'm going to change my shirt."

"I think you had better change your trousers as well, Father - you've been sleeping in them all morning," David, teased.

William nudged David. "Hey, Punchinello, leave Dad alone, will you?"

Sophia stepped on deck. "Good morning, John."

"Aye, good morning, pet. I'm just going to change out of these crumpled clothes."

"That's fine, dear. John, while you're below, could you possibly check that Geordie's washed behind his ears?" There was a roar of laughter from the crew, as they looked indifferently about the ship. "John, what's going on here... have I missed something?"

"Don't bother yourself with them, pet. They'll laugh at almost anything when they get together."

"Father, the chief's almost on the beach." Richard stressed as he wrung his hands.

"Alright, son, I'll only be a few minutes." I rushed below deck, checked on Geordie, and then quickly changed my attire.

My wife, Geordie and I, stepped off the ship just as the chief arrived.

"Good morning, Captain Rigger." Chief Bantu stood with outstretched arms. "We have come to bid you farewell." The whole tribe had come to see us off.

"Thank you, Chief Bantu, for your entertaining hospitality." We embraced.

All around us, the natives began to sing a beautifully sad, farewell song. The deep plaintive tones did nothing to alleviate the pain inside our hearts.

Geordie spoke sadly, with a tear in his eye. "Thank you for making us welcome. This portrait is for you, and this book of early reading lessons is to help you further your English."

"Thank you, Geordie; the portrait is a good likeness of you - I shall keep it always. And the English reading book I will enjoy very much. I will treasure them both until your return."

Sophia held out her hand. "Goodbye, Chief Bantu. Thank you for all the warmth and kindness you have shown us."

"It is my pleasure. May the wind speed you safely back to us."

Chief Bantu and the rest of the tribe lined the beach and watched as we set sail. Their beautiful melodious singing still echoed in our ears as we headed towards the horizon with a favourable wind in our sails.

CHAPTER V

THE JOURNEY TO INDIA

By late December, we reached and passed the Algoa Bay, the 'arm of the Indian Ocean'; then, on to Natal. On Christmas Day, we put to shore at the seaport of Kilimane, founded by the Portuguese in 1544; it has one of the world's largest coconut plantations.

We loaded up with fresh water, fruit, coconuts and vegetables. We stayed for the festivities, and set off on New Year's Day, eighteen hundred and seven. Early January, we reached Mozambique, another Portuguese colony - three hundred and fifty miles north of Kilimane. On February the fifteenth, we landed at Mombasa, eight hundred miles north of Mozambique, mentioned in John Milton's book *Paradise Lost* as existing as early as 4000 BC. We left there on the twentieth day of February. Then on April the twelfth, eighteen hundred and seven, we reached the hot, sunny port of Calicut, on the southwest coast of India, which basks in the idyllic setting of the serene Arabian Sea. It was a trader's paradise. The shore was crammed with noisy merchants plying their wares. As we docked among the many cargo ships, we were approached by a number of native boats.

"You buy? You buy?" They called up to us, holding high their merchandise.

An hour later, a dozen of us strolled about the shore, exploring the multitude of colourful market stalls. The air was filled with an inviting aroma of spices: clovers, nutmegs, ginger and pepper. Geordie was captivated as a snake charmer sat upon a bed of nails with a pipe in his mouth, which he used to tempt a cobra from its basket with a fetching tune.

"Granddad, is he really doing that?"

"Yes, sonna. The world's a curious place; India itself is an experience."

"Oh, dear! What's he doing?" Sophia placed her hand on her mouth in shock, as a native walked with unhurried dignity across a fifteen foot trench of burning coals - so hot that the men tending the fire had to douse themselves with water. The heat made it impossible for the crowd that was gathered to get any closer than about 30 feet, yet the man emerged from the fire unscathed.

"It's alright, dear - he's a holy man, known as a fakir. Walking on coals is his way of celebrating the feast of a Hindu deity."

"But John, it doesn't conform to normality."

"It doesn't conform to your idea of normality, pet. To him, a lady showing her face in public is outrageously abnormal. What's normal to one people, may not be to another. *Fakir* is the Persian word for Indian. Their religion, *Sanatana*, means *ageless and eternal*; for in their mythology, 4,320,000 solar years are equal to one cosmic cycle; and one thousand of these cycles is equal to one single day of *Brahma* - their god, and creator of everything. These holy people reach '*Brahma*' or essential self, by following ten or so *yoga* paths of self-discovery. The eighth stage, *Samadhi*, cannot be taught; it is instinctively revealed when it is reached. And, as you have seen, physical control and supernatural abilities are then achieved."

"Granddad, now I understand what Chief Bantu meant, when he said, 'when the unimaginable is imaginable, then you are truly wise.'"

I put my hand upon Geordie's shoulder in a kind fatherly way. "Geordie, sonna, you're a philosopher and a gentleman. If you keep on the way you're going, then one day you'll be immortal."

"Well, if I do become famous, I'll mostly have you and Grandmother to thank."

"Thank you, Geordie, my love; I agree with your grandfather, implicitly, you're patient, wise and stoical."

David, laughed, as he playfully ruffled Geordie's hair. "Yes, Mother, I agree with the word 'patient'. Anyone who can take a tortoise for a walk must be tolerant!"

We laughed, along with Geordie.

Just then, the fakir walked up to us. He stared deeply into Geordie's eyes, and then stood transfixed for a moment.

"You walk fire with me?" He held out his hand to Geordie.

"No!" Sophia held Geordie back, protectively.

"You come with me... you 'can' walk fire," recapitulated the fakir, enticingly.

"Yes, I can." Geordie was confident. "Granddad, I'd like to have a go."

I knew it could be done, but I was unsure of Geordie's willpower; I had seen people badly burned after losing confidence half way through a walk.

"Are you sure you want to do it, Geordie?"

"John, what are you trying to do?" Sophia challenged, just as the men tending the fire threw on a few handfuls of dried leaves, which instantly exploded into flame.

"Have faith, pet; Geordie knows what he's doing. If he wants to prove his ability of self-control, then this may be his only chance."

We stood and watched helplessly as Geordie was escorted towards the glowing coals. We willed him on, though inwardly our thoughts were consumed by doubt.

THE JOURNEY TO INDIA

"If you show your spiritual supremacy over the fire, it cannot harm you." Spoke the fakir, to Geordie, as they stepped barefoot onto the coals.

Sophia placed her hands over her eyes, as the coloured flames breathed around Geordie's feet. Nearer the centre of the trench, the flames began to dart about more intensely. Geordie looked as composed and content as a poker in the fire. A large crowd had gathered. A white firewalker was a rarity.

"White Siddhis!" They called. We later found this to mean 'white fakir'.

Geordie didn't flinch; his strength of mind unwavering. It seemed he was relishing in his newfound ability, unaware of our pending feelings. As they stepped, unblemished and unperturbed from the burning coals, we give out an unrestrained sigh of relief. We moved forward to meet Geordie, but were embraced by the awed crowd pressing to meet him. The fakir spoke a few commanding words in Indian, and the crowd parted down the middle, leaving a wide aisle. The fakir brought Geordie to us through this passageway.

"Well done, Geordie!" we chorused.

"Thank you. Uncle Dave, you're very strong, do you want to try walking the hot coals?"

"Ha! Geordie, I'd rather head-but a brick wall till it collapsed!"

"Follow me." The fakir kindly beckoned us.

We followed willingly, leaving the crowd behind us. A while later we reached a secluded, sunlit building, situated between a clove of palm trees.

"This is the dwelling-place of our guru."

Sophia calmly looked round. "It's very peaceful, here."

"It is a holy place, memsahib." He kissed an image outside the door, sounded a bell and then entered. A moment later, he reappeared at the door, shading his eyes from the sunlight with his arm. He bowed his head. "You are welcome. Come in, come in."

We thanked him and entered the large, cool, poorly-lit room. A mature smell pervaded our nostrils, not unlike that which is often found inside old pianos. The main wall adjacent to the louvre doors was lined with tall, wooden bookcases. Many worn volumes and scrolls occupied the shelves. The other two walls were furnished with richly patterned drapes - covered here and there with scenes from the Mahabharata. To our right - near a shuttered window, positioned upright and cross-legged upon a pile of cushions - sat the guru: a venerable looking man indeed.

"It is said that you walked the hot coals." He inquired of Geordie, as he slowly opened his eyes.

"Yes, I did," Geordie replied in an unassuming, matter-of-fact way.

"I would like to speak with you privately."

Geordie looked at me with questioning eyes. I nodded. The fakir walked over to the louvre doors and opened them, allowing brilliant sunlight to flood in. Geordie and the guru walked out of the doors onto a veranda and disappeared slightly out of view. While we waited, the fakir offered us tea to drink and a hookah to smoke. We declined the latter, as marijuana doesn't agree with us. An hour or so later, Geordie and the guru came in from the veranda.

The Guru spoke directly to Sophia and I. "If it is possible, I would like to speak with your grandson, every day."

"You are welcome to visit us on board our ship," said I.

The guru visited us every day. Geordie learned many things from him, including yoga.

One month later, we set sail. The people gave us a magnificent send-off.

THE JOURNEY TO INDIA

The guru had kindly presented us with a beautifully decorated box - about a foot square - filled with precious jewels and gems, and implored us to call again on our return journey.

A while later out at sea, Peter turned to me woefully. "Dad, you'll have to turn back... Sammy's gone!"

"Peter, we're three miles from land, man. You don't think we can just turn around and head for shore, just for a parrot, do you?"

Peter started to sob. "Mam, my parrot's gone. It'll be sickening for me. Tell my dad that I need my Sammy." Peter was now prostrate with grief. His face was wet and red with hot tears.

"John, please do something." Sophia pleaded with me as she stroked Peter's hair, trying to console him.

"But dear, we can't just sail back after an impressive send-off like that, and say 'has anyone seen a parrot that answers to the name Sammy?' It just isn't done. It would be insensitive; and anyway, it would make me feel quite self-conscious."

My voice must have carried, for just then, Peter stood up and ran towards the stern of the ship, shouting 'if no-one will help me find my Sammy, then I'll find him myself!' So saying, he pulled himself up onto the taffrail and leapt down into the sea. Sophia gave out a scream and then fainted.

"Man overboard! Lower the life-boat!" I shouted.

As quick as a wave, William slipped off his jacket and shoes and then dived into the water. As you know, William is the only one of my lads that can swim - and what a strong swimmer he is. He cut through the water as powerfully and fleeting as a ship's keel. Before the lifeboat reached the water, William had his arm around Peter's neck, bringing him back to us.

"That was a dangerous and stupid thing to do!" said I, to Peter, as he lay recovering upon the deck. "You've shaken your mother something terrible. If it hadn't been for William's quick actions, it's awful to think what might have happened." I couldn't help but hug him. "Oh, you silly thing."

"I'm sorry, Dad; but I miss Sammy." Peter smiled a pitiful, forlorn smile, as he looked up at me, his head upon my chest.

"We've dropped anchor. If Sammy doesn't come aboard in the next few hours, then we'll go ashore. Is that fair enough, son?"

"Yes, Dad!" His eyes brightened up. "That's fine!"

I scoured the horizon through my telescope; there was no sign of Sammy, just a glimmering outline of the coastline. Peter sat up and looked at me from the deck, optimistically. I shook my head. He lay back down, crestfallen.

The lads were busy cheering William, as I walked onto the quarterdeck.

"Well done son, we couldn't have done without you today, you know? You've proven yourself, immensely."

"And so say all of us!" the lads cheered proudly.

"By the way, William, your mother wants to thank you; she's down in the cabin, recuperating."

"Alright, Father, see you later."

"Aye, son - see you later." I made my way back to Peter.

"Hello, Granddad." Geordie was holding up Charlie for Peter to stroke. "Everything's going to be fine, now, Granddad. I remember Chief Bantu once told me that animals can talk to each other with their sixth sense. Uncle Peter and I have asked Charles Methuselah to call Sammy home."

"And you think it's going to work sonna?"

"Without a doubt." they replied.

Peter looked much healthier now. He sat laughing with Geordie, totally confident that Sammy would return.

"Is Sammy coming?" Peter asked Charlie. The tortoise lifted its head and widened its eyes.

"What's happening?"

"It's Charlie's way of letting us know Sammy's coming, Granddad."

"But how on earth do you know that, sonna?"

"I'm not sure Granddad - I just do. It's a bit like the feeling I get when my body tells me I'm thirsty; but this time it's telling me what Charlie feels."

"Absolutely amazing!" Just then, Sophia and William joined us.

"John, dear, is something puzzling you?"

I explained to her the reason for my bewilderment.

"I'm beginning to think anything is possible now dear." She replied, with a mystified countenance.

William was just as bemused. "Mother, the feeling's mutual."

Peter shouted the lads over and told them about Charlie.

"Ha! It's a load of old tripe!" said Thomas - doubting as ever. "Tortoises know nothing; and anyway, your stupid parrot's probably lying dead somewhere!"

David raised his index finger and gave Thomas a certain look. "Hey, our Tom, shut your mouth, or I'll shut it for you!" Thomas held his tongue.

"Hey, Tom, it might be true, as I had déjà vu, once." Richard spoke as if it meant everything, and seemed very pleased with himself.

Thomas looked at Richard and then mumbled to himself.

Just then, James shouted from up in the riggings. "There's a bird flying towards us!" Peter stood up and walked towards the stern. We all followed.

"Is it my Sammy?"

"I can't tell; it's too far away," replied James. Geordie was standing, looking overboard with Charlie in his arms.

"Look at Charlie!" called Sophia, in astonishment. Charlie had pushed his head out full stretch, and his little legs were thrashing about with excitement. He looked just like a wind-up mechanical toy.

"It's Sammy. I just know it is."

"You're right, Geordie, sonna." I held my lens steadily to my eye. "It is Sammy. Well who would believe it?" As Sammy came closer, we could make him out with our naked eyes.

"Come on Sammy. Come on my beauty!" cried Peter. A minute later, Sammy fell onto the deck, exhausted.

"Take him below, out of the heat," said Geordie; "he needs some cool water." Peter and Sophia took him below.

William shook his head. "What do you make of that, Father?"

"William, the world's a wonderful place that has many unexpected secrets to reveal. You learn something new, everyday."

William lifted his eyebrows. "I can't disagree with that, Father."

Just then, the doctor joined us.

"Good afternoon, gentlemen." He waved his arm like an artiste.

"Oh, drunk again, I see," William sniffed.

"I beg to differ." The doctor's glazed eyes struggled to focus through heavy eyelids. "I've only had a wee dram."

"A wee dram is it?" William sneered. "You've had drop enough to pop the pennies off a dead man's eyes. Your breath could liven a corpse!"

"Do you hold that against me, Sir?" Replied the doctor whimsically, as he stood holding his lapels, his eyebrows raised in question.

"A doctor needs sober fingers." William held out a steady hand in response. "And yours, Doctor, are quivering like topsails in a gale."

"Tell me, Doctor," I interjected, abruptly changing the subject. "What do you think of the sixth-sense?"

"It's a load of superstitious nonsense. Now if you'll excuse me, gentlemen, I have some unfinished business to attend to."

"Aye, a bottle of red rum, I bet," whispered William, as the doctor walked unsteadily away.

"William. I'd prefer it if you didn't talk so explicitly to the doctor."

"Dad, it makes no difference how I talk to him; it goes in one ear and out the other. The other day, I apologised to him because of my abruptness, and he told me that he couldn't ever remember me being uncivil to him."

"William, you might have mastered the sea, but I think it's about time you mastered this." I tapped William's forehead with the stem of my pipe. "It was his way of forgiving you, man."

William shook his head, gravely. "But, Father, man, he's a menace when he's had a drink... and that's almost every waking moment!"

"William, I know you're the captain, but that's no reason to act disrespectfully to Doctor Pearse. I know he drinks, but for the grace of God, it could have been you instead of him. You have to have sympathetic understanding. Learn to walk in his shoes, and see things through his eyes. Life can be so cruel - for some people it can be a living nightmare... especially for Doctor Pearse."

"Doctor Pearse? What do you mean, Father, Doctor Pearse?"

"Well, son, Doctor Pearse - who, I have recently learned, is the eminent author of *'The Heart and its Whereabouts'* - began to drink heavily seven years ago. He told me, that just before that time he had a thriving medical practice, a beautiful wife and three adorable children. They owned and lived in a prosperous house-cum-surgery in Saville Row, Newcastle."

"What ended this blissful existence, Father?" William furrowed his brows pensively.

"He told me that late one dry, thundery night, a man rapped heavily at the surgery door, urgently seeking him. A Magistrate had been run over by a runaway carriage. In his haste, the doctor unknowingly knocked over one of the lighted candles in his study as he left the house, while his wife and children slumbered upstairs in their beds. On his return home, he met with a raging, uncontrollable inferno. By the time the fire fighters had arrived, the house was razed to the ground along with his ill-fated wife and children. Ironically, two-minutes later, the thunderclouds burst and the heavens poured. The embers sizzled and were quickly extinguished. Doctor Pearse, said, 'A more sombre sight could not have been imaginable. I was stricken with grief; my heart broke that night, my hopes all gone. My whole life went up in smoke before my very eyes. I died, but my body just didn't know it yet'. When he was informed of the fire's place of origin, he almost went mad with self-condemnation."

"Hey, Father, I never could have guessed. You know, I'm a colossal insensitive fool."

"I wouldn't say that, son, but you could champion the losing side, now and again; stand up for the underdog."

"Ich dien, from now on, Father... Ich dien."

"Life's an experience, son." I patted his arm, comfortingly. "When you've lived your life, you might have some."

"I agree Father." William smiled, his feelings now lighter.

"Come on, son; let's see what the lads are doing."

The lads were standing around a barrel, which was filled with chilli powder.

"Go on, Davy," cheered the lads, "put it in your mouth, man." David held quarter of a teaspoon of chilli powder hesitatingly near his mouth.

"Here goes." He popped it in. He was calm for a second, and then the heat hit him. He tried to look relaxed as tears rolled down his tense, reddened cheeks. "Right, lads... who's next?" he said, bravely through a braced mouth, his body stiffening in sympathy. The lads looked at each other for a volunteer.

"Hello lads; Sammy's feeling much better now." Peter smiled as he approached us with Sammy in his arms. David then left us.

Thomas was acting mischievously; which was odd, as it didn't agree with his usual nervous, caring, sober values. "Peter, come here; see if you can eat some of this lovely, red chilli powder... it's a little bit hot, mind," he said, with a furtive grin.

"I wouldn't if I were you, son, it'll burn your ruddy mouth off!"

"It'll not be too hot for me." Peter boasted. He gently lifted his arm and Sammy took to the air. "Go on, Sammy, stretch your wings."

"Come on then, Peter." Thomas pointed into the barrel. "Are you going to have some of this, or what?"

"Why-aye, man, 'course I am." Peter scooped chilli powder from the barrel with both hands.

The lads gathered around excitedly, like bloodhounds at the kill. They incited Peter "Go on then Peter, eat it." Peter put his laden hands to his mouth.

"Don't do it, Peter, son - you'll be sorry," I cautioned. My words were unheeded. Peter almost devoured the lot. At first, he coughed and spluttered, intermittently, because of the dry powder. Then, he thought that it wasn't really that hot after all, so he smiled and looked around triumphantly. But, then, the reality hit him! His mouth was on fire and it wouldn't go away! His face distorted and his eyes bulged out with shock, as tears burned contours into the chilli powder on his face. How could anything be so painfully hot?

David re-joined us. "What's going on here?"

"Our Peter's just tried to eat two handfuls of chilli powder!" Thomas laughed out loud. "Look at his face, man!"

Peter's face turned as red as beetroot. He gasped for air. "I need a drink of water." He mouthed in distress.

David shook his head. "No! It only makes it worse!"

"How do you know that?" Thomas questioned. The lads looked at David, curiously. He looked down, shame-faced; his hard man image slightly tarnished. Just then, the doctor appeared. William gained his attention.

"Doctor, we need your help."

The doctor weighed up the situation. "There's nothing I can do apart from advise him to eat plenty fresh tomatoes."

"What will that do, Doctor?" William asked. "Cool his mouth down?"

"Yes; it's the best thing."

David dashed to the galley for some tomatoes. In the meantime, Thomas offered Peter a drink of fresh water, which he willingly accepted. As he drank, the heat from the fiery chilli intensified ten-fold. It seemed as if his head was about to explode. He screamed out and ran frantically around the deck, his eyes pleading for help. Then, the pain became so severe that he fell to the deck unable to scream. He seemed to have become traumatised - beyond pain. David rushed back with a bowlful of sliced tomatoes, with which he began to fill Peter's mouth. Surprisingly, he didn't choke. The remedy began to take immediate effect. Peter sighed with relief.

"Thank you, Doctor." William nodded. "Is he going to be alright?" The doctor nodded back his agreement.

A few days later, the swelling had completely disappeared, leaving nothing but a memory. A month later, with the chilli hot episode behind us, we headed to the East, briefly calling via the headland of India into the British colony of Ceylon: the Island of tea and once home of Solomon. We passed through the pigmy-inhabited Andaman Islands on our route to British ruled Malaysia.

Then, we did as all ships do that pass between the Indian Ocean, and the South China Sea: we sailed through the pirated straits of Malacca - a major port along the Spice Route - and landed at the Dutch trading port there. Its harbour bustled with the sails and masts of Chinese junks and spice-laden vessels from all over the globe. Chinese merchants advertised their wares from their homes with bright red characters - each home being no more than twelve feet wide, as the Portuguese taxed any buildings over that size. Open-air markets sold fruit, vegetables and fish. It seemed as if time had stood still. I cannot imagine it to have changed much since the Portuguese first landed there. We stayed three days, and then set sail for the South China Sea.

CHAPTER VI

THE JOURNEY TO CHINA

We rounded the coast of Vietnam, passing Saigon and Tourane, before heading northwards to the Chinese Island of Hainan. The whole journey from Calicut, India, to Hainan, China - including ports of call - had taken us seventeen weeks. As we moored at the small, quiet, relaxed fishing village of Haikou - an island dominated by staggering mountains, which shelter the wide valleys below - Sophia and Geordie were immediately attracted to the mystery of the place.

"John, I must be dreaming." The freshness, freedom and farness of the place impressed Sophia. "The beauty and stillness fills me with a great wonder and peace."

"I suppose that explains how the natives are so simple and cultivated," said I.

Geordie watched a few working natives, dotted among the beautiful, green, stepped plateaux.

"Granddad, I love this island - it seems older than history."

"I'm sorry, Geordie," I laughed; "but you can't take it home with you."

Eight of us readied ourselves for shore. We alighted from the ship as the setting sun radiated a brilliant crimson and gold. The mountains were magnificently silhouetted as the sun dipped warmly behind them; the shadows lengthening fast across the lush wide plateaux.

"What a beautiful sight," said Henry, as he stood at his easel with pencil in hand, sketching the scene as it was. When the paint was applied, Richard turned to me meekly.

"God is the true artist;' we mere mortals can't emulate the flowers, the sunset and the trees."

"I don't wish to blaspheme, son, but Henry's come a close second."

Just then, an old Chinaman, in a long silk robe, came shuffling towards us in the twilight.

"How you do, Captain Rigger?" He bowed his head in greeting. "I never forget man of honour."

"Thank you, Chief Haikou," I returned the bow, "but it is I that is honoured to be in your noble presence."

"I notice three delightful new faces." The Chief looked for introduction.

"This is my wife, Sophia." The Chief moved towards her.

"Your husband speak highly of you."

"He also speaks highly of you." Sophia acknowledged with a gentle bow.

"This smart lad, here, is my grandson, Geordie."

"He has a knowing look." The Chief looked soothingly into Geordie's eyes.

"Yes, many have remarked."

I moved towards Henry and announced him, cordially. "Henry, here, is a good friend of the family. He is a botanist, and has come along strictly for pleasure - as a guest - to paint and explore the scenery."

The Chief acknowledged Henry with a gentle nod. "There are many people here who have the same interests; you should meet them; but in the interim, you must all come along to my home and indulge in the nutritious delights of the East.

"Thank you very much, Chief Haikou; we'd be honoured."

"Granddad," Geordie whispered as we walked the long path to the village, "do you know how old the Chief is? He seems as old as Methuselah."

"Yes, Geordie, I do - he's one hundred and eighteen years of age."

Sophia was amazed. "He must be the oldest man in the village. I'm surprised he hasn't a haggard old face."

"Maybe he hasn't a haggard old face, because he hasn't haggard old thoughts." I whispered.

The Chief's home was a wide, wooden, bright and airy bungalow, with many sliding doors. We were met in the perfumed garden by his pretty great-great-granddaughter, Hai-linn, who was aged about thirty six. She had sandalled feet, and was wearing a matching blue silk jacket and trousers. Her wide, cream coloured, conical hat rested lightly on her back, and her black hair was neatly tied back, making contrast with her wan face.

"Good evening, Captain Rigger." She beckoned us with a wave. "You may come in and make yourselves at home."

"Thank you very much, Hai-linn." We entered. Inside the main room, there was a low table, surrounded by intricately embroidered cushions, onto which we were ushered. Four of the Chief's great-great-grandsons entered the room, carrying steaming dishes of noodles, rice and food fish. A second course followed, which turned out to be just as delicious as the first.

"You have an extensive family." I nodded to the Chief.

"The families of this village are all related to me."

"Are you really one hundred and eighteen?" Geordie gasped.

"Eeh, Geordie!" Sophia tried to suppress her embarrassment. "Please don't be so forthright."

"It is perfectly alright. He is my guest, and is welcome to ask me whatsoever he wishes. You are hugely charismatic for such a young boy."

"Thank you, but I think charisma is inherent in all people, and is only aroused by divine influence and a healthy mind."

"Well put, Geordie, sonna."

"Your grandson is as wise as he looks."

"He's had the best education money can buy in Newcastle. We're so proud of him."

"That is a wise choice. In yoga, one finds piece of mind and divine influence."

"I have been practising hatha yoga for some time now, Chief."

"Then, you will have to join us in our daily exercises, Geordie - beginning tomorrow morning at sunrise."

"I'd be delighted, Chief."

Two hours later, our appetites fully sated and the evening over, we thanked Chief Haikou and his family for their gracious hospitality.

As we stood in the moonlit garden, saying our farewells, I spoke to the Chief. "You and your family are welcome to join us on board ship tomorrow afternoon, where we will show you our warm gratitude for the benevolence you have shown to us tonight."

"Thank you, Captain Rigger. We will be honoured."

"I must say, Chief, even at night your garden conveys an aesthetic beauty."

"I am an avid collector of beauty. I planted the garden to yogic, esoteric specifications - similar to the garden at the nearby Wugong Temple, reputed to be the 'first building under the heavens'. I believe one's feelings are empathetically endemic of his surroundings."

"Ah, symmetry of the mind, lovingly broadcast," I added with feeling.

"That is so." The Chief caressed a bloom. "I appreciate the beauty of a rose more now because there is no reason for it to be so beautiful... it just is."

We thanked Chief Haikou and his family once again for the warm reception they had shown us, and then bade them good night.

"I will see you at sunrise, Chief," said Geordie, happily, as he held Sophia's hand. "Good night."

"Good night, Geordie. I look forward to your next visit."

The pathway was brightly moonlit as we made our way back to the ship. A warm zephyr sang comfortingly through the trees, as a night bird chirruped softly in the distance. Ten minutes later, we reached the ship.

"You're back early." Andrew greeted us as we climbed aboard.

"It's *early to bed, early to rise,*' around here, son. Has everything been quiet in our absence?"

"Aye, Father - nothing to report."

Sophia tiredly stroked Geordie's hair. "Come on Geordie, it's time for bed."

"Yes, Grandma', I have to be up at daybreak." Geordie stifled a yawn.

The next morning, at sunrise, David and Andrew escorted Geordie to the village.

Meanwhile, back on board, Henry turned to Thomas, and then looked up to the heavens. "Ooh. . . what a lovely morning! Thomas, can you see that solitary white cloud? If you use your imagination, you can create images. To me, that cloud looks like a graceful bird."

Thomas tilted his head back and squinted his eyes. "Yes, I can see what you mean - it does look like a bird... a storm-petrel."

"A storm-petrel?" said William, from nearby; "how can it look like a storm-petrel on such a cheerfully, optimistic day as this?"

"William, you know I live on the defensive, and see life through sombre eyes - that way I'm always prepared for the worst."

"But that way you become depressingly predictable, man."

"It has its advantages William." Thomas sounded almost optimistic. "Most times, things don't turn out as bad as I think, and that cheers me up."

"You have a strange way of thinking, our Tom," William laughed. "You must have been born with three parents, because you don't take after either Mam or Dad."

"Morning, lads! Anyone for a stroll and some fresh air?" I interrupted.

"Eh... yeah, why not?" said Henry and Thomas, and off we went.

As we trekked along the footpath, I noticed that Henry was holding his side, as if in agony.

"Henry, are you feeling alright? You look quite ill."

"I woke up this morning, with a dreadful sharp pain in my lower right abdomen," said he, with a hand on his brow. "And now, I can feel the blood pounding heavily in my head; I think I'm going to vomit." Henry's breathing became unnaturally quick.

Thomas was concerned. "Would you like to go back to the ship, Henry?"

"No, thank you, the fresh air might do me good."

Just then, we met with the doctor, who was heavily inebriated, so we persuaded him to come along with us to the village.

"Thomas, son, carry the doctor's medical bag." Thomas picked up the doctor's bag and off we went.

A minute later, Henry cried out and fell to the earth, clutching his stomach in agony. I took off my coat and placed it gently beneath his head.

"Henry, are you alright?" I anxiously felt his hot forehead.

"I need a doctor," he pleaded - his face covered with perspiration. Henry's only hope of deliverance from agony sat drunkenly beside us, having just slid down a tree. I shook the doctor, trying to sober him up, but my efforts seemed futile.

Thomas looked at me with hope in his eyes. "Father, the only way to liven up the doctor, is to give him another drink. He usually keeps a bottle or two inside his jacket pockets."

"Well, it's worth a try, son." I looked at Henry's pained face, and then placed my hand beneath the doctor's coat and pulled out a bottle of rum.

"I need a doctor," Henry cried urgently, as Thomas comforted him.

"Here Doctor, drink this!" I placed the bottle to his lips. The doctor drank instinctively. It wasn't long before he was sitting up, talking to me semi-coherently.

"Thank you, Captain, I needed that."

"Doctor, we need your help, urgently. Henry's in agony."

The doctor made a quick examination, then, turned to me sombrely. "It's serious, Captain... he's going to die."

"Is there anything you can do to save him?"

"Captain, I have learned much from the mortuary and the battlefield."

"Yes, I hear the corpses speak volumes there; but how can that save Henry?"

"He has inflammation of the worm-like structure, which lies at the junction of the small and large bowels, which ultimately ends in death. I know from experience, gained as Ship's Surgeon, at the battle of Copenhagen, that this worm-like structure is not essential to healthy life, and I have thought of a revolutionary way to remove it."

I turned to Henry, who was vomiting violently, then back to the doctor, who had sobered considerably.

"Doctor, if there's any chance of saving Henry, please try."

The doctor picked up his leather medical bag and took out some fearful looking instruments. In the meantime, I plied Henry with drink.

The doctor put a piece of wood in Henry's mouth and ordered us to hold him down. He lost no time in getting to work. He picked up a scalpel and made a large incision in Henry's lower abdomen. Henry cried out some inarticulate words; it was a very distressing moment.

"Now, if I make my way through the subcutaneous layers, like this, I can then reach the inflamed organ."

"I'd appreciate it Doctor, if you wouldn't be so descriptive."

"Oh, I'm sorry Captain... it's just that it helps me concentrate."

"In that case, carry on."

I was appalled by the amount of blood. My blood pounded and my ears hummed as the doctor talked us through the gruelling operation.

"That's the inflamed part removed." He threw a blood-covered object to the earth, then, proceeded to thread a peculiar curved needle, of his own design. "Now to sew him up and hope for the best."

Thomas lowered his head and sighed. "He was a good mate." Thomas exasperated me. "Give the lad a chance to fight, man." I turned my attention back to the doctor, as he continued with Henry's stitches. "Do you think he has much chance of surviving, Doctor?"

"As I say, Captain, it's a novel operation, and my experience tells me that he has a good chance. He needs plenty of rest."

We made a makeshift stretcher and carried Henry towards the village. As we approached the Chief's bungalow, he and Geordie were sitting on cane chairs in the garden, discussing the morning's yoga session, as David and Andrew chatted to Hai-linn and her brothers nearby.

"David! Andrew! Here, quick!"

"What's happened Father?" They ran towards us.

"I'll tell you later; get hold of the stretcher."

We took Henry into the garden. Chief Haikou and Geordie met us at the door. The Chief took one look at Henry and ordered us to bring him inside.

We did so, and laid Henry on a low bed near a wall. We explained in detail the awful malady Henry had experienced.

"Please make room." The Chief took control.

We all stood around him, attentively, as he knelt down beside Henry, and placed his hands two inches from the painful wound. Henry cried out in agony.

"It will feel hot for a while, but you will recover."

Henry opened his eyes and sat up.

"What happened? What am I doing here?" He seemed quite groggy.

The doctor spoke sternly" Henry, you need plenty rest! You are confined to bed until further notice!"

"But, why? I feel fine, except for a little light-headedness."

"You've just undergone a life-saving operation. Lie still, or you might open your stomach wound."

"I haven't any stomach wound Doctor!" Henry laughed with conviction.

"That can't be so. I'm a doctor, and it is my opinion that you have the fever."

"But there isn't any wound! Pray look!"

The doctor pulled back Henry's clothing. "It's incredible!" he added - transfixed by what he saw. "I've never seen anything like it in all my years in medicine; the wound has completely disappeared!"

Thomas and I stood bewildered.

Thomas pointed to Henry's unmarked skin. "It's beyond belief! You had an operation scar just there!"

"I will explain," said Chief Haikou. "Many people cannot walk fire, see the future, or heal people, because they have not reached their spiritual potential. People are not surprised when their fingernails, or even the arms of starfish grow back; and it is of no surprise to see a wound gradually heal; but to see it heal instantly, alarms them; and that is so in this instance.

The doctor raised his eyebrows. "Do you mean you healed him with your hands... without instruments... without medication?"

"Yes, I healed him with psychic energy from my hands."

"I'm seeing it, but I don't believe it." The doctor had to sit down.

"You have a problem I can help you with." The Chief looked knowingly at the doctor.

"My problem is beyond anyone's help. How do you mend a broken heart?"

"If you would but let me try."

"Go on, Doctor, you have nothing to lose," said Henry, with confidence; "look at me."

We all backed Henry's request, encouragingly.

"Well, I suppose it will be an experience."

"That's the spirit," said Henry.

"Are you sitting comfortably Doctor?"

"Yes, Chief."

The Chief began by placing his hands above the doctor's head, whilst asking pleasant questions.

"What do you feel?"

"I can feel an intense heat in my head, and I have a beautiful calm feeling throughout my mind and body."

"That is good. Can you see any colours?"

"Yes, I see many colours, but predominantly white."

"That is very good. You are very good subject to work with."

An half-hour later, the Chief had finished his healing.

"How do you feel?"

"I can't ever remember feeling so calm and relaxed. I'm so happy; thank you Chief, from the bottom of my heart."

"My gift is from God; thank him."

A remarkable change came over the doctor - he beamed with well-being.

"I'll never touch another drop of alcohol." He spoke with clear sincerity.

An hour later, the excitement had diminished.

"Excuse me, Doctor. It seems a good time to ask; I wonder did you see Lord Nelson when you were at Copenhagen?"

"Yes, Captain; I was there when he famously, and deliberately put his telescope to his impaired right eye, making it impossible for him to see Sir Hyde Parker's signal for withdrawal.

"This is surely an historic day for us."

"Granddad, Chief Haikou told me I have the makings of a great healer."

"Geordie, sonna, that doesn't surprise me one bit."

"Refreshments?" Hai-linn walked towards us with a tray of tea.

"Yes please - I've forgotten what it tastes like." The doctor chuckled, and we all laughed along with him.

"Chief Haikou, I thought I had seen the wonders of the world, yet you

have shown me a miracle more wondrous than I could ever have imagined. To me, you are a disciple of Christ; a living testament to the works of God; thank you."

"I am an old vessel, Captain, topped up with the love of God. My hands exude a loving, regenerative force."

"You are an extraordinary man. I am sorry to seem impolite, but we shall have to leave you now; time has passed quickly, and my wife will be expecting us."

"I will see you this even time. Take care."

We said our goodbyes, and headed cheerfully along the path to the ship. A more agreeable walk I cannot recall.

Back on board, the air was filled with excitement as Henry and the doctor told of our incredible adventure.

"It's true, man," Thomas insisted to William.

"Thomas son, now *you* know what it's like to be doubted.

Peter pointed his thin finger sarcastically. "Aye, now you know!"

The Chief and his family came to visit us that evening; we had a wonderful time. The next day, as usual, Geordie went to visit the Chief.

"Chief Haikou, I have learned many things from you, but sadly, tomorrow, we must set sail."

"Geordie, when you are lonesome and afraid, your pleasant memories will be a great source of comfort to you. So gather as many affectionate feelings as imaginable."

"So the feeling of solitude is only a negative frame of mind?"

"That is so," replied the Chief.

The next day, we said our farewells, and reluctantly set sail.

"Oh, Geordie, sonna, I'm going to miss this place. Geordie, are you alright?"

"Yes, Granddad." Geordie looked sadly towards the shore, his face set like granite.

"You don't seem to be affected by our departure, sonna."

"Granddad, I'm trying to think positively about it." A tear trickled down his face.

"Ah, come here, sonna - give me a big cuddle." With a smile, I tenderly wrapped Geordie in my arms. "Go on, have a good cry - you can be positive some other day."

Geordie gave up the fight, and succumbed to his true emotions, letting his feelings flow.

CHAPTER VII

THE RESCUE – WILLIAM RIGGER DISPLAYS HIS COURAGE.

After four months travelling south-east through the South China Sea, we decided we would call into one of the small Philippine islands in the Sulu Sea. An hour before we arrived, William took two maps from his cabin draw, and pressed them straight with his hands upon the table. He placed his finger on the chart.

"There, Father, I suggest we stop at that island."

"Yes, I agree, William; it's an excellent choice for supplies."

A moment later, there was a tremendous thunderous explosion, followed by a scream.

"Father!" shouted David, from above. "It's pirates! They're attacking an English merchant ship."

William and I rushed above deck and quickly scanned the situation. The merchant ship was listing badly, about a mile from us, closely followed by the pirate ship. William put down his telescope.

"All hands on deck," he ordered. "Helmsman, turn the ship north-west - we're going in."

Geordie watched with interest. Sophia and Peter stood together, anxiously holding each other, as the crew ran about, feverishly securing the ship.

"James, take them below, son." Just before they stepped below deck, Sophia turned and impressed me deeply with an affectionate, lingering gaze.

William planned to distract the pirates' attention, by luring them away from the badly damaged cargo ship. As we neared them, a few warning volleys came menacingly close to starboard.

"William, son, they're trying to intimidate us. Our light swivel guns are no match for them.

"Andrew, son, put this keg of powder with the others safely below the waterline." He took it from me, and headed quickly below deck.

"Father, look!" William was excited. "They're biting!" The Pirates had changed course and were slowly heading our way.

"William, we have the advantage; we can easily outdo that great lumbering ship."

"Father, man, we can sail rings around it." Just then, an overwhelming barrage of cannon fire, ripped through our sails. "Helmsman, turn to larboard!" shouted William, above the roar of cannon fire. We moved quickly out of firing range. "Father, that shook me up!" laughed William, holding out a trembling hand.

"I must admit, son, you were a little cocksure there. You've a head on your shoulders - keep it there."

"Don't worry, Father, I've learnt my lesson; I'll not do that again in a hurry."

"The sails are a mess, but we'll still outdo them."

"Hey, Father, I wonder if our Robert saw this coming?" William looked up to the riggings with a grin. "Why else would he have given us so much canvas?"

"You silly sot." I laughed feebly. "The shock must have turned your brain."

By now, we were about two miles from the cargo ship, with the pirates close behind us. William walked up to the helmsman and spoke to him. "When I give this signal... " He lowered his arm. "... I want you to head back towards the cargo-ship as quickly as possible - keeping well clear of the pirate ship."

"I think our slow speed's fooled them, William."

"Yeah, Father, I think it's about time we showed them what we can really do; Helmsman, starboard." We turned slowly starboard in a wide arc, keeping up the slow pretence. We could see that the cumbersome pirate ship was now locked in a slow wide arc behind us. Now was time to act. "Helmsman, now!" William lowered his arm.

The ship made a sharp turn, putting us on a straight course for the cargo ship. The riggers were busy at work, charming every breath of wind into the sails. We quickly picked up speed, leaving the pirates some distance behind us.

"They might be slow, son, but they're still a threat. We've yet to rescue the crew from the battered cargo ship."

As we reached it, it was listing alarmingly to the larboard side. The captain, leaned over the port side, and spoke to us.

"Ahoy there, I'm Captain John Arkwright, master of what you see left of *The Golden Explorer*: a battered wreck, dangerously close to sinking. I wonder - do you have room aboard for twelve healthy people?"

"Of course, Captain - come aboard; but you had better hurry, for as you see, the pirate ship is close on our keels."

We put a few boards across the bulwarks to assist the doleful dozen in their flight from plight. Then, everyone safely on board, we pulled back the planks.

"Welcome aboard *The Turtle* Captain; I gave him my hand; I'm Captain Rigger." I reverted to the title captain to save confusion.

"Father, we'll have to go," William urged.

We set off with the pirate ship in close pursuit. Five minutes later, we watched, horrified, as *The Golden Explorer*, rolled over and sank beneath the deep - many a sailor's nightmare.

"You must have had quite a cargo, Arkwright?"

"We had the richest cargo you could ever have wished for - gold. The pirates don't realise it, but they are chasing a *red herring*."

"What do you mean?"

"You see, the ship went down minus its cargo, and the pirates most likely think that we have rescued it from my ship."

"Oh, I see." I glanced passed the stern at the ensuing ship. "But what became of the cargo?"

"Well, we started out from Portsmouth, England, with a cargo of gold bullion. Our object was to travel to Siam, and exchange our gold for sapphires, rubies and precious stones."

"What frustrated you in your venture?"

"When sailing through the Straits of Malacca, we decided to call into one of the many ports there, as the crew were becoming restless. They were a motley bunch of ruffians, who looked as though they could handle the job. I enlisted them at Portsmouth, and would rather my hand had withered than sign my name to such a revolting party. I had taken eight passengers on board, bound for Australia: four married couples in their late forties. Apart from my two officers and the cook, that was the whole crew. From the onset, the crew began to harry the passengers, especially the women. I had no charge over my own ship. By the time we had reached port, the passengers were in fear of their lives."

"What did you do then, Captain?"

"I tried to pacify the crew with rum, but that only made them worse. The ringleader - known as 'Brand', because he has an awful habit of branding his initials onto people with a hot blade - is a brute of a man, who is best kept clear of. One day, he interfered with one of the ladies, having knocked her gentleman husband to the deck, unconscious. I was fraught with peril and outrage. I could not tolerate any more. I had taken to the habit of carrying a concealed flintlock about my person, and the thought of using it lay heavily on my mind. The lady screamed out as Brand tore her dress. I walked up to him, cautiously, then quickly pulled out the handgun, cocked it, and placed it to his head. 'What's this?' said he, grinning feebly. 'Come on Captain, I'm only having a bit of a frolic'. He looked at his men for support, his eyes wide and fearful. 'I don't take kindly to anyone who maltreats my

Passengers,' said I, gravely. 'Now, move along, and get about your business'. As the mob disbanded, they looked back menacingly. An ominous feeling loomed over me; our fate was sealed. When we landed, the passengers stayed on board with the cook and the second mate. We were desperate for provisions. So the first mate and I followed the crew ashore. They had disappeared in search of drink. An hour later, we tried to find them, in order to help us carry the provisions, but to no avail. My only recourse was to hire a few locals to help us with the menial work. We carried the supplies back to a quiet and eerie ship. Our welcome was lonely and still. We rushed below deck to check the cargo. The hold was open; the locks and bars had been wrenched from the door. My heart sank as I looked around an empty room; the gold was gone! We found the passengers hiding in my cabin room, with my huge oak desk barring the door. After letting us in, they told us that twenty minutes after we had gone ashore, Brand's villainous crew came slinking back, showing murderous looking weapons and intentions - so they immediately hid away from them. Brand and his band of ruffians found them locked away in my cabin, and yelled menacingly through the door to them that they had taken the gold, and would be back after a few drinks to take the women. I was fearful, as it was now likely that the depraved crew would be back soon, as they knew we couldn't move without them; so it was a case of hell or Australia. I hired a few trustworthy looking men to help us set sail, paying them handsomely to work swiftly. Two hours later, we thanked them, said our farewells and then headed out of port. While on shore, Brand and his mates must have drunkenly discussed the wealth of our cargo within earshot of local buccaneers. For, as we left the harbour, we were slowly followed by a suspicious looking craft - the same craft which dogs us now."

"I see. And what happened next?"

Captain Arkwright sighed pitiably. "Well, they chased us relentlessly through the South China Sea. If I had a crew, we could have easily out-sailed them. But as it was, we barely kept ahead of them. My insufficient company couldn't keep up with my demands. It was then, as we sailed - tired and weak - into the Sulu Sea that they gained on us. They fired a salvo into our starboard side, which immobilised us - allowing water to sluice in alarmingly through the wide open breach. Just as they closed in for the 'coup de grâce', you distracted them - as you know, Captain - luring them away from us and preventing a catastrophe. And now, thanks to you, Captain Rigger, we are survivors aboard your ship. How can we ever repay you?"

THE RESCUE – WILLIAM RIGGER DISPLAYS HIS COURAGE.

"I'm sure you would have aided us if we were in the same position." I assured him. "Besides, we're still in the thick of it; we're not off the hook yet."

William sent Thomas below deck to fetch the sea charts from his desk. He intended to plot a new course for Australia. Two minutes later, Thomas came running on deck.

"Father! William! The rats have eaten Australia!" He wildly and frantically waved a few gnawed fragments about.

I took the fragments from him and placed them on the deck, trying to make sense of the unintelligible jigsaw.

"It's useless." I brushed away the crumbling fragments with my hand. "The rats have taken half the world away with them, and left the rest in tatters."

Captain Arkwright looked at me apologetically. "I wish I could help you in some way. But apart from a small dog, and our present attire, the maps, provisions and everything else on board, went down with the ship to Davy's graveyard."

"Please don't feel so responsible, Captain; our fate is in God's hands, not yours."

I excused myself, and went below to check on Peter, Geordie and Sophia. As I entered the cabin door, they turned to me attentively.

Sophia was visibly shaken. "Oh, John, is everything alright?"

"My Sammy's frightened," interjected Peter, as he held the parrot to his breast; "but Geordie's Charlie's not."

Peter's undertones became evident, as I looked at Geordie, who was sitting calmly with Charlie on his knee.

"There's no need to worry now." I calmly patted Peter's shoulder. "The pirates are far behind us; there's no chance of them advancing on us now; we're too fleet for them. You can all come up on deck any time you like." I walked over to Sophia, and hugged her.

"John, I'd like to stay below until it's all over."

"Of course, pet, I understand."

"Granddad, is the other cargo ship alright?"

"Oh, I nearly forgot to tell you -" I pointed upwards with my index finger. "- we have twelve extra passengers on board... the cargo ship sank."

"Oh dear;" Sophia held her hand to her chest; "what happened to the rest of the crew?"

"They all mutinied while ashore."

"Granddad, did any of the passengers bring pets on board?"

"Yes, Geordie;" I placed my hand on his shoulder; "one of the ladies has brought a small dog on board."

"Ladies?" Sophia leaned forward in joyful surprise.

"Yes, pet - we rescued the captain, his two officers, the cook, four ladies, four gentlemen... and the dog; you'll meet them soon enough. I'm afraid I'll have to leave you for now, my dears, and get back to my duties." I left them in a lighter atmosphere, as I headed up on deck.

I walked over to William. "Father, the sea wolves are still hounding us."

I raised my eyebrows. "Aye - as long as they don't bait us to the end of the world!"

"Captain Arkwright - you, your passengers and crew, may go below with James, who will show you to your cabins, where you may see to your toilette."

"Thank you very much." He smiled self-consciously. "It will be gratefully accepted - that is, if it won't be an inconvenience to you and your crew."

"It's perfectly alright, Captain - it's not the first time my lads have bunked up together."

"Well, if you insist Captain Rigger, then in the circumstances we'll be delighted to take up your offer."

"And, if your cook would care to join ours, later, in the galley, then we'll eat dinner all the sooner." Arkwright's cook nodded his approval.

As Captain Arkwright went below with his company, my sympathy went with him. He looked a broken man - nothing like the man he once must have been. The thought of the gold must have been a great incentive to the pirates, for they chased us for another incredible nine weeks, back and forth, through the Philippine Islands, and then out into the vast Pacific Ocean.

One night, a week later, I was awoken from my bed at the hour of three, by a thrust of knocks on my cabin door. "Come in!"

The door opened and a light broke through, filling the room. Andrew stood silhouetted in the doorway, his hand partially over the lamp, protecting my eyes from the glare.

"Father, the ship's at a standstill... we've hit a lull."

"I'll be with you in a moment, son." I put my legs over the side of the bed. "Just give me a minute to get my trousers on."

"Aye, Father." Andrew closed the door softly, and hurried up on deck.

While I was the captain, I always slept fully clothed - it's a custom difficult to ignore. It seems ironic, that tonight of all nights, I slept without my trousers. I dressed in an instant in the dark, kissed my sleeping wife upon her cheek and quickly followed Andrew above.

THE RESCUE – WILLIAM RIGGER DISPLAYS HIS COURAGE.

On deck, the ship was in semi-darkness; our lamps had all been screened. The moonless night was warm and dark, and the sails sagged heavily from the masts.

"Ah! There you are, Father!" Andrew turned and looked out to sea. "The pirate ship is calmed over there, about two miles to the west." His eyes showed the way. "It's barely visible."

"So, it's a case of stalemate, son?"

Thomas looked overboard despairingly. "Father, the wind's never going to come - we're going to die here."

David put the fingernails of his left hand between his teeth, feigning nervousness, then, put his right hand on his cheek, sarcastically mocking Thomas. "Eeh, what are we going to do? We'll never outdo them - they've stolen all the wind!"

"Shut up, our Dave; leave me alone!"

"Well, you stop yapping on so fatalistically; anyone would think we were on a ruddy extended death-watch with you, man... you're brainsick."

"That's enough, lads." I frowned. "Are you trying to tell them exactly where we are?"

Thomas stared at David, caustically. "Aye, are you trying to tell them exactly where we are, or what, man?"

David clenched his teeth. "Father, you'd better tell him, before I do him some damage."

I tried to lighten the mood. "Now lads, if you don't stop this bickering, I'll set you both on peeling potatoes with one hand tied behind your backs... well?"

Five minutes later, they were as calm as the ocean; the verbal storm had passed.

We looked out to sea in silent vigil, as the ship groaned echoingly around itself. A wide band of light had crept over the horizon, heralding the sun, leaving us exposed to the watchful eyes beyond.

"Well, I suppose I can light my pipe up, now." I tiredly took the baccy from my waistcoat pocket.

Andrew groaned as he gazed eastwardly out to sea. "Father... look! That's all we need!"

As I raised my eyes and looked overboard, my heart sank; for there, coming steadily towards us, was a slow, thick, white fog, but still no wind. I whistled lowly and threw a coin overboard to entice the wind to come and take away this gloom.

David nudged my arm. "Father, look - the pirate ship has caught the wind and is heading this way."

"Thomas, son, call all hands on deck."

A moment later, our ship was completely enveloped by the fog, limiting our visibility to just about six feet, if that. The deck became congested with bodies, as the whole ship stirred eagerly from their beds, anxiously searching for news of our present situation.

Captain Arkwright appeared before me from out of the gloom. "Good morning, Arkwright; how do you feel?"

"I feel quite well," he said, as he inched his way to the rail.

I gave him a brief account of the night watch; he listened intently.

"What are your plans now, Captain?"

"We keep silent, and wait for this cloud of confusion to lift."

It was an intense moment. A feeling of malaise lay heavily upon us as we all listened in deadly silence, waiting for the blind approach of the oncoming ship. Twenty minutes past by - in heartbeats that's a very long time.

"Father," whispered Thomas, painfully, "I can't stand this not knowing what's going to happen; it's driving me insane."

"We're all in the same boat, son."

Then, unexpectedly, the wind began to turn. We could hear the sails filling up with air.

James looked overboard. "Thank providence; we're moving!"

Thomas lent forward and peered apprehensively out into the fog. "Aye, but what I'd like to know, is… where's the pirate ship?"

The great, wide wall of fog gradually began to leave us and head westward. Twenty minutes later, it had moved about a mile out from us. The sky elsewhere was bright and clear.

"The pirate ship must be concealed somewhere behind that far-off haze."

"You're right, Father!" shouted David. "There it is!"

The pirate ship came out of the fog and headed our way. We easily out-sailed them. In one hour, we had increased the distance between us by about another mile.

Thomas looked doleful. "Father, at this rate we'll end up in the New World."

"Don't worry, son, we'll soon lose them."

"I can't believe it;" Andrew leaned overboard joyfully; "the pirates are turning back."

Thomas followed suit, excitedly, straining his neck to look overboard. "Where?"

I viewed the sea with the aid of my telescope. "Yes, it's true! They've given up the chase!"

The news spread quickly about the ship, as everyone on board came hurriedly to the stern, eager to see the marauders head away from us in a southerly direction.

"Father," William enquired of me, "why do you think they turned back?"

"Well, William, apart from sheer tiredness, and diminished supplies, maybe their willpower ran out?"

William stroked his chin as we watched our antagonists sail away into the distance. "Yes, I suppose you're right, Father."

A few hours after the pirates had gone, William walked up onto the quarterdeck and gained our attention. "Silence please," he smiled. "I think that after all we've been through, we all deserve a cheer. I wish to say that I am proud of every single one of you; and tonight, as reparation for our vanquished nerves, we will reward ourselves with a revivifying celebration. Hip-hip!"

"Hurray!" we cried.

The celebration was wonderful; we danced, sang and made merry - though it was odd to see the doctor refuse a drink of ale. We mixed in easily with our new guests, and came to know them quite well. There was a good feeling of camaraderie between us.

CHAPTER VIII

THE ISLAND OF DREAMS

Two days later, I was standing on the sun-baked quarterdeck, talking to William. The sea was calm and the wind was a sailor's dream.

"The lads have done a grand job of the sails."

"Aye, Father," William look up into the riggings, "they've had a perfect morning for it."

"Land ahoy!" shouted David, from up above.

William and I walked to the bow, put our telescopes to our eyes and scoured the horizon.

William grabbed my arm. "Over there, Father!" He showed the direction excitedly with his eyes.

"Oh, yes, now I see it."

It was a small dot, barely visible through the turbulent waves of heat coming from the sea. We were off course and needed supplies, so we thought it best to head straight for the island.

William raised his eyes and pointed up to the riggings. "If it hadn't been for our 'eagle-eyed' Dave, I think that we would have passed that island, unbeknown."

"Yes, I agree totally, son."

Everyone seemed filled with anticipation, as we slowly neared the large, mountainous, lush green island; we circled it for security reasons.

"We'll drop anchor a half mile from land and then go ashore in the lifeboats!" ordered William.

Just then, the ship shuddered alarmingly as we struck something just below the surface, near the south side of the island. Seconds later, we were free of it. The lads above were hanging on for dear life, anticipating another strike.

I urgently put my hands to my mouth in the shape of a cone, and called out. "Thomas! James! Go below and see if there's any damage!" The rest of us looked over the sides, searching for any telltale signs of weakness. A short while later Thomas and James came back on deck soaked through.

Thomas was frantic. "Father, there's water sluicing in through a great hole in the port side - way below the water line, in the powder store!"

"Can it be fixed?" I looked anxiously at Thomas.

"Not while we're in the water," James answered. "The ship's copper plating has pushed the boards so far inwards, and to such a jagged degree, that it's impossible to affix new planks."

A LIFETIME'S JOURNEY

Thomas stood there, wet and despondent, squeezing water from his shirtsleeve. "We stopped the gap temporarily with mattresses, but the water's still rising. It's about three feet deep now. Oh, and we found this, jammed between the copper plating." He handed me a piece of sharp, jagged rock.

"It's volcanic rock. See how it is mottled with variegated streaks, not unlike marble; the hull didn't stand a chance."

Thomas was fearfully. "Do you mean we're floating above a volcano?"

I held up the metamorphic rock. "Thomas, there's no need to look as petrified as this. What we have just passed over, rising from the seabed, is the beginning of an island. The island we are heading for seems to be an extinct volcano, and if we begin to sink, it may save our lives."

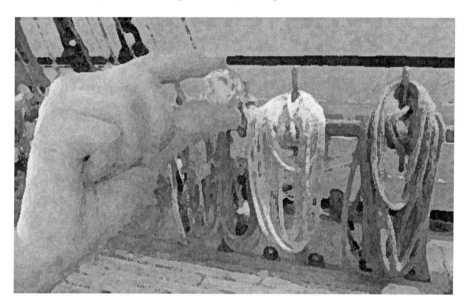

William looked at me tensely, with seawater dripping down his face.

"Father, I've just checked the damage below deck. The water level's rising alarmingly; I think we should abandon ship. What's your opinion?"

"Obviously, we have no thought of sending anyone overboard to plug the hole from the outside, as the volcanic rock would most certainly cut them to ribbons, and the conditions below deck are now just as hazardous; there's no hope, son." I looked grievously at William and shook my head.

"Lower the lifeboats!" he shouted. "Abandon ship!"

As I looked over the port side, pockets of air bubbled up from below the water line - a sure sign that time was running out.

David was very agitated. "Father, if we could just get the ship to the shore we'd have no problem putting the damage right - we're so close!"

"I'm sorry, son. The ship could turn over at any moment and pull us all down with it; it's too risky. As you know, there are only two things on a merchant ship that matter: the crew and the cargo - the one exists for the other's benefit. In this instance we can sacrifice the cargo, but would you have it that we risk our lives for the sake of a sinking ship when land is at reach?"

"When put like that Father, absolutely not."

We quickly filled one boat with animals and any other essentials we could salvage. The other two, we crammed into - some of us carrying personal belongings. Then we tied the three boats together in a single file - one behind the other - and then off we rowed, heading towards the island. We left the sails up on the ship, in the hope that it might be blown towards the shore; but, as we watched, it once again shuddered, violently.

"Ooh! That must have done some damage," sighed Thomas. "Look at the huge air bubbles coming up; the ship's beginning to list."

In an instant, the ship turned over and sank beneath the deep. The silence was exaggerated as the lads stopped rowing. My senses were extremely acute. The grief almost choked me as the ship's life flashed before my eyes.

Thomas sadly turned to William. "One minute a captain, the next... no ship."

"Aye, Thomas, that's life. It's sad, but it must be doubly so for Dad."

The oars started up once again, quietly lapping the water, as we headed dejectedly towards shore.

Once we had beached on the golden sand, an incredible change came over us.

"It feels so wonderfully safe here." I gazed happily around the beautiful island; there was luscious vegetation almost everywhere, and even the plants seemed happy.

"Yes, John, I agree;" Sophia breathed in deeply and calmly; "the air's so clear and fresh."

Everyone affirmed in their own way, how tremendously well they had become since stepping ashore. Even the animals showed signs of vivacity. Ben-Sandy barked excitedly, as Sammy flew freely over the island. Charlie gazed up at the view - his neck fully extended as Geordie held him high. Captain Arkwright, and his remaining crew opened up to the auspicious surroundings; their former anxieties melting away into the air, like ethereal vapours.

Doctor Pearse pronounced how glowingly healthy he felt.

William looked with hope around at the eager faces. "Who would like to volunteer to go on a reconnaissance mission? I need twenty men."

"We four would be more than happy to oblige ourselves," said Girdlestone - one of the gentlemen from the Golden Explorer - as his three companions nodded in assent. "We have never done any menial work before;" he continued; "but this is an opportune time to change that."

Although their hearts were in the right place, William needed hardy men, not gentlemen with delicate fingers. Though, ironically, it was William's 'delicacy' which prevented him from turning them away. In the end, so many volunteered, that William had an embarrassing choice.

Andrew, and Captain Arkwright's two officers, led the 'elite' on their chosen assignment, while the rest of us sat about happily, awaiting their geographic intelligence. It was around noon, four short hours later that they returned. Andrew walked towards me, merrily holding out a small basket of assorted colourful fruits. "Father, I don't think we'll have any problem ensconcing on this island - we've found the horn of plenty. The land here has no need of hands to plough it - nature alone provides all cultivation."

"That's wonderful news, son." I put my hand upon his shoulder. "We've surely landed in Eden."

"Yes, Father, it fits that description precisely."

James looked at William and I - one, then the other - and smiled. "Does that mean we can empty the boats now?"

"Of course you can, son; go ahead."

Firstly, they unloaded the animals from the first boat, and set them free to roam the island, grazing at their leisure. Then, from the same boat, they carried our supplies and other essentials. From the other two boats they emptied our personal belongings. Henry was happy to be reunited with his paintbox. Away he went, on his pictorial adventure - spoilt for choice - Richard not far behind him.

I bent down to pat Ben-Sandy the small dog. "Well, I guess we'll have to make ourselves some kind of shelter."

"There are some canny big trees over there, Father." James nodded in the direction.

"What?" Andrew shook his head vehemently. "That would be sacrilege, man. There's enough bamboo on the island to build with; besides, it's just the material we need in this heat."

"Excellent, Andrew," I said; "we'll build seven bungalows in that large clearing over there: five medium sized for us married couples, and two larger ones for you lads."

An old fallen oak tree was found in the wooded area, so some of the carpenters hastily set to work building a cart to carry bamboo. It was a crude vehicle, but sufficient for its purpose. It was ten feet long and seven feet wide, with solid wheels. It had two long shaft handles at the front, and a three foot square board on each of the two sides.

Soon, Andrew led the lads away to fetch bamboo, pulling the cart as they went.

"Yahoo!" Peter leapt onto the cart with Sammy the parrot. "Wait for us!"

"John," said Sophia, happily, as the cart trundled away, "is there anything we ladies can do to help?"

"Yes, pet, if you'd like to, you can go out and collect some fruit and vegetables."

The four ladies had taken to my wife like a brood of chicks to a mother hen.

"May I go too, Granddad?" Geordie looked up at me with pleading eyes.

"Of course you can, sonna. You can leave Charlie here with me; I'll look after him."

"Thank you, Granddad." He then prudently placed Charlie in the cool shade of a large tree.

As they headed out on their errand, with their shawls, tin basins and baskets, one of the ladies looked back and beckoned Ben-Sandy, her small dog - it followed enthusiastically.

Those of us left on the beach began carrying everything up to the clearing.

"Phew!" William paused, mopped his brow and placed down his side of chest, taking his sweaty hand from the rope handle. "I wish the lads had left the cart behind - this tool chest weighs a ton! Can we not just leave everything until they bring it back?"

"Hey, William, you're getting a bit soft in your old age, aren't you?" I joked, as I put down my side of the chest.

"No, man, Father, it's this heat - it makes me so lethargic. I'm much more at home with the British climate."

"Alright then William, we'll just move the lighter things, until the lads come back."

"Great, Father - I feel better already!"

Two hours later, I was sitting calmly in the clearing, smoking my pipe, as I talked to Captain Arkwright. It was the mixture of joyous singing and the heavy rumbling of wheels that made us look up. The sight that met our eyes was most remarkable indeed. The cart was precariously stacked about ten feet high with bamboo. Some lads pulled at the front, and some pushed at the back. But, most unbelievable of all, was the sight of Peter, standing on the very top without a care in the world, shouting 'Look at me! Look at me!' Now if it had been Richard up there, I would have been worried. But, Peter is a rigger, and riggers are famous for their ability to balance at great heights. Yet this wasn't a solid yardarm, fifty feet up, but an insecure looking stack of rope-bound bamboo.

"Hello, Father!" Andrew wiped his brow and looked down at the sweat in his leathery hand; "we thought we'd save a bit time by carrying more."

"Save a bit time?" I laughed. "It's a good job the wheels can't buckle!"

Peter climbed gleefully down from the cart and walked towards me. "Dad, there's loads more bamboo left. It's all cut down and ready to cart away."

"Yeah, but before you go back for more bamboo, you can go down to the beach with William, and fetch the heavy items up here."

"Come on then lads," Andrew laughed, tiredly; "let's go, before we seize up completely."

It didn't take the lads long to fetch back the cart and unload it. Then off they went again for more bamboo.

William pulled a chair up beside Captain Arkwright and I.

"Father, here's my mother."

"Ah! The food gatherers return." I took a banana playfully from Ben-Sandy's mouth.

"Hello, John!" Sophia held out her basket of fruits. "This is surely paradise, here." The other ladies nodded in silent agreement, showing forth their fresh decorative fruits and stimulating vegetables.

"Granddad," Geordie looked up at me piously, "God keeps a beautiful garden here."

"I appreciate that, Geordie. We should never take for granted the love and beauty that God has bestowed upon us… we are well provided for."

"Amen, Granddad…" Geordie bowed his head, respectfully. "… just like the animals… they toil not… neither do they spin… but the heavenly Father feeds and clothes them… providing them well."

"So very true, Geordie."

"Hello, everyone!" Richard smiled, as he and the botanist returned.

Henry strolled towards us and put down his paintbox and books, while glancing over the delectables before him. "Ooh, what an interesting array of colourful flora. Oh, it almost slipped my mind, Captain," he added, tapping his head, "we have a rich supply of Triticum vulgare, hordeum vulgare, saccharum officinarum and humulus lupulus."

"Wheat, barley, sugarcane and hops," said Geordie, happily translating from Latin.

"Bread and beer," said I, translating into Geordie, through a dry-mouthed smile; "manna from heaven indeed."

| Triticum vulgare | Hordeum vulgare | Saccharum Officinarum | Humulus lupulus |

That evening, we had a wonderful meal. As night fell, we finished stacking the last of the bamboo cane below the bright moonlight, for the morrow's labour. That night we bedded down beneath the stars.

The next morning, we awoke to another wonderful day. The ladies began by rekindling the fire. After breakfast, the lads set to work preparing three raised cane foundations for the bungalows.

Geordie lay awake on his blanket with his eyelids closed, while the tortoise licked his face.

"Ha-ha!" giggled Geordie. "That tickles."

"That's right, Charlie," Sophia laughed; "tell Geordie to get up."

"I am up, Grandma," said Geordie, sweet and innocently; "I'm just daydreaming."

Just then, Peter whizzed past us, almost naked, ripping off his clothes as he went, shouting, 'It's too hot... I can't stand it anymore... I'm going for a dip!'

"May I go too, Grandma?" Geordie rolled over to view the beach, just as Peter entered the cool, enticing water.

"Yes, Geordie," Sophia smiled; "but don't go swimming, mind."

"It's alright, Grandma, I'll be careful." Geordie happily and eagerly hopped about rolling up his trouser legs as he followed Peter down to the beach.

The sight of Peter and Geordie splashing joyfully about in the water with the dog, was so tempting, that within half an hour we had all joined them. William was out in the distance playing with the dolphins, as Sammy flew overhead, attracted by the excitement.

A LIFETIME'S JOURNEY

"Eeh, Grandma, my Uncle William's a dead good swimmer, isn't he?"

"Yes, Geordie, he swims like a fish."

Some folk think swimming should be a prerequisite for sailors... looking at William out there, it looked more like a Perquisite... a perk.

A few hours later, everyone calm and refreshed, we headed back to the clearing. After refreshments, the lads strolled back to work, singing as they went. Geordie played with the dog, as the ladies sat around me knitting. The echo of pots and pans rang out, as the chefs busied themselves at their nearby post. Doctor Pearse and Captain Arkwright were fishing contentedly out at the lake.

Frolicking in the water had made me tired. I sat relaxed in my wicker chair, drawing mental stimulation from my pipe. What was our destiny? When would we be rescued from this beautiful island? Did we want to be rescued? Maybe it was the memories of our families, and the quaint old familiarities that beckoned us home, nothing else. But Eden is home; according to the good Bible, it's where it all began. Home became a paradox. My religious thoughts were in a quandary. Leaving Eden would be sacrilege - a slight to the Holy Bible. Being a fatalist, I left it in God's hands and submitted my mind to another ounce of baccy.

The air was still, as the sun beat down on my face. Eyes closed, I could hear the nearby clack of bamboo, and the low hum of voices as the lads worked merrily together. By noon, the bungalows were beginning to take shape. I decided to stretch my legs. Placing my weight upon the arms of the chair, I pushed myself up.

"Would you like a cup of tea, pet?" Sophia gently reached for the pot, as I placed my hands upon my knees and stretched my legs.

"Oh, aye, thank you pet, I'd love one. I'm going to stretch my legs. I'll take it with me if you don't mind."

As I walked around the clearing - cup in hand - I chanced upon Richard and Henry, as they inspected a beautifully coloured plant.

"Hello, Captain." Henry gave me a warm smile. "This place is a botanist's dream. I have recorded at least two hundred species of plant that are currently believed to be extinct. I was wondering, as I have collected many and varied plant seeds from many different lands, should I not promulgate half of each strain about the clearing?"

"Go forth and multiply," said I, dramatically brushing the seeds from a tall twelve o' clock.

"Thank you, Captain;" Henry gathered up his equipment; "I will."

Ben-Sandy barked, as Geordie ran playfully ahead of him, dangling a piece of rope. "Come on, Ben-Sandy, let's find Charlie!"

"He's shading beneath my wicker chair!" I pointed back to where the ladies were.

"Thank you, Granddad!" Geordie then quickly ran off with Ben-Sandy in tow.

My peaceful stroll was cut short by the wild clanging of the dinner bell. My stomach moaned loudly as the delicious smell of food led me on. My mouth began to salivate at the thought of its salvation. I quickened my step. As I reached the dining area, Geordie and the ladies were busy laying the clean white tablecloths onto the grass, in preparation for the meal. Ten feet away, there was a glowing ground fire, ringed with large white pebbles collected from the beach. From this, the chefs carried pans of appetising food to a makeshift bench, assembled from a few planks of wood laid between two sea chests.

Ralph nodded - his chubby round face reddened by the hot coals. "Has your constitutional given you an appetite, Captain?" He smiled from behind his bench, as he stirred the contents of one of the pans.

"I'm famished, Ralph." I placed down my empty teacup. "What have you prepared for us today? The smell is driving me wild!"

Ralph placed his hand upon his younger colleague's shoulder, "Today's speciality, Cap'n, was recommended and lovingly prepared by Tam, here."

Tam was a tall, shy, red-haired Scotsman, who stood silently with his head down.

"What is it Tam," I peered into the pot, "broth?"

"Aye, Captain," said he, quietly, as his eyes met with mine for the briefest of moments, and then darted away again beneath his bushy eyebrows. "Translated into English, it means 'thin soup'; it's the ideal thing to cool us down in this hot weather."

"Splendid. I can't wait."

Just then, my attention was arrested by the sound of the cart, as it wheeled towards us. As I turned, William nodded towards its canvas-covered contents with the unfeigned air of a gentleman.

"Father, we lads were thinking of how undignified it was for Mother, and the other good ladies, to eat their meals while sitting on the grass; so we thought it of the greatest importance to set a few lads to work building these priority items." So saying, he and a few others pulled back the canvas, revealing four long bamboo cane tables and eight benches to match. In the situation, to see, and be privileged with such necessities, seemed like luxury.

"Well done, lads; thanks to you, we'll eat our meals in a civilised manner."

The tables and benches were instantly lifted down from the cart and laid end to end. The ladies gathered up the white cloths from the grass, shook them and then happily re-laid them on the tables. As they were laying the cutlery, Doctor Pearse and Captain Arkwright returned. They set down a large basket before us and drew back the green canvas from it, showing us their enormous catch.

"There's no competition Captain," said Arkwright. "It's too easy; the nets just wouldn't hold any more fish."

"Easy game or not, Captain, you've still procured a wonderful supper. I've never seen such large red salmon."

The captain nodded modestly, then knelt down on one knee and replaced the canvas.

Doctor Pearse glanced over the new furniture, his eyebrows raised in approval. "I see were not the only ones who've been busy."

"Aye, the lads, thought it would be honourable to respect the ladies' dignity."

Arkwright winked. "That's just like the lads - ever courteous." He then put the catch to one side, and joined us at the table as the chefs served the meal.

No sooner had Peter sat down, he was up again, wriggling like a worm on a hook. "Oh, let me past, our Tom!" He bit on his lower lip with his little black teeth. "I need to go!"

Thomas moved to one side, allowing Peter enough space to clamber over the bench. Peter dashed off in the direction of the bushes. A few minutes later, he came back with an expression of relief upon his face. He washed his hands and then rejoined us at the table.

"Hey, our Tom, give me my space back, I want to sit beside our Dave. If you don't, I'll slaver all over you, mind!" Peter's words seemed to have more effect than slings and arrows; or maybe, it was the discreet cough, and the embarrassed look that Sophia directed at Thomas, that made him move up to let Peter squeeze in.

"I must say, Tam," said I, quickly changing the mood, "this soup tastes as delicious as it smells."

"Hey, I'm not eating it if it smells!" Peter peered into his soup bowl with a ghastly expression.

It wasn't only Peter's mind that was affected by his childhood accident - his olfactory nerve was damaged too, leaving him with anosmia: that is, a lack of sense of smell. "I'm not eating stinky soup," said he, adamantly, pushing his bowl to one side; "Ben-Sandy can have this bowl as well!"

Peter's untimely outburst turned his mother pink; but it needn't have, for

THE ISLAND OF DREAMS

as I looked at Tam, he counteracted in a way that I would never have expected - he burst into laughter. Everyone followed suit; that was it - the ice was broken. As the laughter subsided, so did the formality. The years of compulsory, ritualistic ceremonies instilled into us for generations at the dinner table - although difficult to shrug off - had abated. Being the eldest among us, I was looked upon as the patriarchal father. This honour privileged me to a seat at one end of the table, the other being reserved for Doctor Pearse and his *wooden leg*. Captain Arkwright, who was nearest to me on my right, sat upright with a jolt and a mystified expression upon his face.

CHAPTER IX

AN HUGE HISTORIC DISCOVERY

"Captain Rigger, it almost slipped my mind; as Doctor Pearse and I were fishing in the lake over yonder, we saw the most extraordinary thing."

"What on earth was it, Captain?"

"There, lying just beneath the surface of the crystal clear water," he continued, "is one of the most unusual objects I have ever come across. It has a smooth, flat, stone-like surface, covered with unfamiliar markings. But the most remarkable thing about it is that it is perfectly round, about thirty-five feet in diameter, six inches thick, and made of a strange, unknown, greyish coloured material."

I leant forward, pushing my empty bowl to one side, enrapt by the captain's fascinating narrative. "Please continue, Captain."

He looked in the direction of the lake. "I don't know if we imagined it, but there seemed to be a slight glow emanating from that monumental stone, which shone iridescently onto the underbellies of passing fish."

"It was no product of the imagination!" said Doctor Pearse, excitedly, rising from his wicker chair. "Please excuse me," he added, and then hobbled away towards the bushes.

By this time, Captain Arkwright had attracted everyone's attention.

"Captain Arkwright," William leant forward with his hand poised forward, to give weight to the question, "do you think it's a natural formation?"

"Oh, definitely not;" he shook his head; "it's so well dressed that it must have been finished by human hands."

"Or godly hands," interjected Doctor Pearse, as he walked back towards us and retrieved a book from beneath his seat cushion.

"Do you mean to say it's a meteorite, Doctor?" said William, in amazement. The doctor raised his eyebrows and shrugged his shoulders in acknowledgement, and then headed back towards the bushes.

"That's neither fish, nor fowl, William," said Captain Arkwright, shaking his head. "The question is, 'who shaped it, and for what reason?'"

"Can we go and see it, Granddad?" Geordie stood up eagerly.

"Aye, Father," David nodded approvingly, "Geordie's right; the best way to solve a mystery is to view it first-hand."

I looked around at the empty bowls - even Peter's. "Well, I can see there were no complaints with the fine soup; so, if everyone is ready, I'm sure Captain Arkwright will show us the way."

"Of course, Captain," said Arkwright, as we rose from the table, "I'd be only too glad to."

As we passed the fire, we placed our tin basins into the two cauldrons of simmering water thereon, and then headed on our way. Shaded from the sun, we followed the newly cut route through the sugar cane - then on through the banana trees. The trees eventually gave way to a large, beautiful expanse of open terrain. Not long after that we reached the lake; at most, it must have taken fifteen minutes. From where we now stood the view was even more stunning. We were surrounded by lush green grass, blanketed here and there with beautiful perfumed flowers. A shallow stream - so Andrew informed me - traverses the distant wood to the left of the lake, on its way to the sea. Nearby, a few sheep drank peacefully from the clear, still water. A slight rumble came from the lake's snow-capped benefactor: a waterfall, cascading down from the distant mountain. In the centre of the expansive lake - east of the island - lay another island; smaller, but just as beautiful and alluring - like a wheel within a wheel. As if this sight was not enough, it was clearly mirrored in the lake.

Geordie ran ahead of us with the dog, following the water's edge until he came to a tall stick placed into the earth, whereupon he stopped suddenly and pointed excitedly into the water, about three feet from the edge.

"Granddad, here it is! Here's the stone!"

Captain Arkwright trudged to a halt and pointed to the stick in answer to my thoughts. "Yes, this is the marker I left."

We stood at the lake's edge, looking down upon the immense circular stone, overawed by its radiance, beauty and size.

"Father," David nodded to the water, "shall a few of us lads go in and take a closer look?"

"We can all go in, son, but be mindful not to disturb the bed of the lake too excessively."

The ladies decided not to enter the water, so we men bared our feet and rolled up our trouser legs. As we walked gently into the water, little clouds of silt puffed up around our feet, and graceful fishes darted in and out between our legs. We stood around the part of the stone nearest to the bank - leaning over - our faces suspended inches above the water.

William ran his index finger across several ancient looking symbols, almost obliterated by the action of the water. "Father, they look somewhat like armorial bearings."

What could it mean? What mystery lies beneath this relic, and why this particular shape?

Andrew looked up at me. "Hey, Father! I think this would make an ideal conversation table; especially as the cane tables will be needed indoors soon."

"Yes, Andrew," said Sophia, "it could easily accommodate everyone at one sitting; but how on earth would you move it?"

"Ingenuity and brute force, Mother," Andrew grinned confidently.

"Aye, man, our Dave and Alf Bennet could lift it between them." Peter stood miming the action in all earnestness.

The lads were determined. Once they had set up a challenge, they would not relent. They gained my consent, and then headed off to the bungalows to bring back equipment. As we awaited their return, we were so enwrapped in our own thoughts, that we hadn't noticed Charlie had joined us. He was at the water's edge, drinking the cool, refreshing water.

"So this is where you get to, Charlie." Geordie chuckled, as he knelt down beside him on all fours. When Charlie had finished his drink, Geordie picked him up and carried him over to where we now sat.

"He's a bit hot, Grandma."

"Why don't we make him a leaf sunshade?"

"Ooh, yes, Grandma - Charlie would love that!"

They gathered together a bundle of large green leaves, and began to seize them together with tendrils collected from a nearby shrub.

"There you are, Geordie, one new sunshade, fit for a tortoise."

"Thank you, Grandma," Geordie placed the large sunshade lightly onto Charlie's shell, "he'll not get too hot with that on."

"Not if he doesn't lose it." Sophia brushed a piece of tendril from Geordie's hair.

It wasn't long before the lads returned. They were carrying all manner of things: ropes, levers, wooden blocks and long lengths of bamboo cane.

"Right, Father, shall we get started?" William rubbed his hands enthusiastically.

"Yes, son, let's give it a try."

We began by digging silt away from beneath one edge of the stone - making a hole great enough to take a large block of wood, on which we would operate two levers. Then ropes were placed around the stone, ready for towing it. We placed a stone fulcrum upon the solid wooden block and then pushed in two levers. Twenty of the lads manoeuvred them, pushing downwards with all their strength.

"It's moving, Captain!" Henry, the botanist nodded, keeping well clear of the levers in case they snapped.

"It's true!" I looked on in astonishment as Geordie pushed home a wedge.

In went two more levers - inching up the stone - followed by another wedge. But then something awful happened. Just as Geordie was pushing in the last of the wedges, the lever slipped from the fulcrum, dislodging the wedge, allowing the full weight of the stone to press down on the little finger of his right hand, slicing it clean off. A passing fish snapped it up before it had time to hit the bottom. Geordie didn't cry out; he just stood there in the water, calmly weighing up the situation, as blood poured profusely from his wound.

"Neptune's ocean, wash away this blood," said he, deeply.

I asked David to go and find the doctor. He ran like the wind - not once looking back. If anyone could find the doctor in a hurry, he could. In the meantime, I covered Geordie's wound with a clean handkerchief, and applied a rope tourniquet to his arm, constricting the flow of blood considerably. Everyone showed concern, especially Sophia.

The doctor was with us within twenty minutes - which is good going for a man with a wooden leg.

"What's happened to Richard?" The doctor quickly knelt down beside him with his medical bag. "Oh, it's alright," he continued; "he's only fainted." In the confusion, no one had noticed Richard swoon.

"Oh, all that blood in the water!" Richard sat up groggily; "it was horrible!"

The doctor left Richard in a comfortable state and walked over to Geordie, who was sitting silently on the grass with his arm raised - supported by his grandmother.

"How do you feel, Geordie?"

"I feel well, Doctor." Geordie flinched slightly as the doctor examined the bloody wound.

"You don't feel drowsy at all?" He continued.

"No, Doctor - not at all."

"Amazing!" The doctor pulled a threaded needle from his medical bag, applied a few stitches, cleaned the wound, and then dressed it. Then off came the tourniquet. "Now, we only need to support your hand." He wrapped a sling around Geordie's neck and arm.

"Thank you, Doctor," Geordie looked calm and content.

The doctor took me quietly to one side. "We had better keep an eye on him, Captain. His wound will heal in a week or two, but he doesn't feel any dizziness or pains; I believe he may be suffering from delayed shock."

"Of course Doctor; we'll do so; thank you very much for the advice."

The doctor laid his hand compassionately upon my shoulder. "I'll take first watch Captain." He then walked over to Geordie, and sat down beside him on the grass.

Sophia came towards me showing obvious concern.

"John, is Geordie going to be alright?"

"Of course, pet, he's a bit overcome, but as well as can be expected in the circumstances."

"I knew I shouldn't have let him assist you." She lowered her head and placed her right hand onto her brow.

"Why-no, pet." I tenderly held her left hand. "He's adventurous. He'll feel proud to have received a wound in the call of duty."

"Do you really think so, John?" Sophia removed her hand from her brow and looked up at me with relief.

"Yes, pet. Anyway, what's so uncommon about a sailor with a few fingers missing?" I added, holding up my left hand, exposing two small, rounded stumps where my middle and annular fingers used to be. Sophia smiled. We both looked over to where the bustle was. Geordie was being showered with attention.

William caught my eye, and then came over. "Father," he glanced back at the activity, "Geordie seems to be as right as a trivet, now."

"Aye, son," I looked over at Geordie's happy, smiling face, "he seems as well as ever."

"Well, I was thinking, Father, would it be so inappropriate if we went back to moving the stone?"

"I think Geordie would be only too pleased to see it raised," I smiled. I was right; Geordie was delighted at the idea.

Geordie came and sat down at my feet. "Granddad, I'm sorry for being a nuisance. I do hope you can lift the stone out of the water."

I patted him softly on the shoulder. "Don't worry, sonna, you're the one we're concerned about now; we'll see if we can get this stone out, just for you."

Ten minutes later, we were back in the lake. The huge stone disc was as we had left it, raised up upon the wedges. The cloud of blood that had earlier permeated the water was gone. Geordie and the others sat quietly on the water's edge, watching us intently as we pushed the levers into place. As the stone went up, Peter pushed the last wedge home, as Geordie had previously. Then Thomas and James fed bamboo rollers into the spaces at each side of it. Once the rollers were in place, the wedges were removed, and then the long ropes around the stone were pulled taut.

"Right, Thomas!" William ordered. "We want to keep a momentum going here. When the stone begins to move, make sure you and James get all the rollers underneath. Have you got that?" Thomas and James nodded in agreement. "Right, is everybody ready?" William looked round for dissension. "Right then... after three, I want everyone to pull on the ropes as if your lives depend on it!"

The moment was tense, but exciting. As we held onto the four ropes - ten men to each one, we dug our heels in and waited for the count.

"One... two... three... Pull!" shouted William.

It seemed the ropes would snap at any moment. For the stone proved adamant - held fast for unknown centuries in the silt.

"Keep pulling!" yelled William, hoarsely. "Don't relent!"

Suddenly, the stone broke away from the past, and was borne into the future. Our morale was heightened as the stone glided ever more easily over the rollers. As the stone broke through the water onto the beach's edge there was a cheer.

"Hold it!" cried William, raising an arm; "that's far enough for now; take a breather!"

We all let go of the ropes and rested our aching bodies on the grass.

"William, I've had enough."

"It's alright, Father," he smiled down at me and rubbed his neck soothingly, "I know how you feel. Anyway, it's a straight run to the village clearing now; we should manage without you."

"Thanks son - you're a good one."

William joined the others as they gathered around the stone. The lads were still cheering, and patting each other on their backs for their achievement.

"Right, lads!" William hollered cheerfully, rubbing his hands excitedly. "Lets get this thing moving again!"

Geordie and Doctor Pearse came over and sat down beside me, closely followed by Sophia and the other ladies.

"You did a grand job, Captain."

"Thank you, Doctor." I nodded whilst removing my pipe from my waistcoat pocket; "I only wish I could have followed it up!"

The lads readied themselves once again, waiting for William's orders.

"One... two... three... Pull!" he shouted.

This time, there was no hesitation; the stone was light and moved as easily as a sleigh on snow. It was lovely to see the precise operation, as the rollers were fed at the front, collected at the back, and then fed at the front again, ever so smoothly.

"Granddad, I think sailors are 'dead' strong. And I love it when they all sing together, when they work."

"So do I, sonna." I joined in with the chorus of the shanty the lads had just begun.

A while later, as the lads went out of view, we could still here them singing, as they rolled away the large, mysterious, lightweight stone.

"Granddad!" Geordie pointed in astonishment to where the stone had rested. "What's this in the water?"

I stood up and went over to investigate. My eyes darted over the unsettled murky water.

"Where, sonna?"

"There, Granddad!" He pointed through the gloom; "something's glistening on the bottom."

I just caught a brief glimpse of it before it vanished beneath a cloud of yellow, silted water.

"What is it, Granddad?"

"I don't know, sonna, it may have been a large fish."

"Granddad, to me, it looked more like a golden dish."

"You could be right, sonna, but let's leave it for now and come back when the water's settled."

Although the long respite had refreshed my body, my mind was worn out, cogitating over our unexpected find.

"John, shall we head back to the clearing now? I'm sure we could all do with a nice refreshing cup of tea."

"Why-aye, pet," I picked up my shoes, "that's a splendid idea. There's nothing better to clear the head."

On our way back, we met Alf, Thomas, Richard and David, as they wheeled the cart along.

"Where are you going now, lads?"

"We're going to the mountain, Father." David nodded over to the snow-capped heights. "According to Andrew, there are some sandstone boulders there. William wants us to cut four of them into blocks, to rest the table top upon."

"Is it soft sandstone?"

"Aye, Father;" Richard sliced his hand through the air; "Andrew believes the saw will cut through it like a knife through butter."

"Ah, well, that's not too bad. What are the lads doing now?"

"Andrew and William are marking out an area in front of the bungalows, ready to put down the stone blocks," said David. "The rest of the lads are busy with the bungalows. They'll be starting on the roofs soon."

"Will you be back for tea?"

"I doubt it, Mother." David pointed to a basket on the cart. "Anyway, we've brought some with us."

The ground began to rumble again, as the lads began moving the cart.

"Well, good luck, lads," we said; "we'll see you later."

Once the lads were out of sight the rest of us decide to make our way back to the campsite, to see how the others were getting on with the building work.

The weather was wonderful - not a cloud in the sky. The grass was lush and green beneath my bare feet. I had forgotten how much it tickles as it squeezes between the toes.

"Granddad, will you carry Charlie for me, please? My arm's aching."

"Why of course, sonna;" I immediately took Charlie from him; "I should have realised."

Sophia embraced him. "Are you alright now, Geordie? Would you like to take a rest?"

"No, Grandma," Geordie smiled, "I feel fine."

"All right, Geordie, come along then."

It wasn't long before we reached the campsite. It was quiet and deserted.

"Oh, look!" Sophia pointed towards the kitchen area. "Someone has had the forethought to put the kettles on."

Ten minutes later, we were sitting in our wicker chairs, drinking tea.

Ralph walked towards us, closely followed by Tam. "Ah! The tea's brewed already."

"Yes," I lifted my cup in acknowledgement, "it's been mashed for a short while."

Ralph placed a row of cups onto the table. "The lads are looking forward to a fresh cup, *an' tha's* a fact."

Sophia sat forward. "Here they are now!"

The lads sat down noisily at the table while Ralph poured the tea.

"Well, we're getting there, Father," announced William, proudly; "there are just the roofs to finish now."

I tilted my head and looked over at the distant bamboo erections. "Yes, they're coming along nicely, son."

Ralph stood up courteously from the table. "If you'll excuse us, Tam and I will get on with preparing the next meal."

Peter licked his lips. "It's alright with me - the sooner the better!" Ralph smiled genuinely. "Thanks for the compliment, Peter." He then walked over

AN HUGE HISTORIC DISCOVERY

to the dining area, with Tam.

The lads finished their drinks, and then headed back to work.

"Ah! That tea was delicious," said I, as I finished off my second cup.

Geordie was sitting on a wicker chair, leaning over, dropping a handful of pebbles, one at a time, into a wooden bowl between his feet. I could tell he was anxious to get back to the mystery at the lake.

"Do you think we should check the lake now, Geordie?" I winked mischievously.

"Yes, Granddad," Geordie leapt out of his chair, "it should have cleared up by now!"

"Ha-ha, come along then sonna, let's go."

"You'll be back for your tea, won't you, John?"

"Aye, pet, don't worry; we'll not be long."

As Doctor Pearse was deeply engrossed in a heavy medical book, I thought it very unlikely that he would be in favour of a walk, so, Geordie and I set off on our quest without him. We talked so much that we reached the lake before we knew it. We followed the water's edge until we found the bamboo tracks, and then stopped.

"Look, Granddad!" Geordie pointed to the water. "It's clear!"

"So it is. It's brilliant!"

"Can we go in now, Granddad?"

"Yes, sonna, but take care not to drag your feet."

"I won't, Granddad," whispered Geordie.

We entered the water cautiously, breathing slowly, as we watched our every step. We had almost reached the place of interest when we heard a most unsettling sound - a bark. Ben-Sandy was running towards us playfully. I looked at Geordie, pleadingly.

"Get the dog. If it comes into the water it will ruin the whole adventure." I've never seen anyone move so slowly, so quickly in all my life. It was so unbelievable that it was on the point of being hilarious. The silt wasn't even disturbed! He was out of the water and onto the land in a flash.

"I've caught him, Granddad." Geordie knelt down on one knee and held Ben Sandy lovingly with his good hand.

"Well done, Geordie. But, I'm afraid you'll have to stay there with him."

"It's alright, Granddad, I can see from here."

I raised my thumb in acknowledgement, and then made my way towards where the stone had lain. There was definitely something metallic glowing beneath the silt; part of it was exposed. I reached down and grasped it in my hand, and slowly pulled it upwards. As the water washed away the yellow mud, I was totally astounded by what I saw - too elated to think straight. For there clasped in my hand was a heavy golden sword, the handle encrusted with jewels. I pulled it out of the water, and held it up high in the dazzling sunlight so Geordie could see it.

"Geordie, isn't it magnificent?"

Geordie leapt up and down, keeping a tight hold on the dog.

"Granddad, I cannot believe it!"

I placed it back down softly on the bed of the lake, and then ran my fingers lightly through the silt. Almost immediately, I came upon a solid object. It was a leaden cross, inscribed, but alas, indecipherable - probably due to the weight of the stone. I held it up to Geordie - he cried out with excitement. I put it down, and searched again through the soft clay. I felt a cup-like object in the palm of my hand; it was smooth and light, and glowed brightly beneath the water. I shook it lightly to remove the clay, revealing a beautiful golden goblet. As I showed it to Geordie, his face lit up. Then, all of a sudden, there was a blinding flash, and I dropped the goblet.

"Did you see it, Geordie? Did you see the light?"

"Yes Granddad, I saw it!"

I felt the water getting shallower around my ankles, as I inched my way towards the lakeside. I found my way onto the grass, and fell down on all fours.

"Are you alright, Granddad?"

"I've been struck blind, Geordie!" Ben-Sandy muzzled up to me comfortingly with his nose. "Go and get Doctor Pearse! If your grandmother asks why I want him, tell her not to worry, she'll find out soon enough. Hurry Geordie! Hurry!"

I could hear Geordie's rapid footsteps leaving me, as I held on to the dog. I was blind and frightened. I have never felt so alone. In the past, I thought that closing my eyes for a few minutes was a good conception of blindness, but oh, how dreadfully wrong I was; now I was also mentally blind. I mulled over the situation in terror and isolation. I don't know how long I had sat there with Ben-Sandy by my side, but it seemed an age before Geordie returned.

"I'm here, Granddad!" Geordie panted. "Doctor Pearse is right behind me!"

I heard the heavy, familiar thumping of the doctor's wooden leg, as he hurried towards me.

"What is it Captain? What on earth's happened?" he panted.

I communicated to him the events leading up to my blindness.

"Incredible!" said he, as he finished inspecting my eyes. "Geordie, did you see this light?"

"Yes, Doctor, it was a very bright light - more pure than the sun. It came from a figure dressed in white that was standing on the water beside my granddad. I couldn't see a face, as the glow was so bright."

"Being that I am a trained physician, my medical training only allows me to see things scientifically. I am sure that there is a rational explanation for what you have experienced Captain, but I am hard pressed to find it."

"Will I be permanently blind, Doctor?"

"There are no physical signs of injury, Captain; you have temporary blindness."

"When will I recover my sight?" I grasped his arm.

"One cannot tell. I've known some cases to last weeks and yet others to last minutes."

"Thank you, Doctor, that's of some consolation to me."

"We had better get you back to the others; you need plenty of rest."

"No, Doctor! I must make you believe. I must show you the evidence in the lake. I'll never rest if you have doubt!"

The doctor paused for a moment. "Alright then, Captain - if it'll will ease your mind."

''Thank you Doctor."

Geordie and the doctor each held an arm and led me into the shallow water.

"Is this the place, Geordie?"

"Yes, Granddad but there's nothing here."

"What do you mean, Geordie, 'there's nothing here'?"

"Everything's gone, Granddad. The sword, the cross and the goblet have all vanished."

I was frustrated by blindness. I waved my body in agitation, willing myself to see.

"Calm yourself, Captain!" The doctor stood in front of me and shook me by the shoulders. "Pull yourself together man!"

The jolt seemed to wake me from an awful nightmare. It was then, ever so slightly, that my sight began to return.

"I can see!" I stared at the blurred vision of the doctor. "I can see!" Colour here, colour there, vivid colour everywhere.

"Thank God for that, Captain; it must have been the jolt that did it."

"Thank you for delivering me from purgatory, Doctor."

Geordie then looked up at me, and hugged me tenderly.

"Granddad, can we go back and see my grandma, now?"

"Yes, sonna; anyway, there goes the dinner bell!" I took one last look about the lake, thinking of the arcane mystery that had eluded us. Who or what was the brilliant figure standing on the water? What happened to the sword, the cross and the goblet? And what was their significance? I thought of the round table back at the village - and then it dawned on me. The hairs stood up on the back of my neck.

"Are you alright, Granddad?"

"Yes sonna - I can see clearly now. I was blind before, but now everything is crystal clear."

We reached the village, just as the meal was being served. Sophia turned to me with concern.

"John, whatever is the matter? You look as if you've seen a ghost!"

"You may be right, dear;" I took my place at the dinner table; "you may just be right."

During the meal, we held everyone spellbound as we recapitulated our adventure.

"Father," James stroked his chin, as I finished my narrative, "maybe a solitary holy man landed on the island centuries ago, and decided to bury his treasure here for safe keeping?"

"Whereupon he picked up a stone disc with a diameter of thirty five feet, and placed it on top?" Thomas sniffed sarcastically.

"Oh, I forgot about that." James looked down while scratching his head.

"Thomas," said I, gravely, "James might be more near the truth than you think."

"What do you mean, Father? Why would someone travel all the way to this remote island just to bury a few old artefacts?"

"Think of it, son - does the significance of the objects not suggest anything to you?"

Thomas thought for a moment, and then turned to me. "I'm sorry, Father, but it doesn't suggest anything - except of course, the legend of King Arthur."

"Exactly, son." I smiled knowingly. "Did not Joseph of Arimathea bring the Holy Grail to Glastonbury? And was it not Sir Galahad, the purest knight of the Round Table, who found it? And in the end, when Excalibur was thrown into the lake, was not the wounded Arthur escorted away to the island of Avalon?"

"Yes, Father, they're indelibly linked; but what does it all indicate?"

"Thomas," I whispered piously, "I think Geordie and I have witnessed a revelation."

Everyone bowed their heads and crossed themselves implicitly. A moment later, the suppositions began.

"I wonder if the island in the centre of the lake could be Avalon." James gazed out romantically.

"Or even Nod." Henry nodded dreamily. "For does it not say in the good book: 'And Cain went out from the presence of the Lord, and dwelt in the land of Nod, on the east of Eden'?"

These assumptions caused quite a stir. And if it hadn't been for William's direction to go back to work, I'm sure the lads would have talked all day.

The excitement had fatigued me, so I relaxed into my wicker chair, and fell into a deep slumber. I awoke several hours later to the sound of Sophia's sweet, comforting voice.

"You've slept well, dear. Would you like a cup of tea?"

"Yes thanks pet," I groggily shifted my position in the chair, "that would be delightful."

A LIFETIME'S JOURNEY

I observed Sophia as she made the tea. Her movements were graceful and sweet; she was, and is, the embodiment of womanhood.

"Here you are, dear." She placed the teacup down on the table in front of me.

"Thank you, pet," I smiled up at her, "my world revolves around you."

After tea, I sat in my chair, pipe in hand, running my tired eyes over the exquisite scenery. In the background, to my right, way beyond the trees and bushes, stood the almighty mountain - bordered in the foreground by the enchanting lake. Straight ahead, about two hundred feet to the north, stood the seven bungalows, almost in completion. Beside them, lay the colossal circular stone, resting upon a log. The lads were up above, working on the roofs. To the west, lay the 'Garden of Eden': hundreds and hundreds of plants, bushes and trees. And one hundred feet behind me lay the wide golden beach - dotted here and there with palm trees. As I looked over my shoulder, I espied Doctor Pearse, walking with the dog across the sands; then Geordie, as he sat beneath a palm tree, showing Charlie the ocean. On the table in front of me, Sophia and the other ladies busied themselves, reading, knitting and sewing.

It was almost sundown when the lads came back from the mountain, carrying four sandstone blocks on the cart.

"Granddad, are you going over to watch the table being laid?"

I knocked the spent ash from my pipe. "I wouldn't miss it for the world, sonna."

We followed Doctor Pearse and the ladies over to the bungalows. David and Alf were lifting the four, two-and-a-half foot square stone blocks from the cart. The lads stopped their work on the bungalows and came over to help lift the tabletop.

"Hey, man, Father, this stone's excellent to work with; we could build a mansion with it!"

"No thank you, David," said Sophia, "the mountain looks nice enough where it is." We all laughed.

A few minutes later, the stones were set solidly into place upon the pebble-reinforced foundations - ready to take the weight of the table.

"Heave!" said William, as the table was inched higher. "Okay, swing it round and slide it onto the blocks." Some of the lads were raising the table with levers, as the others manoeuvred it gently into place with ropes. "That's it, now lower it." They then did the same with the other side. "Left a touch... hold it... down... perfect!"

"Well done, lads, you've done a grand job."

"Aye, Father, a couple of pints would go down well." David grinned cheekily.

"Why don't we christen the table now?"

"There'll be plenty of time for that when the roofs are finished."

The lads looked at each other thoughtfully, and then David held his throat, thirstily, and gulped.

"Let's get back to work, lads."

They worked quickly, for that night, we slept indoors, and the table was well and truly christened!

The next morning, after breakfast, we moved the rest of our belongings into our respective bungalows. Sophia and I decided it best for Geordie to move in with us, as - so Sophia put it - the lads can get a bit too surly when they get together.

Geordie and I carried a small chest of clothes into his bedroom.

"Granddad, do you remember last night, when you told us all that there was no ascendancy at the round table - the table with no beginning and no end? Well I was thinking... it doesn't matter where 'you' sit, that place will always be the head of the table."

Geordie's candid words humbled me. His expressions were honest and agreeable.

"John?" Sophia stood measuring a picture up against the bamboo wall, as I entered the living room. "Do you think this portrait of Geordie goes well here?"

"Aye, pet, that's just about right."

Sophia was very pleased with the bungalow. The other married accommodations were of exactly the same design - rectangular in shape. This rectangle was walled down the middle - lengthways - to make two more rectangles: one being the living room. The other was walled again; but this time across the width, making two pleasant size bedrooms with north facing windows. Each living room had four windows: one on each side of the central door, facing the ocean, and one on each of the remaining walls, facing east and west. Our living room was barely furnished. Standing on the floor beside one of the windows, was my old sea chest, which contained - apart from other nautical memorabilia - the logbook of *The Turtle*. We had three chairs, and a table from which to read the Bible.

"John, if the lads could bring us some coconut fibre, I'm sure we ladies could make some matting for the floors."

"Yes, pet, that's a splendid idea."

It was around noon, when everyone had finished transferring their

A LIFETIME'S JOURNEY

belongings into their bungalows. The lads' bungalows didn't have any separate rooms or partitions. They were just shells, almost like army billets. But they didn't complain; in fact I'm quite sure they enjoyed it.

Later, we all walked over to the round table and sat down upon the specially built, wooden bench that encircled it.

"Hey, Father," David held his head in his hand, "that was some drink you gave us last night!"

"Oh-aye, son - I made that one double strength."

"Double strength?" said Peter, pulling a bemused face. "Does that mean that when you have one pint, it's the same as having two?"

"Yes, man, Peter!" Thomas scoffed arrogantly. "Of course it does!"

"Well, there must be something wrong with me."

"How's that then, our Peter?" Thomas challenged.

"Well," Peter raised his brows in bewilderment, "I didn't go to the bushes twice as much!"

Everyone laughed, including Thomas, even though he felt cheated.

"Hey, Peter," Ralph laughed, "that was a corker! When the new ovens are built, I'm going to bake you a cake – an' tha's a fact."

Peter grinned from ear to ear, and his glistening eyes widened so much, that I thought his eyebrows would surely disappear beneath his hat.

"Thank you Ralph, I can't wait - does anyone know how to build an oven?"

It was only then, when everyone sat around the table, that I realised its true magnificence. It seemed to have a presence of its own - an aura of mystique. I sensed a feeling of power. Then it happened, the strangest feeling of déjà vu I have ever experienced - déjà vu of the future.

AN HUGE HISTORIC DISCOVERY

"Doctor Pearse, an odd thing has occurred. I have just had a feeling of déjà vu, in which the past, present and future, all co-existed.

James looked at me thoughtfully. "Father, I had a premonition you would say that!"

"Yes, I know you did!" I replied in astonishment.

My mind was spinning. How could anyone have a premonition of déjà vu? It seemed to be some sort of innate remembrance. This was the state of reality as we knew it. Doctor Pearse interrupted my wild thoughts.

"These things happen, Captain. Alcohol can play strange tricks on the mind... I should know!"

I found this to be a feeble explanation - an anticlimax to such a ponderous culmination of ubiquitous thoughts. I tried to put these thoughts out of my mind; so, after dinner, I went for a walk. As I turned the corner of the bungalow, I bumped into Henry, who was separating a large bunch of seedlings from a tray, for replanting.

"Hello, Henry; it's nice to see you back at the pastime you love."

"Yes, Captain; thank you;" he held up the tray; "I've found a beautiful place for these."

"I don't doubt it," I smiled. "When it comes to horticulture - or garden design - you have impeccable taste." And with that compliment, I left him, and headed back towards the beach.

Time seemed to pass quickly on the island, as days turned to weeks, and weeks turned to months. We began to settle down, and accommodate ourselves to our new surroundings.

In their spare time, which seemed indefinitely infinite, the lads had busied themselves, creating things to make life a little more comfortable: heated pools, showers and cooking ovens, etcetera.

The next morning, whilst sitting at the round table, having morning tea with Captain Arkwright, I looked up from the logbook in surprise, at how long we had actually been on the island.

"Six months, Captain! Doesn't time fly?"

Just then, Geordie came towards us, holding out a sheet of paper.

"Granddad, I've written a poem about our stay on the island - would you like to hear it?"

"Yes, Geordie," I said, with a quick acknowledging glance from Captain Arkwright, "we'd love to."

Geordie placed the sheet of paper down on the table, verso side up, and then began to recite the poem aloud from memory:

A LIFETIME'S JOURNEY

"Fifty men, five ladies, one boy and their pets:
one tortoise, one dog and a parrot happy and content.
All together on a beautiful island of dreams,
where the sun glimmers by day, and the ovens glow by night.
Granddad made the river flow into wine.
Doctor Pearse walked straight and sober through a river of alcohol, with his newly fitted leg.
Cricket in the clearing, boating on the lake and yoga on the beach; fitness and health are the name of the game - not winning."

"Well done, Geordie;" Captain Arkwright lightly tapped his hands together in appreciation; "we have a poet among us."
"And a philosopher," I added, proudly.
It was then, as the words of Geordie's poem resounded in my mind, that I thought of the brilliant future that awaited him in England.
We knew it would have taken a while to build a boat big enough to carry us all. But quite frankly, we've never actually been all that keen to leave the island. In this Eden, there is no serpent and never will be. We were twice shy - our yoga and prayers went hand in hand to keep us from the slithery path. We'd wait half-heartedly for a ship to answer our SOS - none ever has.

It has now been four and twenty years since Geordie wrote his poem; and the logbook entries - although perfectly informative - have become quite sporadic, listing only matters of importance. My illness now has the better of me. Therefore, it is today, in the year of our lord, the twenty first day of September, one thousand, eight hundred and thirty-two, that I, John Rigger, Master Mariner, and former captain of *The Turtle*, do hereby formally hand over the logbook of the above mentioned ship, for safekeeping and updating, to my grandson, Geordie Rigger, officially known as George Thomas Barnfather.

22nd. Sept. 1832: It is with honour, duty and respect, that I Geordie Rigger, place my first entry into this logbook. For during the early hours of this morning, my dear grandfather, Captain John Rigger, did pass away quietly in his sleep. May God rest his soul.

AN HUGE HISTORIC DISCOVERY

17th. January, 1890: My grandmother had been right; she had told me that being so young, if I stayed here I'd see a future of solitude. Being the youngest by twenty six years, I watched all the others pass away, one-by-one. My grandmother had re-united with my grandfather once again. Captain Arkwright passed on the year after. Doctor Pearse, William, Andrew and Fenwick, all died octogenarians. Everyone else died septuagenarians, except for Peter, who lived into his one hundred and fifth year, passing away in the year one thousand, eight hundred and sixty-nine. I am now alone, but not lonely; my pet tortoise being my only source of company; Ben-Sandy and Sammy having crossed over many years ago.

2nd. July, 1896: Celebrated my one hundredth birthday.

1st. January, 1900: Celebrated the new century with a small drink of wine. Feeling extraordinarily fit.

22nd. October, 1901: An unusual event occurred today. While I was passing by an old fallen tree trunk, my pet tortoise - Charles Methuselah - crawled out from beneath it. The strange thing being that his huge shell had been cleanly truncated, rather like the top from a boiled egg. The remaining thick hard shield of carapace now glistened like brilliantly polished jet, as black as a pool of ink.

2nd. July, 1917: Celebrated my one hundred and twenty-first birthday. I don't know how, but for some reason, my finger has grown back

CHAPTER X

THE JOURNEY HOME

"And that, gentlemen, is the last entry."

Captain Wiseman looked up from the logbook, as if from a dream. The rest of the crew looked up at the old man in disbelief.

"It can't be!" gasped the ship's younger security officer. "It ain't possible!"

"It is possible," the captain replied; "the old man is Geordie!"

The crew looked at each other in confusion.

"But wait a moment!" said the elder security officer; "if he celebrated his 100th birthday in the year 1896, then that now makes him an incredible 210 years old!"

The bosun shook his head. "Strewth! No wonder the old cobber didn't converse with us - if Peter died in 1869, then he hasn't spoken with anyone for about one hundred and thirty-seven years! He must have been a lonely bloke!"

The captain patted the logbook. "As Geordie said himself, loneliness is only a negative frame of mind. He must have lived with memories fresh in his mind, undisturbed by people and events."

"But Geordie and the others must have been at least homesick?" said the younger security officer, looking pitifully at Geordie.

"They were forgetful of the world by which they were forgotten," replied the captain.

The elder security officer raised an eyebrow. "You mean they chose to forget, Captain?"

"You could say that."

"Look, Captain!" the bosun pointed out through the window in amazement. "Look at that!"

Geordie's pet tortoise had come into view as it passed by the veranda. There was a clamour at the window, as eager heads fought for viewing space.

Captain Wiseman could not conceal his feelings. "What in tarnation? Why, that tortoise must be over six feet long!"

"Captain," the bosun's jaw dropped, "look at its back... it's just as the log-book said!"

"Yes, Bosun... black as ink!"

Charlie unknowingly caused a scene, just by being there. He had grown spectacularly large. He was just over six feet long, two feet six inches high

- with his truncated shell - and slightly over one hundred and fifteen stone.

Captain Wiseman turned to Geordie, and spoke softly to him. "Geordie, being here is like being in a dream. Can you understand me? Geordie?"

Geordie was obviously induced; he had learned to communicate beyond words; yet to him, the American dialect seemed remotely cognate.

"I think we had better get you home, friend." The captain warmly placed his hand upon Geordie's shoulder. He then radioed the ship, informing the Security Personnel of their imminent arrival. "... And have the crane ready," he added; "we have an unusual guest coming aboard." The bosun looked curiously at the captain. "Well!" retorted the captain, "we can't separate them after all these years, can we?"

The captain and his crew stayed on the island a few more hours, filling in the missing details. Then, with Geordie and the crew aboard the lifeboat, they headed back to the ship. Charlie was quite content to be towed behind on a raft, like a small island. Once safely on board the ship, the captain handed the staff captain the logbook of *The Turtle*.

"Put that in the safe room, Captain." His expression intimated the importance of the document.

"Right away, Sir!"

Hoisting Charlie aboard caused quite a stir. The ship's passengers were not satisfied with just watching - they wanted to be in on the act. To pacify them, the captain gave them a general report of the adventure on the island. As soon as he had finished his account, one of the passengers - a fat, ruddy-faced male reporter, with a white Stetson - took a photograph of the new arrivals and dashed furtively away.

Geordie and Charlie were once again the centre of attention. But this didn't at all perturb Geordie; he was so engrossed by the modern marvels around him. Now it was his turn to be cast into another world. He wondered at the miracle of a 'metal village floating on the sea'. The ship had six decks, weighed 41,000 tons, and had a length of 643 feet. It had 115 private apartments, each one containing a dining area and 3 to 4 bedrooms with en suite bathroom. The 225 crew and staff kept the whole ship running 24 hours a day. All requirements where catered for.

Geordie walked around knocking on walls in wonder. The sheer size of the place awed him. He marvelled at this new wonderful world - surprised by almost everything on board: electric lights that switched on and off; running tap water; television; telephones; convenience foods; cigarette lighters... and of course, the ship's helicopter, which he later described as a 'giant man-eating dragonfly'. His ancient thoughts were revolutionary and refreshing.

THE JOURNEY HOME

That evening - with the aid of fax - the papers were rife with stories of Geordie and Charlie complimented by a supplementary photograph. 'The oldest man captured on film', said one New York newspaper. 'Woman has healthy baby to 210 year old man', said another.

Sitting in his quarters, the captain waved a fax in the air. "You're famous before you're famous, Geordie." Geordie moved his lips, and gave out an inaudible sound. "What's that old man?" The captain looked kindly into Geordie's face. "Never mind, we'll have you talking again before you know it. In America, we have some of the greatest speech therapists in the world."

If the ship was incredible, then America was awesome; for, after docking in New York Harbour, Geordie was given the greatest welcome that anyone could remember in living history. The harbour was filled with all kinds of small boats and ferries, filled with cheering and waving people that had taken the liberty to come and greet him. I'm sure if she could have, the Statue of Liberty would have winked at Geordie. He was honoured as a living legend - an age-old phenomenon. On Liberty Island there was a large police presence as the crowds were so overwhelming. Geordie stopped for a moment, to try and take in his surroundings. It would be difficult to imagine what was going through his mind as he looked up at the towering buildings above his head - some of them over a thousand feet tall; or, what he thought of such a huge amount of people in one place - even Captain Wiseman was overwhelmed. The police then ushered Geordie and the captain through the crowds to the awaiting vehicle. As the car began to move there was a tremendous cheer from the swarming spectators. The streets of Broadway buzzed with life as the small group made their way to the New Yorker Hotel - people cheering all the way. As Geordie later described, 'The ticker tape came down from the houses that touched the clouds, and landed on the horseless carriage in which we sat'.

At last, now in their hotel - which had one thousand rooms, each with cable TV - they had privacy at last, with the added bonus of a fantastic view of the Empire State Building. Later, they unpacked their belongings and settled into their rooms.

As time went by, Geordie began his speech therapy at the Hotel. A few weeks after treatment, Geordie's voice was audibly soft and low - so sweet and gentle on the ear.

Meanwhile, scientists agreed that Geordie had the physique of a very fit man in his early sixties, and feared he must be mistaken about his claimed age of 210 years, especially as no man on record had ever lived above one hundred and twenty years. The scientists were eager to do tests, but Geordie declined saying, 'I am what I am'.

Many theorists and philosophers also studied Geordie's claim; and, after much deliberation and reading of religious texts, came to the conclusion that his age had not broken God's law, and was not as sacrilegious as it had first seemed. They explained that just as a caterpillar changes into a butterfly, that Geordie, when 120 years of age, had transmuted from man into Angel; Geordie was no longer a man - he was an immortal. The theorists agreed that at some stage Charlie had transmuted too.

It was then that Geordie's new world came alive. He was inundated with offers of television and radio interviews - public speeches, and the like. Captain Wiseman had taken immediate early retirement from his work to be a constant and loyal companion to Geordie.

"Go for it, Geordie!" enticed the captain; "take the bull by the horns."

"Yes," whispered Geordie, in a sweet, cheerful tone.

The tour of America was a success; Geordie and Charlie took America by storm.

"What a month!" said the captain, to Geordie, as they stepped from the 'metal bird of magnitude'. "What a month!"

People were amazed at Geordie's great age. 'Imagine having the good fortune to see the future', said some. 'Nostradamus guessed the future - you're living it', said others.

Sitting in their New York hotel room, Captain Wiseman turned to Geordie.

"Well, old fellow, we'll be leaving for your beloved England, tomorrow; I guess you'll be feeling mighty glad?"

"Yes, Captain; but firstly I have a great desire to visit a place in Africa, called Mossel Bay. I promised I would return one day."

"Ah, Mossel Bay…" the captain reflected, "… I know the place well.

"Can we go there?"

"Anything you say old boy. If that's what you want to do, I'm at your disposal… you're the man!"

The next morning, they boarded a ship bound for Africa - Geordie, Charlie and the captain - during which, Captain Wiseman observed Geordie's expressions. The years of solitude had caused him to become rather devoid of outward physical emotions; yet, the captain distinctly detected a hint of a smile on Geordie's face, and a glimmer in his eye. The captain wondered what reception Geordie would receive. So far, Geordie's fame had preceded him everywhere he went. He healed the sick, the lame, the deaf and the blind; and once brought a dead child back to life. He now became an international asset.

THE JOURNEY HOME

When they arrived in Africa, the harbour at Mossel Bay was crowded with all and sundry. The weather was glorious, as myriads of happy, brown, smiling faces greeted them with song. Geordie surveyed the scene.

"It's just as I remember it."

The banana plantation was still there, as were the fishing boats laden with nets, resting on the warm, golden sand. But, best of all, was the sight of the natives standing on the beach and harbour, in their brown leather loincloths, singing a welcoming song.

Geordie and Captain Wiseman stepped eagerly ashore. Ever so gradually, the singing quietened to a hush and the crowd parted down the centre, creating a clearing, through which an age-old, white-haired African man, stepped slowly forward with the aid of a walking stick. He was wearing a white Sengalese kaftan: an ankle-length robe with long bell sleeves - over a pair of white cotton drawstring trousers.

A LIFETIME'S JOURNEY

"Good morning, Geordie," said he, emotionally, straining to see through his white, cataracted eyes, all watery and sad; "we have been expecting you; it was foretold that one day you would return. My name is Dr Khal Chakka Bantu, doctor of farming, and head of my tribe, and great-great-great-grandson of Chief Bantu."

"Is he still alive?"

"I am afraid not Geordie; he passed on many years ago."

Geordie now realised that all his old friends were most likely long gone; and so his intended visit to India, or even a visit to China, would be futile.

"That is unfortunate. I have belatedly brought along the books he so longed for.

"We would be delighted to receive them in his honour," said the doctor, piously - for they looked on Geordie as a god.

"Chief Bantu was a great man, and I so much wanted to meet him again. I am overjoyed that you will receive the books in his absence."

"Thank you," the doctor bowed his head; "you are now welcome to visit our village."

"It will be a pleasure." Geordie returned the bow.

As they entered the village, the air was filled with an appetising, fruity aroma. Makeshift tables were piled high with an array of sea foods, meats, fruits and vegetables. It was almost as if Geordie had never been away; it was a place where time had almost stood still: a place remote from the twenty-first century. Chief Bantu's ancient throne, the mud huts and the Witch Doctor's livery - although in current use - all stood out as images of a time gone by. The setting was the same; only the characters had changed.

"Please follow me." The doctor led Geordie and the captain into his hut.

Hanging on the wall, side by side - as they had done for centuries - were the portraits of Geordie and Chief Bantu. The doctor put his face close against the portrait of Geordie, his hand gently following the contours of Geordie's face.

"You look like your image."

"Thank you." Geordie then eyed the other painting. "And you have a very strong resemblance to Chief Bantu."

Geordie walked forward and embraced the doctor, placing his hands about his person. "I do this out of love for Chief Bantu and his people." So saying, he placed his hands gently about the doctor's head - covering the eyes. A few natives stood in the doorway, their brown heads thrust inquisitively into the cooler innards of the hut. A moment later, Geordie removed his hands; the doctor opened his eyes and blinked.

THE JOURNEY HOME

"I can see clearly!" He waved his hand across his face in wonderment. The white fog-like cataracts had gone - his eyes were as clear and healthy as a young man's - and his legs too. The natives, and Captain Wiseman, looked on in astonishment. "Thank you, Geordie;" the doctor held him by the hand and then pointed with his redundant stick to a battered radio that lay upon the floor; "the stories we hear of you are true. At my age, I thought I had seen it all, but I have never witnessed anything so spectacular. I am now in my ninety eighth year, and I never thought I'd see the day you would return. We will now celebrate."

The doctor led the way out into the sunshine. He clapped his hands and the sound of tom-toms filled the air. The natives all about began to dance.

"What an incredible reception!"

"People are always welcomed this way, Captain - it is the Bantu custom."

The reception lasted two whole days; at the end of which - due to Captain Wiseman's influence - the entire village was invited aboard the American cruise liner. Doctor Bantu and the natives were intimidated by the technology aboard ship. This surprised Geordie.

"What are they afraid of, Captain?"

"They are afraid of technology, because they don't understand it."

"How is this? And why do they live in mud huts without technology?"

"It's because they can't afford to live any otherwise," sighed the captain.

"They live in the past because they cannot afford the future?" asked Geordie, in disbelief.

"Yes, Geordie." Here in Mossel Bay - as like many other places in Africa - the natives grow food crops for transportation abroad. This, they sell to a middleman, for a pittance, leaving themselves barely without a profit. They can see the wealth, and dream of it, but they can't ever touch it"

"How frustrating!" Geordie was visibly moved. "The doctor is an educated man; can't he and his people do anything about it?"

"The middleman keeps aloof, and keeps the village people subdued by ignorance... they're more-or-less bondsmen."

"It's an indignity, Captain!"

"I'm very sorry, Geordie." The captain lowered his tone. "Sometimes the truth hurts - but you did ask me."

"The world is not the place I thought it would be, Captain."

The captain of the ship came over to greet them.

"Hello again, Robert!" said he, to Captain Wiseman. They gave each other a mutual handshake and nod. "So this is the celebrated Geordie I have heard so much about? Hello Geordie, I hope you and your guests enjoy your evening of entertainment. We have an excellent show lined up for you, concurrent with a multi-course... a six course meal."

"Thank you very much." Geordie nodded in appreciation. "I'm sure we'll enjoy it immensely."

The evening went smoothly and everyone had an enjoyable time.

Alas, the next morning, as Geordie, the doctor and the captain stood upon the sunny shore, surrounded by the natives, it was time to say farewell. The doctor spoke to Geordie and the captain.

"It was a wonderful evening you gave us. We will never forget it - especially, Geordie, when you healed our sick."

"I only did what I could. When I arrive in England, I will send back a consignment of the necessary equipment that I spoke to you about."

"You are a pure man, Geordie." The Chief faced Geordie and they gently held each other's forearms. "Never enmity between our blood!"

"Yes, doctor; let wisdom prevail!"

"Thank you, Geordie. We are privileged to have met you. And you too Captain Wiseman; goodbye!"

Later, as the ship sailed out of port, Geordie heard once again, the plaintive singing of the Bantu people.

One hour into the journey, Geordie went below ship - down in the cargo bay to check on Charlie. He had paid a crewmember handsomely to keep him comfortable, watered and fed. Forty minutes later - satisfied that Charlie was feeling as well as should be - Geordie headed back up on deck.

The journey to England was smooth. Portsmouth Harbour finally came into view. For over 800 years this harbour has played a key role in the history of Britain and the world. The Historic Dockyard is home to three of the greatest warships ever built: Mary Rose, HMS Victory and HMS Warrior, and offers a complete Royal Navy experience, past and present.

Geordie and the captain stood on deck as the ship docked. The shore was swarming with waving, cheering people - many having waited hours to see Geordie. "It looks as if the whole world has come out to see you," the captain smiled.

Geordie seemed overwhelmed by the crowds, but gladly waved and posed for photographs, and kept his admirers happy and content. Later, he and the captain said their goodbyes to the adoring fans, and climbed into an awaiting police escorted limousine. Captain Wiseman had reserved a rented accommodation in Harrow, Middlesex, for the first week in June. He had booked the limousine to take them there, and had arranged for Charlie to follow by truck. This transport, which was selectively driven by experienced men - was hired indefinitely at a very handsome price. Before long, they were on the motorway, minus police escort, heading for Harrow.

Harrow is located in the northwest of London, and is one of London's most attractive suburbs. It is an area which combines the fast pace of a lively business and commercial centre with the peace and quiet of the countryside. It is famous for its boys' school, which was founded in 1572. Many famous historical figures were educated there, including Churchill, Byron and Fox Talbot: the inventor of photography.

When they arrived, they pulled into the drive of a beautiful, remote, sunlit cottage - the nearest neighbour being at least quarter of a mile away.

"Here we are, Geordie," said the captain, as the car pulled to a halt; "I think you'll enjoy it here; it's quiet and secluded."

The beautiful gardens all around were spacious and well cared for.

Geordie surveyed the various multitudes of colour. "It's almost like being back on the island. Charlie will like it here; it's perfect."

Charlie arrived a quarter hour after the limousine had set off to the nearest hotel. The truck was duly backed up to the front of the house, where a ramp was lowered onto the lawn, allowing Charlie free access to the enclosed gardens. The truck then left the drive in moderate pursuit of the limousine.

"Well, now we're alone, Geordie; we can relax, and Charlie can explore the gardens to his heart's content."

"There are things I must do first," replied Geordie, as he seated himself at the garden table. "But I will need your help."

The captain stood smiling in the sunshine with his arms unfurled. "I'm all yours."

"Thank you, Captain. How much money do we have?"

The captain knelt down, pulled some papers from the side of the laptop case at his feet and promptly laid them on the table. "According to the last bank statement, you have just over five million U.S. dollars. Geordie, you're a walking gold mine."

Geordie slid a piece of paper across the table. "Could you please tell me how much it would cost to buy the items upon this list, Captain?"

"Phew! This is some list - probably capable of bringing any small village into the technological age. If you excuse me Geordie, I'll price the items on the Internet." The captain pulled the wireless laptop from the case at his feet, placed it upon the table and set to work pricing up the items as best he could. After some time he stopped typing, took a pen from his shirt pocket and a sheet of plain paper from his laptop case, and then scribbled down some figures. When he had finished, he looked across at Geordie's eager face. "Well, Geordie, including the one year of tuition fees, you're talking in the region of three million pounds sterling - that's not far off a cool five million dollars."

"So we have enough?" replied Geordie; "then let's go shopping Online."

Just then, a red BMW Convertible pulled smoothly into the drive and came to a halt. A beautiful, well-dressed, middle-aged lady, with blonde, shoulder-length hair, climbed out. She closed the driver's door and walked towards Geordie and the captain.

"Hello, I'm Miss Clark! I believe we talked over the telephone?"

The captain closed the laptop and stood up. "Yes, I'm Robert Wiseman - I phoned you from New York."

"I'm sorry I'm late; I've had quite a journey."

"Never mind, ma-am; my friend and I kept ourselves entertained... we took the liberty of exploring your wonderful English garden."

"Actually, it's not my home - it's my sister Anna's. She's presently on holiday in Vienna, Austria, visiting our grandmother Helscher." Miss Clark then removed a bunch of keys from her jacket pocket, and dangled them on the end of her beautifully manicured, long slender fingers. She then waved her arm gently towards the door. "Would you like to see the place?"

"After you, ma-am." The captain stood to one side to let her through.

As she passed him, she turned her head quickly. So doing, her soft, blonde hair floated from her black velvet jacket and brushed across his neck; her perfume engulfed him, making him feel warm inside.

They stopped briefly, looking deep into each other's eyes.

"I just wanted to say... my name's Rose." She ran her fingers tenderly through her hair, brushing it gently back into place.

"A rose by any other name would smell as sweet," the captain replied softly.

Rose unlocked the door, and they both went inside. Thirty minutes or so later, the viewing done, they came back out, laughing.

"Yes, it's ideal!" The captain happily went to his laptop case, pulled out a cheque and handed it to Miss Clark. "I think that that should just about cover the rent for one month."

Rose looked back at him over the cheque "You're very generous, Robert. My sister Anna will be pleased."

A few minutes later, they were all sitting at the garden table, drinking coffee.

"Your friend's face looks familiar." Miss Clark reflected. "Now where could I have seen him before?"

"I'm sorry I didn't introduce you; I feel so impolite; but my friend here is so famous that he cannot venture in public without being recognised and mobbed by adoring followers. We came here, to this secluded cottage, so he could keep a low profile... I didn't want to betray his anonymity."

"Oh, I'm very sorry." Miss Clark placed her hand on Geordie's. "I didn't mean to intrude."

"Captain, I give you leave to break my anonymity and bring Miss Clark, into our confidence, as she is obviously a lady of integrity.

"That's true." The captain turned to Miss Clark. "My friend here is named Geordie Rigger, and he is two hundred and ten years old; you probably saw him on the news, or in this morning's paper. His pet tortoise Charlie, is at this moment strolling about in this very garden."

"Well I never!" Miss Clark put down her coffee cup in surprise. "Isn't it a small world?" After meeting Charlie, she was given a brief account of Geordie's amazing adventure. "What a remarkable story. I feel quite humbled."

"You're not the only one," the captain smiled.

Soon it was time for Miss Clark to leave. She said her goodbyes, then climbed into her car and wound down the side window.

"You will phone me, Robert... to let me know if you need anything?"

"Yes, I have your number here." He tapped the phone on his belt. "Goodbye."

The car tooted as it left the drive. Geordie and the captain waved.

"You would make a nice couple."

"Do you really think so, Geordie?"

"Most certainly."

The captain espied Geordie's list and picked it up with a smile. "Well, now... where were we, Geordie? Oh, yes, we were about to make some orders." The captain reopened the laptop and reconnected to the Internet, while Geordie relaxed back into the chair opposite. The captain spent a good few minutes, happily tapping at the keyboard, before turning his attention back to Geordie. "That leaves only the power generator, Geordie. I guess it's time for a telephone call."

The call was successful; Captain Wiseman had arranged for an adequate sized power generator to be delivered to Portsmouth harbour within the week; and from there, to be shipped directly to Mossel Bay, South Africa, along with all the other equipment.

"Well, Geordie, I think that just about wraps it up?" The captain then logged off the Internet and put away his Laptop. "I think it's about time for tea."

"Yes, Captain, the food we've brought should be sufficient."

Within half an hour, he and Geordie were eating their evening meal at the dining room table. When they had finished, they went into the living room to watch television. They switched on just as a photo of Geordie flashed up on the screen.

"... Our second report is about Geordie Rigger, a two hundred and ten year old man who is now believed to be living somewhere in England." As the report continued, Geordie looked on with interest.

Meanwhile, in the living room of a house in Hebburn, in the North East of England, there sat a young man named Tom Rigger, who was cosily watching the same evening news on television.

"Hey, Father, man - look at this!" He called his father in from the kitchen. "There's a two hundred and ten year old man on the telly, called Geordie Rigger; he's believed to have originally come from Newcastle!"

Tom's father, Davy, entered the living room, just as Geordie's photograph flashed up onto the screen once again.

"Hey, it's uncanny! It's our John's double!"

"Aye, Father, you're right! Look at that nose, man! Hey, I should have taped this! Wait till our John sees it, man!"

"Well, surely it'll be in tomorrow's paper?

"Oh, why-aye, of course it will, man!" Tom punched the air cheerfully.

Back in Harrow, Captain Wiseman picked up the remote control and switched off the television.

"Well, Geordie, if they want a story, then let's give them one."

"Yes," Geordie gazed thoughtfully at the empty screen, "television is a valuable medium - I'm ready to talk."

This resulted in a five day spate of nationwide TV chat show appearances; culminating in a visit to Buckingham Palace.

"Hey, Geordie," said the captain, as they sped through the night streets of London, on their way back to Harrow, "that prince of yours seems a mighty swell guy."

"Yes, he is. I could see in his eyes the signs of compassion, integrity and wisdom - gained only through familiarity, humility and experience. He is the one person I have so far met that knows the true value of the past."

"You must have had some conversation with him?" The captain glanced at his watch. "You were in there for three hours. Before he joined you, I asked him if he felt excited, meeting someone who had met one of his forefathers: George III of England, no less. 'Oh,' he answered, instantly, 'my grandfather to the sixth generation... yes'. 'Ah, you're well versed in genealogy,' I said. 'Royal pedigrees are a particular interest of mine,' he replied with a wry smile while feeling his cuff."

An hour or so later, the limousine pulled into the cottage drive.

"Oh, by the way, Geordie," said the captain, stepping from the car, "did you get to meet the Queen of England?"

"Yes," replied Geordie; and that was that.

"I wonder what Rose is doing now?" The captain paused and looked dreamily up at the moon, as the limousine pulled out of the drive.

"That's the fifth time you've asked me that in as many nights. It must be love, indeed."

Indoors, Geordie sat on the sofa, drinking a nightcap, as Captain Wiseman stood in the hallway, oozing out sentiment over the telephone. Geordie wasn't one to eavesdrop, but he distinctly heard the words 'love', and 'soon', mentioned frequently.

An hour later, Geordie decided to retire. He walked quietly by the captain, caught his attention, and then put his hand up to wish him good night. The captain nodded back in acknowledgement, and then went back to his telephone conversation; a while later he gently replaced the receiver and headed contentedly to bed.

The next morning, Geordie was awoken by the usual dawn chorus from the birds in the trees outside his window. After washing and dressing, and a spot of yoga on the lawn, he and Captain Wiseman breakfasted alfresco, beneath a beautiful, clear, summer sky.

"Well, Geordie," the captain pushed aside his empty bowl and replaced it with his diary, "let's see what we have planned for today."

"It's the eighth day of June," replied Geordie, matter-of-factly; "I believe you'll find that I'd like to visit the county of Leicestershire, today."

"That's absolutely true;" the captain looked up from his diary; "how on earth could you remember that?"

"I never forget." Geordie picked up his teacup. "And the matter of the date... well, the calculation is a simple one. While on my maiden voyage on *The Turtle*, my grandmother taught me certain memory techniques - one of them being the art of calculating the day of the week for any given year. The ability has never left me."

"That's unbelievable!" The captain shook his head. "Do you mean to say, that you never ever forget a name, a face, or anything else you ever see, hear, or read?"

"That is correct."

"Would it be okay if I put your memory to the test? I'd like to ascertain your capabilities."

"Yes of course - it would be my pleasure."

The captain hesitated a moment to procure pencil and paper. He then proceeded to jot down a few questions.

"Now then, Geordie, what are the days of the week for the following dates: 4th of July 1776; 22nd of November 1963; 4th of April 1968 and 21 July 1969?"

"Tuesday, Friday, Thursday and Monday, respectively," Geordie pronounced fluently.

"Astonishing!" the captain looked across at Geordie, "your answers are exact beyond belief; those are four of the most outstanding dates in American history; I'll never forget the days, or the dates." The captain looked admiringly at Geordie. "You know, old fellow? I thought I knew everything about you, but the dark horse keeps on coming back - you amaze me; your inspiration gives me aspiration."

"You think I'm highly perceptive; maybe it's so; but any person with an ounce of determination could become as capable as I. A person who acts like a psychic sponge is sensitive to other people's emotions. And if the absorbed emotions are negative, then that person could soon become deeply sad."

"Yes, Geordie, it's so easy for people to join the stress arena; and once they do, they're on an uphill struggle; with symptoms like depression and lack of concentration; i.e. bad memory."

"That is true, Captain. But the person with a positive attitude has a stronger aura, and is therefore more resilient to disease."

"But how do you get this positive attitude, Geordie?"

"Love - love and you shall inherit the earth, along with good health and peace of mind. On the contrary, you shall quickly become the earth - antipathy causes misery."

"There's one thing that puzzles me, Geordie; if your memory is infallible, how did you forget how to speak?"

"I didn't. If one gets pins and needles in ones leg, one can't walk on it; this doesn't mean that one has forgotten how to. Similarly, when one has not spoken for one hundred and thirty-seven years, one has not simply forgotten - one just can't."

"Similar to having laryngitis, or atrophy of the muscles you mean?"

"Exactly."

Just then, there was a rustle, as Charlie crawled out from behind a large bush.

"Hello Charlie," said the captain, cheerily, "I thought you were lost out there."

Charlie acknowledged by placing his momentous head upon the table, and sniffing loudly at the two empty breakfast bowls thereon. Geordie placed his right hand upon Charlie's head, and stroked it tenderly.

"Would you like some sugar lumps?" Charlie answered by putting out his tongue. Geordie removed a handful from the sugar bowl and lovingly fed them to Charlie. "There you are; you'll need your energy today, as we're going on a journey; you'll like that, won't you?"

Charlie finished off the last of the cubes, licked Geordie's hand, winked and then moved off contentedly towards the cool refreshing shelter of the nearby willow tree. A moment later, Geordie and the captain went indoors to make arrangements for the journey.

The captain replaced the telephone receiver. "John will be here with the truck at 9 o' clock, a.m., and Martin will be here with the limo at quarter past."

Geordie turned towards the wall clock, just as it struck the hour. "That gives you two hours to pack. Meanwhile, I'll do the washing-up."

Time passed quickly, for within two-and-a-half hours, Charlie, Geordie and the captain found themselves heading north, on their way to Leicestershire, in the Midlands. Leicestershire is a beautiful county in the heart of England, a county where timeless villages really do exist and market towns actually live up to the name. It's a lovely place for those who love the great outdoors, and those with a passion for English history and heritage.

As the roads were quiet, they reached their destination early. Both vehicles pulled into the gravel drive of a mansion house, in the village of Heather. Immediately, the driver opened the truck doors and lowered the ramps, to allow Charlie to descend down onto the driveway. The driver left the truck on the drive, as had been arranged, then closed the driveway gate, and headed off with the limo driver to their nearby hotel.

Ten minutes later, Geordie, and the captain stood with their backs towards the three car garage, tilting their heads back to look up admiringly at the top of the building.

"Wow! This is some place; are you related to royalty, or something?"

"I'm not sure, Captain;" Geordie glanced up at the rows of windows, set neatly into the buildings impressive facade; "my grandfather always claimed we were, but there was never any confirmation to back it up. Besides, my Great Uncle Archibald inherited this house on the terms that he adopt his wife's surname. Although a rich man in his own right, he accepted the name on account of respect; it was a very common practice in those days."

"Your British peculiarities are very thought-provoking. Consequently, this mansion must have seen some history."

"Yes, it has," said the owner, as he entered the drive by the nearby side gate. He was a tall, fit-looking gentleman, with blonde hair, blue eyes, and a healthy tanned complexion. "Hello, my name's Jason!" He held out his hand. "You must be Geordie and Robert... it's wonderful to see you... welcome to Leicestershire."

The captain and Geordie shook hands with Jason, and cordially introduced themselves.

"If you come with me, gentlemen, we'll enter the building through the rear, which will allow Charlie to have free run of the lawned garden there in complete safety."

"Thank you very much," said Geordie; that's very much appreciated.

Indoors was much cooler. The guests were ushered into the large, west wing sitting room, across a beautiful deep pile carpet and invited to sit on a leather three-piece suite. The entire decor was cream-coloured.

Three full-length windows on one wall had their shutters pushed back, allowing in maximum light. On the other walls hung framed family portraits, a huge framed plate glass mirror and a set of golden wall lamps. The centrepiece of the room - a beautiful carved marble surround - was adorned with two beautiful ornaments, while a very large crystal chandelier hung ornately from the ceiling.

Jason offered Geordie and the captain each a cool refreshing drink, as he introduced them to his family. His wife inquired of Geordie's television appearances, and how he had felt living alone on the island. Geordie felt obliged to give a résumé of his adventures. The family sat enraptured as they listened to the exciting narrative. An hour later, Geordie ended his story on the subject with which he had begun - his childhood.

"So your great-aunt was born here, in this very house?" Jason's wife asked.

"Yes," said Geordie, pleasantly; "and my grandmother was born nearby, in the home of her father, the then local clergyman."

"How astonishing!" replied Jason's wife, just as the dinner bell rang; "the way you bring the past to life!"

Presently, they moved from the living room and down the hallway to the dining room, where a sumptuous meal awaited them on a very large wooden table. Before long, the conversation turned back once again to the subject of the house.

"It was built in the tenth century," Jason explained, "and extended in the seventeenth. Some of the original timbers can still be seen inside the house - especially upstairs. The adjacent Anglican Church is named The Parish Church of Saint John the Baptist, and is associated with the Venerable Church of St. John - and formally, The Knights Hospitallers. I think that that, and the fact that this house was once used as a monastery, greatly influenced the writer, Sir Walter Scott. For it was here, in this very house, in a room upstairs, that he wrote the novel *Ivanhoe*."

"I can't believe it! Ivanhoe is one of my favourite stories," the captain marvelled. "I particularly like its portrayal of the English art of chivalry. You Brits sure have an impressive history!"

"Yes," Jason added, "the story also coincides with the local castle of Ashby - the place Mary Queen of Scots was held captive; and with the more prevalent Conisbrough Castle, in South Yorkshire, where the film Ivanhoe was made."

They chatted until long after dinner, whereupon Jason gave Geordie and the captain a tour of the house, then showed them up the winding staircase to their rooms.

Looking down upon the front garden from an upper room window, the captain gave out a whistle.

"That's some tree trunk!"

"Yes, and it was some tree!" Jason pulled back a curtain and peered down onto the lawn. "Sadly, it had to be felled, as it had become weak and diseased and was in danger of collapse."

Later, after having settled in, Geordie wished to visit the cemetery which adjoined the mansion, to pay his respects to the family he once knew. Jason and the captain went along too. It was now late afternoon.

The steeple of the Parish dominates the village. The church itself is of the Norman period. The graveyard is always in a very neat and respectable condition, mostly due to the efforts of the Heather Parish Council.

THE JOURNEY HOME

As Geordie, the captain and Jason entered the churchyard, they came across the rector. He was a small, timid looking man with a round, clean-shaven face, short grey hair and a slight stoop.

"Good day, rector!" Jason gave a slight nod.

"Good day to you," replied the rector, piously; "how may I help you?

Jason explained the reason for Geordie's visit, and the distance he had come.

"Let's see what we can do." The rector removed a large key from his pocket. He unlocked the heavy church door and led them through to the cool, dimly-lit vestry. Inside, he unlocked a large chest, and removed a heavy brown leather-bound book. "This is the record of burials for the date in question. Do you know which name you are looking for?" Geordie gave the names and occupations of his great uncle and aunt. The rector slowly turned a few pages, scouring the names intently. "Ah! Here we are; I think this is what you're looking for?" It was indeed. Geordie's great uncle and aunt had died in the year 1822, both aged eighty nine. The rector removed an old chart from the chest, which showed a full plan of the graveyard. "If you follow me gentlemen, I'll show you the whereabouts of the grave."

They found it near the south wall of the churchyard. Geordie knelt down and spoke in soliloquy, as he read out the words from the headstone. When he had finished, the rector spoke to him.

"That was very sweet my friend; you have feeling indeed."

"The feeling's mutual." Geordie rose to his feet and then shook the rector by the hand. "By how much is your church fund in deficit?" He added, nodding over towards a donation sign on the church door.

"Three thousand pounds," replied the rector, turning to look up at the roof.

Geordie looked at the captain with raised eyebrows - the captain looked back with a discerning smile, and proceeded to withdraw a chequebook from his wallet. A moment later, Geordie handed over a cheque for ten thousand pounds.

"But this is way beyond the deficit!" The rector held out the cheque in confusion.

"It is a small repayment in comparison to the love and affection you have shown to the people of this village," said Geordie, warmly.

"Thank you!" The rector then closed his eyes for a second and breathed out joyfully. "Thank you very much; may the Lord bless you."

They said their farewells to the delighted rector, and then headed back to the mansion house. Ten minutes after that, they were sitting in the second of the two ground-floor living rooms, drinking refreshments. The living room was situated on the east wing and decorated in a similar manner to the first, except for the addition of fitted bookshelves, a television and a red velvet three piece suite.

"You're very generous, Geordie," said Jason, sinking back into his plush red armchair.

"I can afford to be;" Geordie set down his drink; "I'm a rich man; besides, I like to help those that help others."

"Do unto others as you would have them do unto you?" said Jason.

"Yes," Geordie nodded, "that's the idea."

The captain eyed the portrait of Sir Walter Scott, which hung upon the wall.

"While we're here, we'd love to see more of your wonderfully, historic county, if possible."

"I think that could be arranged," Jason smiled.

In between their sightseeing, Geordie decided to take up an offer to visit the children at Heather Primary School. The children loved Geordie, and all asked how Charlie was. Geordie went away with a bag full of drawings of himself and Charlie. It is difficult to tell who was more excited at meeting Geordie - the parents or the children. A fun day was had by all.

Some nights Geordie and the captain would join Jason and his wife in the Crown - their local - directly opposite the mansion house. They would talk for hours. The landlord told Geordie and the captain about the Heather Music Festival, based around three venues in the village: The Crown Inn, The Queens Head Public House and Heather St. Johns Football Club - a great crowd-puller in late July, early August and an excellent standard of local and national established live music. He also told them about 'The Heather Scarecrow Festival'. This event is such a fun time for the villagers. They dress up scarecrows in the most original fashion and place them in the oddest places. If you happen to pass through Heather village in late July, early August, you'll no doubt see some of the strangest sights imaginable: The likes of Elvis the scarecrow hanging from a chimney top! Madonna the scarecrow hanging halfway out of an open window! Michael Jackson the scarecrow climbing up the side of a house! This is all covered by the local press. The money collected from the festival is donated to and shared equally between five Heather Village organisations.

Geordie and the captain had a great time travelling around Leicestershire, but suddenly their visit was almost over. They stayed at Heather for two more days, meeting the most wonderful people, before saying a most gracious farewell to Jason and his family. The truck and limousine then headed off to the picturesque village of Ovingham: a village due west of Newcastle, Northumberland, North Tyneside.

They crossed over the River Tyne, on the Ovingham Bridge, from Prudhoe, and arrived in Ovingham, just as St. Mary's church clock struck 10 a.m. A wedding was in progress, and the church bells began to ring.

"Ah, such sweetness!" Geordie closed his eyes and reminisced. "Bells provide a comforting sense of permanence in an ever-changing world. These same bells rang out the day we left here - oh so long ago. Since ancient times, bells have been rung in times of joy and sorrow; and there is something about their peal that stirs up the deepest human emotions."

The limousine turned right at The Terrace and then left into Horsley Road.

Geordie pointed excitedly through the car's near-side window, to a solidly built two-storey building. "There it is, Captain! There's the house!"

It had sash windows and solid grey stone walls, dotted here and there with ivy, and surrounded by a perimeter wall overhung with branches;

"This is the house your grandparents owned?"

"Yes!" Geordie pressed his face to the side window as they drove into the courtyard; "this is the house where I spent some years growing up."

As they stepped from the car, they were met by a jolly looking fat man in a tight brown suit, with a fat, shiny, bald head and a huge grey bushy moustache.

"Hello!" he squeaked, enthusiastically. "Welcome; my name's Septimus; I'm glad you could make it." Septimus oozed happiness; his eyes were round and expressive, and his small ears stuck to his large head like quavers on a pumpkin. His smile was infectious; when he laughed, it was from his stomach upwards, and his ruddy cheeks shook on command.

We had prearranged with the property owner for the truck to be left on the drive; so after Charlie was set free to roam the enclosed garden, the drivers both headed off in the limousine to their nearby accommodation.

"If you'd kindly come with me, gentlemen," Septimus beckoned us cheerfully, "I'll show you indoors. My brother Hugo awaits us in the reading room."

As Septimus turned, he noticed the front door was shut. "Oh, that's a silly thing... I've locked myself out. Now where did I put the key?" He looked through each of his pockets, in turn, fumbling with peculiar, little jerky movements. "No, it's not there," he laughed to himself; "I wonder where it could be!" He opened a few shirt buttons and then peeped inside his vest.

THE JOURNEY HOME

"Hmm!" he placed his finger on his lips. "I wonder if it's in my shoe." He bent down to have a look. As he did so, his face turned crimson; his fat red neck squeezed ever tighter over the top of his white shirt collar; it looked as if he would choke, or at least pass out! He replaced his shoe, fastened his shoelace and stood upright, holding a single piece of jigsaw between his fingers. "How on earth did that get there?" He laughed, placing it in his trouser pocket. "Never mind, Brother Hugo will know - Brother Hugo knows everything."

Even though Geordie and the captain were aware the key was in the lock, they didn't have the heart to tell Septimus, as he seemed to be having so much fun.

A second later, Septimus noticed the key in the door. "Ah, look! The key wasn't lost at all; it was in the lock all this time; it's amazing what you can find when you know where to look!"

The captain looked at Geordie with an expression of constrained laughter, and then back to Septimus.

Septimus turned the key, opened the door and led them through a hallway to the door of a room. "Would you wait here a moment, please? Hugo has been very engrossed in his hobby for the past few weeks." So saying, he disappeared into the room, closing the heavy door behind him.

"What an exuberant character!" The captain laughed. "He's the first true English eccentric I've come across. You couldn't ever find another like him; he must be unique."

Just then, the door reopened, and out stepped Septimus.

"Please come in, gentlemen; Hugo is ready to see you now."

As they entered the huge room, they looked around. The walls were panelled with oak; one adorned with a fancy array of no less than 49 ornate clocks - each one perfectly synchronised with the others. Beautiful old oak furniture filled the room; into each piece was carved a single mouse - each one caught in the act of play - giving a quaint look to the place; and a pile of old books lay haphazardly on the floor. And, although it was summer, a roaring fire blazed in the grate.

"Over here, gentlemen!" a familiar voice spoke from the far side of the room. Geordie and the captain made their way across the heavy carpeted floor towards it. They could make out two figures standing by the window - outlined by the summer sun - the faces shadowed and unrecognisable. A moment later, their eyes became accustomed to the light. The captain looked at the brothers with utter disbelief, and almost cried out with laughter. He glanced at Geordie, to reassure himself that he wasn't dreaming - Hugo and

Septimus were identical twins!

"Good morning, gentlemen!" Hugo beamed with the same enthusiasm as Septimus. "You're welcome to stay here for as long as you wish; your rooms await you upstairs."

"Thank you very much," the captain drawled.

Just then, the clocks on the wall began to whirr simultaneously, before striking the half hour. Hugo looked at his pocket watch, then the three wristwatches on his left arm, then walked to the window and checked the church clock - nodding to himself as he did so. He then walked over to the door, rattled the knob, and then walked back to his desk. He opened a drawer, took out a £50 note, scribbled an address onto it, stuck a first-class stamp in the top right-hand corner, then pushed it towards Septimus and said, "Don't forget to post that!" Then he quickly sat down, put his head back, and stared up at the ceiling, as if in deep thought.

The captain looked down at Hugo with concern. "Are you alright, Sir?"

Hugo put his head down, and then laughed to himself.

"Yes," he squeaked, excitedly, "I am now! You see, gentlemen, the jigsaw which you see upon the table, has taken me almost two weeks of leisure time to complete. And at the end of my toil, I found a single piece to be missing. A week ago, a few pieces fell to the floor, which I immediately recovered... or so I thought. It wasn't until two days ago, that I realised a piece was missing - and all this time my mind has been preoccupied with finding it. I know it isn't on the floor, because I have scoured every inch of it... and it is only just this minute that I have realised where it must be!"

So saying - and before Septimus could utter a word - Hugo leapt up, wrestled him to the floor, grabbed his legs and whipped off his shoes. Septimus squealed with laughter.

"Leave my feet! Oh, no! Holy moley! Not again... anything but my feet!"

"It's impossible!" Hugo laughed, stood up and threw Septimus his shoes. "It's the only place it could have been!"

"You're right!" Septimus quickly pulled the piece from his pocket and proudly held it up. "That's exactly where I found it!"

Hugo grabbed the piece with excitement, and hurriedly placed it into the awaiting space in the jigsaw, looking down at the finished puzzle with pride.

He then immediately helped Septimus up from the carpet; and then - both holding each other at arms length - they began to dance around the floor in fits of hysterics. The captain - a man of strong resolve - lost his self-control and joined the twins in a mad orgy of laughter. This was the entertaining way in which Geordie and the captain met their unusual hosts.

Two hours later, having settled in, and with a hearty meal behind them, Geordie and the Captain decided to take a stroll. In the garden, Geordie stopped beneath a great oak tree and nostalgically caressed the bark, as Charlie and the captain looked on.

"My grandfather planted this tree; it is identical in age to me, and also to three other trees planted elsewhere: one in the grounds of my Aunt Isabella's home at Hebburn Hall, one now just a stump in Jason's garden at Heather and the other at Dents Hole, the place where I was born."

"How did this come about?" The captain asked.

"A few days before my birth, my mother and her sister Isabella, joined my Great Uncle Archibald, his family and my grandparents, on a trip to Sherwood Forest, in Edwinstowe, Nottinghamshire - the place famous for its association with the folk hero Robin Hood. Whilst there, my grandfather, my Uncle Archibald, my mother and her sister Jane, each picked an acorn from the Major Oak, with the agreement that they would each plant them in their gardens along with ten half guineas, on the very day of my birth.

"What a beautiful gesture, Geordie."

A moment later, they headed for St. Mary's churchyard - a short walk - leaving Charlie and the garden behind. There, they found the grave of Geordie's cousin, George. The poignant verse upon the stone, cut deep into Geordie's soul:

'THE BURIAL PLACE OF
GEORGE WILLIAM RIGGER,
OF CROFT HOUSE, OVINGHAM.
THE LAST OF A FAMILY, WHO FOR GENERATIONS WERE
FREE BURGESSES OF NEWCASTLE UPON TYNE.'

THE JOURNEY HOME

Geordie passed out through the lychgate with a heavy heart. "I need to go to Dents Hole."

Dents Hole is on the north side of the River Tyne, about ten miles down river from Ovingham village, and about 8 miles up from the open sea.

The captain phoned the limo driver at the village inn, and within five minutes they were on their way. It should have been a special day for Geordie - coming home at last - but for the first time in his life he felt alone.

Standing at the place of his birth, a few yards from the water at Chandlers Quay, on the River Tyne, he looked around at the modern buildings about him - it seemed as though he was trying to resurrect the last embers of a time gone by.

"It's not as I remember it," said he, sadly; "the contour of the land has changed; not even the river is the same. Gone forever are the scenes of my childhood. It might sound odd, but I thought it would be just as I left it."

"I'm sorry." The captain felt Geordie's pain. "Men can now move mountains and put them elsewhere."

"Where are the old folks?" Tears filled Geordie's eyes. "There are people here... but to me, the place is empty. Where is the village that I once knew? Gone forever, just like the ship that sailed away, never to return." Geordie lifted his teary eyes up to the heavens. "I feel I've failed my grandfather."

"But how, Geordie?"

"I don't have children, and, as my Cousin George's epitaph indicates, I am now the last of my line, Captain." Geordie became overwhelmed by the thought.

"It's a terrible cross to bear, Geordie - but are you sure there aren't any other present branches of the family Rigger?"

"I have no idea! I'm so upset... the stress has swung me... the sadness is stronger than my spirit."

"I feel as though by bringing you here I've deadened your spirit," the captain sighed; "and for penance, I wear the *S. S. Albatross* around my neck."

Geordie looked around at the view, in deep thought. "There's nothing here but sadness and memories. Why stand I here like a ghost and a shadow? 'Tis time I was leaving, 'tis time I was gone."

CHAPTER XI

THE REUNION

When they arrived back in Ovingham, Septimus was at the door to greet them.

"When you were out, a man called for you. He said he was a relation of yours."

"Did you catch his name?" asked Geordie.

"Yes, his name was Davy Rigger." Septimus beamed.

"Davy Rigger?" Geordie clasped his hands with delight."

"Yes, he left this note for you."

Geordie's face showed such happiness, as he flashed his eyes fervently across the paper. He turned excitedly to the captain, and held out the note.

"Great news, Captain... I need to go to this address in Hebburn!"

The captain briefed over the note. "I understand, Geordie; we'll leave at once."

Before the limousine pulled away, the captain turned to Septimus, who was standing at the gate. He kissed the note, and then waved it to him through the open window.

"Septimus, you're the best!" he shouted, with a smile. Septimus beamed with delight.

It wasn't long before the captain and Geordie reached Davy Rigger's address. They parked at the front of the house: a humble semi-detached with a small fenced garden and a tight drive.

A LIFETIME'S JOURNEY

Geordie eagerly left the car, then walked down the drive, closely followed by the captain. The captain knocked on the door. It was opened by a small lady with a kindly looking face.

"Yes?" Can I help you?"

"Hello ma'am. My name's Robert Wiseman, and this here is my good friend Geordie Rigger; I believe your husband may be expecting us?"

"Could you excuse me a moment, please?" the lady smiled timidly; "I'll just fetch him."

A moment later, a pleasant looking, large and powerful white-haired man, in his early seventies, came to the door, wearing black shoes, a white short-sleeved shirt, and dark trousers fastened with a thick, leather brown belt.

"Ah, hello there gentlemen, come in, come in! You must have just missed me at the churchyard." They all walked through the small carpeted passageway, into the modestly furnished living room. "I'm afraid you'll have to excuse my wife," the host apologised, as the lady left the room; "she gets rather nervous in company."

"Oh, I'm sorry to hear that," said the captain, sympathetically; "I hope we're not intruding."

"Oh, not at all - your visit is a pleasure."

"Oh, we didn't introduce ourselves." The captain held out his hand. "My name's Robert."

"And mine's Davy," said the host; "and this must be our Geordie?"

"It's unbelievable!" Geordie stared emotionally at Davy. "You're my grandfather alive again!" Tears began to run down his face.

"Come 'ere," Davy held out two inviting arms; "it's about time someone gave you a cuddle." Geordie opened up to the warmth of kinship - succumbed by enveloping love.

"I needed that," Geordie stood wiping tears from his face. "People usually treat me like a god - untouchable."

"It's your sublime beauty that overawes them." Davy's affection did Geordie well, for within a few moments, he seemed his old self again. "Take a seat Geordie; take the weight of your feet. You too Robert; make yourself at home; you're with family now." He then walked over to an oak sideboard and withdrew a blue folder from the top drawer, from which he took some pedigree charts and a few letters. "This is why I came to see you." He leant over and handed them to Geordie, who was now sitting on the settee. "You see, I'm the family genealogist, and the possibility of meeting you was a chance not to be missed - you're our link with the past. I'm the great-great grandson of Thomas Rigger of Hebburn; you're my 3rd cousin, 5 times

145

THE REUNION

removed."

Geordie put his hand across his mouth and closed his eyes, giving out a sigh of relief. After a moment, he reopened his eyes. "Davy, you don't know how heart-warming and consoling it is to hear that; it's fortifying news indeed."

"I feel just as excited," said Davy, now relaxing into the armchair opposite Geordie.

"But, I don't understand why Cousin George would claim he was the last of the Riggers."

"That's easily explained," said Davy. "Cousin George didn't mean he was the last of the Riggers... he meant that he was the last of the Riggers, who were Free Burgesses of Newcastle."

"Oh, I see," said Geordie. "An ambiguous sentence so easily misconstrued. English grammar has changed considerably over the last two centuries."

The captain looked over from the easy chair by the window. "Davy, how did you know we were at Croft house?"

"Now and again, I journey to Ovingham churchyard, to pay my respects to George and his family; mainly to keep in touch with the past. Today, after doing so, I called into the local pub for refreshments. Whilst there, I overheard two local men discussing your arrival at Croft house. 'Yes', said one - whom I later discovered to be a servant at the house - 'it was definitely Geordie Rigger, the two hundred and ten year old man off the telly'. And as I say gentlemen, meeting you was a chance not to be missed."

"I'm so happy you did, Davy." Geordie looked across from the settee. "To have a family, is to have a future; it's an exhilarating feeling."

Geordie then looked down, picked up an envelope from his knee and studied the stamp and postmark. "Thirty two pence from London to Hebburn... it's incredible! When I was a boy, my grandfather used to send a weekly post via the Newcastle to Sunderland Bye Post, at a cost of threepence per letter. The post boy rode a large grey pony, and carried the Bye letters in a small leather satchel slung over his shoulder. My grandfather used to give the boy a generous tip, and say, 'post haste, boy... post haste!' ah memories."

"Geordie, the habit of charging letters by the sheet was unique to Europe, and ceased in 1839. Writing was quite expensive for some folk, so they made full use of a single sheet with 'double writing': that is writing from left to right on a sheet of paper and then overwriting it from top to bottom. I have examples of letters from that period upstairs."

Geordie smiled, then, once again gave his full attention to reading the letters and charts upon his lap. "You've done your research well; it's nice to see the old names still going strong." Geordie's ability to recall family relationships, plus the dates of their births, marriages and deaths, was at that moment invaluable. He pointed out a few minor discrepancies in the more distant family lineage, and put them right accordingly. Geordie tapped the chart, "I'm sorry, but up to eighteen hundred and six, is as far as I know, except for my family on the island."

"I'm absolutely astounded!" Davy beamed. "The papers were right - you have a phenomenal memory. But how do you know so much about the family history before your time?"

"My grandfather had a fondness for telling me stories of times gone by, told to him by his father, and so on. He once showed me a sea chest he owned, which was filled with old wills, deeds, certificates and the like."

"Did he take it with him on the fateful journey?"

"No, he left it behind at Croft house."

Davy sighed with relief, and wondered if the chest could still be there.

Geordie seemed to read his mind. "I could duplicate everything word for word, and draw any people or illustrations from any time in my memory, if you so wish."

Davy put his head back and laughed out with excitement. "I think I might be imagining this! Geordie, you're a genealogist's dream - a delightful paradox! The past isn't the past anymore, because you are the past - but you're here now - it's wonderful!"

They talked together for an hour or more. Geordie was delighted to find someone that knew his past so well. The scrapbooks, pedigree charts and the videoed news and documentaries were a testament to that: to the past of the miraculous rarity that honoured Davy's home. The captain reminded Geordie of the time, and the patient driver waiting in the limousine.

"It's been an educational visit." Geordie shook Davy's hand. "When do we meet the rest of the family?" he added, pointing to some photographs of Davy's immediate family, placed here and there upon the sideboard.

"Soon enough, Geordie - but I'll have to round them up first."

Arrangements were then made for a private family reunion, in the concert room of the town's Elmfield Social Club, for 2 o' clock the following Saturday. Davy's brother John is an organist at the Club, and an excellent one at that, as many people come from miles around to dance to his wonderful music. This large, flat-roofed club is one of the family watering holes. It has a large bar, a small lounge and a concert room with a very spacious dance floor and high stage - atop which the club organ stands. Each room has many windows.

As the small group stood at the door of Barnard Crescent, saying their farewells, Davy suddenly realised something. "Oh dear, I'm sorry; I was so enrapt that I completely forgot to offer you refreshments."

"That's no matter," the captain smiled; "we can make up for it tomorrow."

"Oh, you'll need directions to the social club." Davy raised his hand, just about to explain the route, when Geordie interjected.

"It's on the corner, where Finchale Road meets Campbell Park Road."

"I know from the newspapers that you were well acquainted with bygone Hebburn, but how on earth could you know of a building that is comparatively recent?"

"The A to Z street atlas."

"You mean you memorised it, page by page?"

"Yes, page 65, E3 of my map book."

Davy stood open-mouthed. "Incredulous! Oh, that reminds me," he added, inquisitively; "as you knew this area and its small community so well as a child, it seems odd - class divisions aside - that you didn't come across your poor relations at some point."

"I'm sorry; my grandfather only mentioned your family briefly, whilst passing Hebburn, on the first day of our fated journey; which Cousin George's words erroneously had led me to believe had become extinct."

"No apologies needed, Geordie. It's just one of those things that has puzzled me for years - how, somewhere along the line, families divide."

Davy followed the captain and Geordie down the drive to the gate.

Before stepping into the car, Geordie turned back and spoke softly, "I'm sorry to hear about your wife's nervous disposition; I'll send out sympathetic healing to her; she'll be well by the morning. Please bring her with you tomorrow; we'll see you at two. Goodbye." The guests waved.

When the car had gone, Davy felt a trifle confused by Geordie's last statement. He went indoors to see his wife, and to ring around the family - rounding them up for the great reunion.

The following Saturday, shortly before two, Geordie and the captain arrived at the car park at the back of the club. They exited the car and made their way round to the club entrance at the front. They were met outside the porch by Davy and his wife, who led them inside, through the double glass doors.

Standing in the passageway Davy's wife looked up at Geordie, reverently.

"Oh, thank you Mr. Rigger; thank you very much!" said she, heartily. "I don't know what you did last night, but whatever it was, it had a tremendous positive effect on me - you couldn't begin to know what you've done for me!"

"Oh, I think he could, dear." Davy put his arm around his wife's shoulder. "Whatever it was, Geordie, my wife and I are deeply indebted to you; thank you very much."

They all walked along the short passageway and then turned right, passing through the double doors into the concert room.

"I thought it was a private function." The captain mused, as he and Geordie looked around the large, crowded room.

"It is!" Davy smiled proudly; "this 'is' the family!"

"Son of a gun!" the captain cried. "There must be at least two hundred people here!"

"Yes, that's true," Davy laughed; "I'm just sorry they couldn't all make it!"

Geordie looked at Davy, contentedly. "And I thought I might be the end of the line! This is more than I deserve."

Just then, the awaiting audience noticed the guests' arrival, and cheered.

"Well, I think I had better say a few words," said Geordie, to Davy, through the roar of the applause.

Davy attracted Geordie's attention and pointed over to two seats on the stage, where refreshments awaited them - nearby, stood two boom mikes and video cameras, operated by Davy's sons James and William. The captain and Mrs Rigger were ushered to a reserved table, near to the stage.

A moment later, on stage, Davy raised his hand for silence. "Thank you. Now we all know why we're here; we're here to welcome back into our fold, the oldest and wisest member of the family... ladies and gentlemen, Geordie Rigger!"

The crowd cheered wildly.

Geordie wiped a tear from his cheek. "You know?" he nodded as he looked around at the happy smiling faces, "some say there's no such thing as reincarnation." The crowd laughed. "Davy, here - the granddad of the family - is the image of my grandfather." Geordie looked fondly into Davy's face. "I thought my nose was all my own, but now I see I have it on loan." The crowd laughed once again.

"You know?" Davy added respectfully, with a warm smile, "I thought I was the granda', but I'm glad to say, you're the granda', now." The audience cheered in agreement.

Geordie glowed with exuberance. "My granddad once said to me

THE REUNION

'Hebburn people are the most charming folk you're ever likely to meet', and with such a reception as this, I most certainly agree... it's still so!" The crowd smiled and nodded to each other shyly, but proudly. "Is there anything you'd like to ask me?" Said Geordie, looking around at the audience as Davy poured him a soft drink.

"Aye!" Davy's son, Tom, spoke up from the front row. "Apart from Hebburn Hall and its old peel tower: now part of St. John's Church; and the Black Staithes: known colloquially as 'steeths', are there any other man-made landmarks in the immediate town area, still extant from the days of your childhood?"

"Alas, no. Trees were the great landmarks back then - of greater significance than they are today. The Hebburn Halfway Tree, that ancient focal point and meeting place, has gone - as are many other trees I climbed as a boy. I have noticed the absence of a greater feature - one which is a 'man-made loss' - the skylark and the peewit."

The older folk looked on thoughtfully, and nodded. "As an eight year old I often visited my maternal cousins at Hebburn Hall, and almost the whole area of Hebburn was our playground. Although  many things have changed since that time, there is one thing that has always remained steadfast - which no amount of physical change could ever alter - that is the wonderful ambience of the town: a feeling that can be sensed most strongly around the present Marina, and will be there for all generations."

Tom spoke again. "Thank you, Geordie, that's a wonderful sentiment. Your mention of the Marina prods me to further ask how you know so much about our recent local history in the short time you've been here."

"Tom, your father is a very clever man, and has kindly filled in many of the gaps in my local history knowledge. And, out of this proud and happy town has sprung two remarkable local websites: oldtyneside.co.uk and hebburn.org;" united as one by mutual consent. The camaraderie between the regulars shines through, and my heart is gladdened to view the interesting messages and pictures they contribute."

"Have you ever posted a message," said Tom; "and do you know any of the regulars?"

"I have posted incognito; and being a daily viewer, I know all the regulars by heart; they have the following diverse and delightful array of names:

A LIFETIME'S JOURNEY

Adam, Adrian, Alan, Alastair, Alex, Alexander, Alf, Alfie, Ali, Alison, Alistair, Allan, Allison, Allyson, Alyson, Amanda, Andrea, Andrew, Andy, Angela, Angie, Ann, Anne, Anth, Anthony, Arthur, Audrey, Azra, Barbara, Barnie, Barrie, Barry, Bernadette, Berni, Bernie, Beverley, Bill, Billy, Bob, Bobby, Brenda, Brian, Bridie, Bruce, Bryan, Byron, Caberdeen, Caine, Carol, Carole, Caroline, Carolyn, Cath, Catherine, Cedric, Charles, Charlie, Charlotte, Cherie, Cherry, Chris, Christine, Christopher, Cindy, Claire, Claudia, Colette, Colin, Colleen, Corinna, Craig, Cynthia, Daniel, Danny, Darren, Dave, Davey, David, Davy, Dawn, Debbie, Deborah, Debra, Denese, Denise, Derek, Des, Diane, Dick, Dickie, Dinah, Doc, Dodie, Don, Donald, Donna, Donnie, Doreen, Doris, Dorothy, Dot, Doug, Dougie, Douglas, Dug, Ed, Edd, Eddie, Eddy, Eds, Edward, Edwin, Eileen, Elaine, Eleanor, Elizabeth, Enid, Eric, Ernie, Evelyn, Faith, Fiona, Fran, Frances, Frank, Frankie, Fred, Freddie, Gail, Gary, Gavin, Gaynor, Ged, Geoff, Geordie, George, Georgina, Gerald, Gerard, Gerry, Gez, Gil, Gill, Gillian, Glenn, Gloria, Glynis, Gordon, Graeme, Grant, Gwerngen, Harold, Harry, Hazel, Heather, Helen, Howard, Hugh, Iain, Ian, Irene, Jac, Jack, Jackie, Jacqueline, Jacquie, James, Jan, Jane, Janet, Janice, Jean, Jeanette, Jed, Jeff, Jen, Jennifer, Jenny, Jill, Jim, Jimmy, Jo, Joan, Joanne, Joe, John, Jon, Joseph, Josie, Joy, Joyce, Judith, Julie, June, Karen, Karl, Kathleen, Kathryn, Kathy, Katie, Katrina, Keith, Kelly, Kelsey, Ken, Kenny, Kev, Kevin, Kirsty, Lance, Laura, Laurence, Laurie, Layne, Leanne, Lee, Len, Leo, Leonard, Les, Lesley, Leslie, Less, Lilian, Lily, Linda, Lisa, Liz, Lyn, Lol, Lorna, Lorraine, Louie, Louisa, Louise, Lydia, Lyn, Lynn, Lynne, Lynda, Mac, Maggie, Mal, Malc, Malcolm, Mandy, Marg, Margaret, Marge, Margie, Maria, Marie, Marina, Marion, Marjorie, Mark, Marlene, Marshall, Martin, Martyn, Mary, Maureen, Maurice, Maxine, May, Meg, Mel, Melanie, Melvyn, Michael, Michelle, Mick, Mike, Moira, Monica, Moreen, Muriel, Murray, Nancy, Neil, Nicola, Niall, Nora, Norma, Norman, Olwen, Pam, Pat, Patricia, Patrick, Patsy, Paul, Pauline, Penna, Pete, Peter, Phil, Philip, Pm, Rachel, Ray, Raymond, Rhoda, Rhoda, Richard, Richie, Rick, Rob, Robbie, Robby, Robert, Ron, Ronald, Ronn, Ronnie, Rosalyn, Rosemary, Ross, Roy, Roz, Russ, Ruth, Sandra, Sandy, Sara, Sarah, Scott, Sharon, Shaun, Shaunio, Sheila, Shelley, Shirino, Shirley, Simon, Stacey, Stan, Stanley, Steph, Stephanie, Stephen, Steve, Steven, Stevie, Stew, Stewart, Stu, Sue, Susan, Suzanne, Syd, Sylvia, Tania, Terence, Terry, Tessa, Theo, Theresa, Thomas, Tina, Tom, Tommy, Tony, Tracey, Tracy, Trevor, Tricia, Trish, Val, Valerie, Vernon, Veronica, Vicki, Victoria, Vikki, Vince, Vivianne, Vivien, Walter, Wayne, Wendy, William, Win, Yvonne and Zeta."

THE REUNION

Geordie bowed his head slightly, and the audience rose to their feet and began to clap and cheer at his incredible memory skills, and his appreciation and love of the town - the same town he knew and loved as a child.

When the applause had abated, Geordie was then asked to talk about his journey - which he did, giving a magnificently accurate recital. As he concluded, he was met once again with a volley of questions, such as, 'were you lonely?' and 'how's Charlie?' and so on. One question, which caused much interest, was, 'Could Geordie heal a mass audience?' Geordie answered that he could, and would be willing to give a demonstration if so wished. Not one person in the room declined. Geordie stood facing the audience with his hands held high.

"Anyone with a malady, please close your eyes, relax, and receive the power, and your ailments will just float away."

As Geordie closed his eyes, a band of light began to form around his head. He lowered his arms and stretched them outwards. As he did so, a surge of intense power left his body, floated silently over the heads of the responsive crowd, and fell upon them like a heavenly mist - absorbed by the sick and infirm. Five minutes later, the mist had gone, along with all sickness and ill-health. Geordie lowered his arms, and sat down. Davy and the rest of the family stirred, as if from a delightful dreamlike slumber.

"You might feel tired," said Geordie, affectionately; "but that will soon pass."

A moment later, there were cries of wonderment, as the crowd became conscious of the miracle that had taken place.

A large lady held aloft her walking stick. "I can't believe it! My leg's healed!"

"I can't believe it either, May," said her cousin; "my back's as right as rain!"

The air resounded with excitement, as the audience laughed and cheered.

Davy smiled, as he turned to Geordie. "You know? I wouldn't have believed it if I hadn't seen it; and now I have, I wouldn't have missed it for the world. Thanks to you, the family has never looked so fit and healthy. My heart feels as good as it did forty years ago, and the future looks rosy and bright. Geordie, you're a godsend - let's go down and meet the family."

As Geordie stepped down from the stage, he was given a rapturous standing ovation, in honour of his 'victory'.

Davy joined his wife and Captain Wiseman.

When the cheering had subsided, Geordie thanked the crowd, and then visited each table in turn, meeting his new family, one by one. By the time his round had finished - at his hosts' table - he knew every name and face in the room, and had systematically matched up every relation, and connected them mentally, with the pedigree charts that Davy had shown him.

Captain Wiseman looked up to the great, white-haired man who was standing by his chair, and reminisced of the time back on the island, when he first came face-to-face with this transcendental force.

"Geordie," he whispered. "Thank you for the compliments you showed me during your narration."

"They were well earned, Captain." Geordie relaxed in his seat.

"Geordie, my wife and I have a gift for you."

Davy's wife pulled an A4 envelope from a brown paper bag, and handed it to the appreciative old man. "You may open it now, if you wish," she smiled; "I hope it pleases you."

"Thank you." Geordie opened up the cover, placed his fingers inside and gently withdrew a picture, which he then laid flat upon the table. "Home! It's just as I remember: the beautiful white cottages and the fishing boats resting on the river. The cottage in the foreground is the place where I was born; and there's the oak tree that my grandfather planted."

Davy raised his eyebrows. "Absolutely amazing... that brings a totally new perspective to the picture!"

Geordie lifted his eyes from the picture and turned to Captain Wiseman. "I'd really like to go home."

"There's no wonder, Dents Hole looked such a beautifully, tranquil place."

"No," Geordie was emotional, "I mean home to the island."

"But I thought you were here to stay," pleaded Davy, with a pained expression.

THE REUNION

"No." Geordie explained softly. "I hope you can understand; I have been reunited with a family whom I never knew existed; loved, honoured and accepted as if I had never been away - what more can a person want? But, this land is not my home now, and it is regrettable to say, that I belong on another island, an island far away."

"I'm surprised." The captain placed his hand on Geordie's shoulder. "I thought it's here you'd settle down. But if you want to go back to the Pacific, it's your prerogative."

"I will stay here with my family for another eight days - at the end of which I will head back home with Charlie."

Just then, Davy's sons, Peter and John, walked up to the table. Peter spoke up confidently.

"Hello Mr. Rigger - I forgot to tell you... my late granda' knew a man older than you."

Geordie looked at him knowingly, with wisdom as great as his age. "That's unbelievable, Peter; are you sure?"

"Yeah. My granda' was born in 1898; and he told me that when he was five, he knew a very old man called Edmund, who had been born in 1795; and as you were only born in 1796, that means he's older than you."

"It doesn't, man!" John bristled with dismay. "You just don't get it, do you? Edmund died about 103 years ago, man! I've told you again and again, but you just can't get it into your thick head, can you?"

"Well, my mam said that 1795 is older than 1796, right! So there!"

"You're illiterate, man!"

"No I'm not, Our John - I've a mam and dad!"

"Oh go away, man, you gonk!"

Davy raised his eyebrows and breathed out a sigh, as Peter and John stormed off in separate directions. "You'll have to excuse them."

"Yes," his wife mouthed quietly, "Peter's a bit slow."

The captain laughed. "What did you say, Geordie? 'Some people say there's no such thing as reincarnation'?"

Geordie nodded and smiled, and then looked at the pensive faces of Davy and his wife. "Please don't be dismayed by your sons' innocuous behaviour, or my imminent departure; but savour the moment for what it is, a charming celebration. Besides, I'll be back."

Geordie's age put doubt on that, but somehow, Davy believed him.

"To Geordie!" Davy raised his glass, as his wife and the captain did likewise.

The party went well, and the thought of Geordie's leaving was pushed aside, to make way for a most palatable afternoon.

For the next eight days, Davy was in his glory, showing Geordie and the captain around the area, with his video camera at hand. This sightseeing adventure included views of aesthetic, as well as genealogical interest: Saint Paul's Church, Jarrow, burial place of the ancient Riggers, and once home of the Venerable St. Bede; All Saint's Church, Newcastle, another family place of worship - witness to many family baptisms, marriages and burials; Saint Nicholas Cathedral, Newcastle; Durham Cathedral, now the resting place of St. Bede; and Penshaw Monument, Houghton-le-Spring - home of the legendary Lambton Worm.

The captain had heard mention of a 'Longship' in Hebburn, and being a nautical man, had longed to see it. He was quite excited about the whole venture, as he distinctly heard other ship names mentioned. Little did he know that they were all names of local watering holes, which Davy's sons were 'only too happy' to show him. So, off they went, leaving Davy and Geordie behind in the sitting room of Barnard Crescent, discussing the website www.donmouth.co.uk: a diverse site, predominantly focused on Jarrow.

Later, after viewing the Hebburn website, Davy felt he couldn't let Geordie leave without offering to show him Hebburn, itself. Geordie was very keen. Together, they wandered on foot over every part, discussing the detailed history of the place, ending the tour at the part of the town known as Hebburn Quay. Standing on open ground, covered here and there by flowers, small bushes and the odd tree, Davy turned to Geordie.

"I don't have much to guide me, but I'd guess that my parents' house was somewhere round about here." He wagged his finger about in the air.

There was a landscape contractor standing nearby, hoeing round a small shrub.

"There's Jimmy, an ex-council worker from the parks. He used to be a neighbour of ours; one of the only ones I'm still in touch with. If you don't mind I'll go and ask him if he knows exactly where our row of houses was. Davy left Geordie and walked over to speak with Jimmy.

"Hello Jimmy; how are you doing?"

Jimmy lifted his head back and leaned on his hoe.

"Oh! Hello Davy; not too bad, you know; especially with my retirement coming up soon." He rubbed his nose with the back of his hand.

"You've worked in landscaping for quite a few years, haven't you?"

"O' aye, Davy... it's coming up to 47 years, now!"

"My goodness, Jimmy, that's a long time, and worthy of anyone's respect

- well done! You must have seen a lot of comings and goings."
"O' aye, I've seen it all!" he laughed.

"Jimmy, I wonder if you have any idea where our street used to be; I've been looking, but can't seem to locate the exact spot with certainty."
"You're standing on it, Davy!"
"Never in the world?"
"You see those bunches of white roses there... placed at intervals in a row?"
"Yes."
"Well, that's where each individual front door used to be... my idea. In fact, most of the doorsteps can still be found a few inches beneath the soil. When the Quay and the Colliery areas were pulled down, we just covered the remaining streets and rubble with a few inches of topsoil."
"You mean the front streets and back lanes we used to play in as kids, and the layouts of our old houses are still there, just below the soil?"
"O' aye, Davy! Many times we hit roads just under the soil while trying to plant trees, and had to send for a drill to make holes. It's astonishing what turns up; we've found just about everything you could imagine to be found - from doorknockers to chimney pots. Like I say, I've seen it all."

"I don't doubt it, Jimmy!"

"I remember one time, while trying to plant a tree - we hit an old white glazed sink. We had to smash a hole through it - it's still there!" Jimmy pointed somewhere over yonder.

"My goodness, some mother probably washed her bairns in that sink."

Just then, the conversation was cut short as a wagon pulled up alongside them.

"Well, Davy, it looks like I'm finished here for the day." He dropped his gardening tools and a few bags of rubbish onto the back of the wagon. "It's been nice talking with you."

"You too, Jimmy; watch how you go; and thank you for the nostalgic touch with the roses - you're a good man."

Jimmy climbed into the passenger door of the cab, pulled it shut, and poked his head through the open window.

"Thanks, Davy; I'll see you!"

When the wagon disappeared from sight, Davy beckoned Geordie, then smiled and made little stabbing motions with his index finger towards the ground. When Geordie came within hearing distance, Davy restarted the history lesson.

"Geordie, in my childhood days, the Hebburn Quay and the Hebburn Colliery were vastly populated tight communities - buzzing with life and excitement. Now that the main industries have gone, these two communities have almost gone too. Many properties were razed to the ground, leaving the Quay and the Colliery looking desolate, underpopulated, and void of life and laughter.

"Where did they go: the friends, the neighbours and the many characters? O', how I miss my companions and the familiarity of those surroundings. We never had a chance to say goodbye. Alas, I'm reunited with many of them through the death columns - it seems so unfair. I miss the old buildings too; they used to hold the memories of my family and friends - many of whom are long-gone. Our old Schools: St. Aloysius, St. Oswald's, the Quay School and the Colliery, are all gone; and so are most of the old friends we went there with. The shop windows we pressed our faces to; the rows of houses where we lived; even most of the public houses - gone! Our whole small world has almost disappeared. The memories in my head are often lost without something tangible to hold on to." Davy moved his hand through the air. "This very spot here is where my childhood home used to be - this used to be the front door."

Geordie placed his hand softly onto Davy's shoulder.

THE REUNION

"Davy; breathe in the past; relax and remember once again your childhood memories." Davy breathed in slowly and then calmly closed his eyes. "Davy, go in through the door and greet your parents."

Davy stepped into the warm, sunlit passage, and was instantly met by his mother. She lifted him gently up off his feet, then hugged and kissed him, and asked where he had been all this time, as she had missed him. She set him back down, and then led him by the hand into the parlour. The familiar aroma of baked bread and other delights filled the room. It was Saturday; the table was set for high tea. Davy looked around. The same oak framed family portraits hung upon the whitewashed walls - walls decorated here and there with light green, hand-painted roses. The sideboard - dotted with ornaments and a crystal wireless set - was backed against the wall opposite the chimney breast. The unlit paraffin lamp sat on the windowsill, framed by a half window net and two heavy green curtains, tied back near the centre. A row of small gold-rimmed tumblers sat atop the pelmet.

Davy noticed the green paint flecks missing from the skirting board, where he had once run his toy truck against it. Joey chirped in his cage near the full-length, dark brown wall cupboard, above which hung the empty clothes maid, pulled up to the cornice, out of the way.

The baking was done, and the fire still burned in the grate. The old black clock sat ticking in the centre of the mantelpiece, accompanied either side by two very old and cracked porcelain dogs.

Then, Davy was overjoyed with emotion, as there, looking over from the dark green, high-backed armchairs, either side of the old fireplace, sat his father and his favourite uncle, Tommy. They, too, were overjoyed to see Davy. They all hugged. The moment was heightened yet further, as Davy's dog, Laddie, appeared with wagging tail from beneath the table and proceeded to leap and jump up excitedly, spreading its paws onto Davy's chest. Davy hugged and fussed Laddie as much as he had ever done. Surrounded by so much love, Davy chatted excitedly, catching up, as his mother happily served tea. Davy was so very happy that he thought he must surely be dreaming.

Just at that moment, out in the open air, Davy opened his eyes, as if from a dream. "What happened? Was it a dream? How long have we been standing here, Geordie?"

Geordie removed his hand from Davy's shoulder. "We've been here but a moment."

"Thank you, Geordie. You must be an angel. I don't know what you did or how you did it, but I'm incredibly pleased you did. To meet my family again has been a blessing. My mother was a big woman, and when she put her precious arms around me, I knew I felt safe; oh how I missed that!"

Davy and Geordie made their way to the top of the Wooden Bridge.

"Dear Geordie, the years are passing so quickly, and it is unlikely that I will see another decade; so before my time is up, I wonder if you will allow me to see one more time, this dear town as it was in my youth."

Geordie didn't speak, he just smiled kindly and placed his hand gently onto Davy's shoulder; Davy was immediately transported to the wonderful, carefree, summer world of his childhood days.

A moment later, Geordie took his hand from Davy's shoulder and smiled; all was as before. Davy was back in the present with Geordie, looking down once again from atop the Wooden Bridge, amazed at what he had just experienced.

"Geordie, that was an exceptional adventure; so incredible that I feel the need to share the tale verbally with someone, just to make it sink in."

"Davy, although I was with you throughout your adventure, I would gladly listen to your narrative, if it would help you set it in your mind."

Davy began to recount his sentimental journey around dear old Hebburn.

"It was a Friday morning, and the summer sun was shining brightly. I was standing alone on the path, near the top of the Wooden Bridge, with one foot on the ground, and one resting on the footplate of my scooter - the one with the fat, white-walled tyres; my hands rested lightly on the handle bars. I was wearing a blue and white striped T-shirt, light brown shorts and black plimsolls. I breathed deeply and took in the familiar view before me. There, ahead of me was Campbell Street, at the bottom of the bridge.

"Before it was decided to build the Tyne vehicular tunnel at Jarrow - the Tyne Cyclist and Pedestrian Tunnel being a separate operation, opened in 1951 - Hebburn Council had put forward a proposal to have it built here. They had widened Campbell Park Road, on the other side of the Wooden Bridge, right up to Luke's Lane, where they had planned for it to join Leam Lane, giving easy access to the Motorway. They had also planned to scrap the present Wooden Bridge: a steel and concrete construction, named after the wooden-built bridge that preceded it, and build a new, wider one, for both vehicles and pedestrians; and Campbell Street would have been the tunnel approach. When I saw the beautiful big cars lined up outside Henderson's taxi office, I was very glad the tunnel didn't come here, and thought of how different things might have been. Walter List's truck depot, with its red wagons, was at the bottom of the hill, to my right; and beyond that, further along Argyle Street, Thubron's Woodyard, Bygate Nursery

School and St. Aloysius Infants' School. To my immediate right, down the bank, stood the allotments: rows of greenhouses filled with fresh-smelling summer bloom, with adjacent patches of land, packed with vegetation. I heard some light banging and tapping as gardeners busied themselves. A young boy was helping his grandfather to take plants and light garden tools from a shed and place them into a home-made box barrow, made from wooden planks and old pram wheels.

"There was much industry in Hebburn, but the familiar noises coming up the banks from the shipyards, dominated the lower parts of the town. The mighty, dependable cranes down at the river, hung over the town like proud, friendly sentinels. They gave off a safe and secure feeling of 'everything's alright'.

"From behind me, I heard an old familiar rumbling - it was the sound of metal-rimmed cartwheels meeting with concrete. I turned around. A man headed towards me pushing a heavily laden flatbed cart, piled high with household furniture - it barely fit through the bridge. He was obviously moving house - a common sight, as not many folk owned motorised transport. I moved off the path to let him pass; as he did so, I heard the sound of an approaching steam train. I was filled with excitement; I lay my scooter down, just off the path, then ran up to the railing, lifted myself up and popped my head over the side, just as a plume of steam rose up and enveloped me with a wonderful nostalgia. Seconds later, I ran to the railing on the other side, to watch the train hurtling away, down past the corn fields. Filled with content, I went back to retrieve my scooter, and stood again at the top of the bridge taking in the view before me. There were many pedestrians on the bridge, coming both ways. A lady passed me, pushing a well-built Silver Cross pram, which reminded me of a fairground shuggy boat. A smiling baby in a sun hat and reigns was sitting up in the pram, happily biting a rattle, which it bounced now and again off the side. It chuckled each time the rattle hit the colourful string of plastic ducks hanging from the canopy.

"At the side of the path, away from the pedestrians, was a well-worn rut, made by countless bicycles and scooters, leading down to the bottom of the bridge. I felt so energetic. I took my right heel from the footbrake, and pushed off forcefully with my left foot. I excitedly whizzed down the bridge with the wind in my face, not afraid of falling in the least... wheeeeee!

"As I neared the bottom of the bridge, at Campbell Street, I noticed a lady up at a top window cleaning the panes, with her legs on the inside and her body outside. Mr Henderson came out of his taxi office - I waved and he waved back. I slowed down a touch and coined left at the old green, swan-necked lamppost and up Ropery Lane, which leads all the way up to the Station Bridge. I passed the heart-warming, old terraced streets to my right: Dumhope, Usway, Swindon, Holystone, Barrow, Wreigh and Coquet; and

THE REUNION

the familiar factories to my left: Miles Druce; then the Electric Power Station, where the Power House - an old dance venue - used to be; and then Frazer's steel yard, which ran to the end of Ropery lane - named after the rope works that once stood there. At the end, I reached the County Hotel - this bit being Bell Street back lane - and made my way to its frontage. I faced this splendid building; the Station Bridge and the very industrious Reyrolles: the electric engineering works, with its winding shops, etc., were now behind me; and behind that once stood the just as industrious Bauxite Works, Tennant's Alkali Works and the Tharsis Sulphur and Copper Works - now home to Reyrolle's associate company, the Bushing Company.

"My thoughts were distracted, as a heavily laden bus, belched black smoke as it struggled over the bridge. There were people all about. Some walked down King Street, to the train station, and made their way over the metal bridge to the Newcastle side - that being the side that takes folk to Newcastle. I wheeled down to the station - the South Shields side - stopped and looked through the railing there. The porters were busy on the platform, as a train was in the station. I watched as bird owners handed over their baskets of pigeons to understanding Porters, who would look after them until they reached their intended destinations, where they would dutifully set them free to race back the many miles to their respective homes. Other Porters wheeled barrows full of parcels and other items to the goods carriage, many from the nearby Bitumastic and Pyrotenax works. Some folk put their bikes and prams into the goods carriage. The head porter came out of his office to oversee the situation, in his neat black suit, black tie, highly polished black shoes and his black, shiny, peaked cap. The big, old trains looked so relaxing, with their private, comfortable sitting areas - the soft, gentle rocking and lilting would soon soothe the commuters, old and young. I looked through the railings up towards the Newtown, on the other side of the tracks. There was the old library at the top of Queen Street to my left; with Craig's paint shop, Ritchie's bike shop, and the Newtown School and other shops beyond. The Station Hotel was just visible over Station Road - the Council Yard behind it out of view.

"I felt so full of life. I turned around, put my scooter over my shoulder and hoicked it straight up the side of the bank, no problem. People passing on the other side of the railing didn't seem to acknowledge my presence. There was a rut, made by my friends and I, which followed the railing down to the bottom of the bridge; it was so long since I had ridden it. Off I went… wheeeeeee!

"At the bottom, I stopped, and bumped softly down, off the small step and

THE REUNION

made my way back to the County Hotel. On the other side of Prince Consort Road I could see the Newtown Nursery School and Lloyds Bank. A bin wagon passed Lloyd's, heading down to the council rubbish tip, and then passed White's Marine Engineering works, with a gully sucker road sweeper not far behind.

"Down the bank to the left, over the road from R.W. Transmissions, was King George VI playing field, where Tyne View Terrace used to stand. Footballers played there, and jazz bands practiced. Many buses lined the bank during competitions in which The Hebburn Heralds, The Hebburn Highlanders and The Hebburn Crusaders took part, against the likes of The Calf Close Kilties and the North Shields Grenadiers, the latter of whom always seem to win everything.

"Ahead of me, across Bell Street, was the Rectory and St. Aloysius Church; and beyond, over Argyle Street, was Martin's Bank. I turned into Bell Street, and glanced into the rectory garden as I passed; I could see the garden surrounded by trees; also the greenhouses - one lean-to; and the bell in its little tower, a relic donated by the old chemical works. I made my way down Bell Street, to the main church entrance, and paused at the big, brown, arched doors, as I felt I had to call in. I turned the heavy ring handle until it clunked, and then entered the church. To my left on the wall was the clamshell-patterned half bowl stoup, half filled with holy water - I dipped my fingers in to wet them and then blessed myself. A low, flat, glass case, full of beautiful jewellery stood before me on my right. Behind it stood a sculpture of the Virgin Mary holding the crucified Christ on her lap - a pietà. I noticed Father Walsh appear at the chancel, at the far end of the church, so I felt obliged to leave.

"Outside, back on my scooter, I quickly headed down bell Street, and turned left into Coquet Street. I could hear children playing in the schoolyard. I peered through the big, metal gates. A few boys were playing football, using their jumpers as goalposts. There were girls playing skips, jumping in and out while shouting out rhymes. Other girls sang rhymes while juggling balls up against the side of a building; they laughed, as yet again, one of the balls became stuck in the cross shaped recess at the top of the wall. A girl came up to the gates and asked me why I wasn't at school - I didn't know. I thought about the repercussions if the school board man caught me, so I scooted off towards Argyle Street - the main road, which runs southwest-northeast. The Police Station - with the turquoise panda cars outside - and the Courts, and the Iona, were ahead of me on the other side of Argyle Street. Old Mr Wright, a retired man, was standing at his usual place

A LIFETIME'S JOURNEY

at the Coquet Street/Argyle Street corner of the school, opposite Audrey's clothes shop; he showed me an amazing sleight of hand magic trick - I was still puzzling over it as I pushed my way down the path, in the direction of the Colliery. I stopped at Swale's shop - opposite the clinic - propped my scooter up against the wall and called in for some spangles and sarsaparilla tablets to keep up my amazing energy. At the counter, I put my hand in to the right pocket of my shorts and felt some coins. I took out a shilling and paid for my sweets. I went outside, collected my scooter, popped a sweet in my mouth and walked to the corner of Wreigh Street. I noticed John Camara carrying his dog home over his shoulder - it had escaped again. Over the road was Albert Street, down which, was the Gem Bingo Hall: formerly the Gem Picture House. Further down was the Albert Hotel and the Co-op Store. Further down still, was Ann Street, with Renee's fish shop at the top left, and the Ballast Hill at the bottom. Back at the top of Albert Street, beside the red post box, was the Surgery of Doctors James Norman Swainston, Michael Norman and Peter Norman. It had a small, dark, oaken panelled waiting room, with long, hard, wooden seating all around the room, and a glass panelled reception area, which reminded me of the TARDIS.

"The Doctors' was fronted on Argyle Street, by Lismore House; then, next door, in the direction of the Colliery, was Stanharken House, then Kulsia House, then the Hedley Schools and then the chemist shop.

"I turned and walked up the front of Wreigh Street, a little, to take a look down the back lane, leading down to the Colliery - it seemed to go on forever. A ragman was walking his horse and cart up this cobbled road towards me, trying to avoid some washing on a line that had been strung across the lane. A lady was using a prop to lift her washing out of his way. The ragman showed me a Donkey Stone and some balloons, and asked me if I had any old lumber... which he pronounced *Loomba*. I told him no, and then sped off, back to the Argyle Street main road.

"The drab colours of the passing traffic matched the battleship colours of the doors and windows of the tall buildings about me. To my right, looking towards the Colliery, was the chapel, the scouts' hut, and then Barrow Street - at the top of which was Fraser's Steel Yard. On the corner of Barrow Street and Argyle Street, was Arthur Cook's, gents' tailor shop. After that was Gamble's paper shop and then the bookies - Michael, the blind man was just going in to place a bet. I crossed the road to the chemist shop, as I really fancied some liquorice root; I went in and bought some. I came out and stood with my scooter on the corner of Argyle Street, looking left, or northwest, down Ellison Street bank. Straight across from me, on the

THE REUNION

opposite corner of Ellison Street was St. Cuthbert's C of E Church. The traffic on both the path and the road was busy, so I walked my scooter down the left side of the bank as far as Lyon Street, passing the Territorial Army building on my left on the way. I was now at the junction of Lyon Street, standing outside the Commercial Club, facing down Ellison Street. The fruit shop was opposite me, to my right, on the south side of Lyon Street; I crossed over to the north and faced the river Tyne down the bank.

"Donohughe's paper shop - formerly Hewison's - was on the corner to my right; and a little further downhill, on the same terrace, was the café - behind which was the old, obsolete pit yard. Further down the bank - behind the offices - was Leslie's shipyard, built by Andrew Leslie in 1853. I noticed Leslie's clock tower, and remembered my father telling me that there was an anti-aircraft gun mounted atop of it during the Second World War.

"On my left, a little way ahead of me, on the corner of Carr Street and Ellison Street, was the Progressive Club, adjacent to St. Andrew's Presbyterian Church and Institute, which stands the next street down, on the corner of St. Andrew's Street and Ellison Street.

"I stood proudly, looking down the long, steep hill before me, ready to 'take the plunge'- as many excited children had done before on their bikes, scooters and go-carts, known locally as boogies. I pushed hard and was away, flying down the bank at a million miles an hour. I felt invigorated. I kept the handles steady with all my might, for the slightest bump could upset them, bring them to a sudden halt and throw me over the top - and at the rate I was travelling, I guess I could have smashed through the 'bomb-proof' wall at the bottom, and landed on the other side of the river! However, as expected, I pushed down hard on the foot brake and came to a steady halt, without dunching into anything.

"I walked up to the railing and looked across the river Tyne - it smelled of seaweed. Although the air was still, the motion of the river traffic disturbed it slightly, and brought to my nostrils a smell of burning from the underground fires at the nearby tip, and a slight pong from the bone yard across the river. There was much industrious noise: clanging, banging drilling and shouting from the workers on the many ships... the Sir Percivale and the HMS Norfolk being two. Sparks flew like fireworks from high up on the decks and down into the water. Buzzers of different pitches and volumes went off at certain times throughout the day, each one having a specific meaning. Ships, big and small, passed up and down the river. I watched as the Tyne Queen ferry came over from Walker, and berthed alongside the ferry landing. The rope lad jumped off, quickly placed the

Hawthorn Leslie offices and main gate

securing rope around the capstan, lowered the gangway, and then unhooked the barrier chain, allowing the many passengers to alight. They came through the style and rushed up the bank.

"Behind the ferry landing loomed the ballast hill - a wonderful vantage point from which to watch the great ships being launched; and there were many: RMS Mauretania1906, and HMS Kelly 1939, to name a couple. At that very moment, a man appeared at the railing and began to take photographs of the ships, maybe with forethought to hold this moment for future generations. I made my way up the bank, stopping for a drink at the beautifully decorated, blue water fountain in the wall near Leslie's gate; I then carried on up to the top of the bank at Lyon Street, and passed a group of children with their teachers, heading down towards the ferry. I glanced left, down the low road, in the direction of Jarrow. I could see the Caledonian pub on the corner of Tyne Street, but the Quay Board School, also on the right, was just out of view beyond the bend.

"I looked uphill again. I was so full of energy, that without a struggle I wheeled myself back up to the top of the Ellison/Argyle Street junction, outside St. Cuthbert's Church. I stopped at the red telephone kiosk and looked down towards the Colliery. I watched as a group of ladies alighted from the bus ahead, and struggled towards me with many bags of shopping in each hand; chatting merrily away about their day out at Newcastle. Community shopping was a common ritual among many friends.

"There were many people going about their business. The roads, as expected, were fairly quite; but at peak times, the busy traffic - especially the buses and lorries - roared, groaned and shuddered past, giving off nasty, unhealthy smelling clouds of smoke. Danby's fruit shop was over the road, on the corner of Holystone Street. I wheeled slowly down Argyle Street, passing St. Cuthbert's Church, and then the adjacent scouts' hut. On the other side of the road, Mr Donnelly, the undertaker, came out of his shop at 58 Argyle Street and headed on foot up towards the St. Aloysius Church. I crossed over the road and rode down to the shop on the corner of Swindon Street - opposite Jack's V.G. shop - for some aniseed balls. I was eager to view the lane at the back of the shops once again - these busy shops and the lanes still seemed never ending - it's a good thing I was on my 'magic' scooter. I pushed myself down the lane a small way and then turned right - I was now in the communal lane shared by Swindon Street and Usway Street.

"A lady came out of one of the back doors in the lane, stopped me and asked if I would go a message for her to the V.G. She told me she'd give me sixpence - it was common for children to be stopped in this way. Without hesitation, I stuffed the money and the shopping note she had given me, into an empty trouser pocket, placed my scooter against the wall and dashed off to Jack's shop, on foot. I was young and fit - there was no chance of becoming overweight.

"Jack was standing behind the counter in his white shop coat. I gave him the money and the note, which had the prices written beside each item. He brought the bread, milk and small tin of cat food and placed them on the counter; there was no change. I picked the items up into my arms, thanked him and then headed back to the lady - she was waiting at her back door for me. She thanked me, gave me a toffee cake and a tanner, and then went indoors, closing the door behind her. I stepped onto my scooter and wheeled slowly down the lane; the sun was warm on my back. I noticed the old coal hatches, high up in the walls of each premises, and similar hatches low down in the walls - signs of where the dry toilets had once been. I turned with surprise, as a flock of pigeons suddenly flapped up out of a backyard, into the air; disturbed by a cat walking silently along the half round capping bricks on top of the wall.

"A few feather foots climbed high, and then began to tumble back down; what a sight! I passed an open back yard door; a man with a familiar face stood beside a cree with a pigeon in his hands, inspecting its wings. At the end of the lane, I turned left into Swindon Street, and then right, back onto Argyle Street.

"I stopped outside Morton's Dairy, on the corner of Dumhope Street, and rested my scooter against the shop wall. A local character named Robin came by, pushing his bike, which he very rarely rode - though when he did, it was in a strange fashion using only one leg. He blurted out to me three times in a manic fashion, 'you got any old tellies?' I told him that I didn't; so off he went, poor fellow, leaning over his bike as he pushed it up the road towards the tip - probably off fighting windmills! I went into the dairy and bought an ice cream... deliciously cooling on such a hot day. Oddly enough, any time I needed more money, it just appeared in my pocket. As I came out of the dairy I looked down Caledonian Street and saw the Quay School, and also the blue star sign, high up on the side of the Dock Hotel - trademark of 'Newcastle Breweries Limited'. I finished my ice cream and then made my way down to the Colliery, passing the Co-op and other shops on the way. I then passed the Bygate Nursery on Bygate Street, and St. Aloysius Infants' School, which was opened in 1929.

"Hebburn was originally made up of three villages, the Newtown, the Quay and the Colliery; all separated by manmade boundaries: the

station bridge parting the Newtown from the Quay; and the railway
barrier gates ahead of me, dividing the Quay from the Colliery.

A LIFETIME'S JOURNEY

"The barrier had just been swung open across the road, when I arrived at the crossing. The signalman popped out of the open door of his signal box, looked up the tracks and popped back again.

"The traffic started to build up as a steam locomotive came slowly down from the main Shields to Newcastle line. The engine was pulling beds full of steel plate, going to Hawthorn Leslie's top shop, or pit yard as it was sometimes called. The engine slowed; the brakes squealed, and the trolleys shunted into each other, then came to a halt. Moments later, the engine began to move again. The chains tightened one by one, clanking as each trolley took the brunt and shook a little before moving off. It took a few minutes before the engine was gone and the gates opened.

"Over the crossing was another world - the Colliery - so separate and distinct from the Quay; here, Argyle Street changed name to Brancepeth Road; I followed it. On my left, I passed Harvey Street and Arthur Street, and then turned next left at Frederick Street. The old, obsolete 'A' Pit was to my right. At the end of Frederick Street, was a T-junction, traversed by Wagonway Road. On the other side of Wagonway Road, to the right, I could see Patrick's shop - known affectionately as Nelly's. I decided to call in. The shop had double doors, with only access through one. I pushed down the latch. The narrow door was heavy, solid and thick. I opened it and entered; even at such a young age, I felt as if I was stepping into a different era. There was little floor space; only standing area for about five adults, as the two counters - one with the till to my right, and one ahead - took up most of the shop area; these counters were joined by a hatch. The high shelves on the walls were filled with wonderful things. For such a small shop, it seemed to sell any and every obscure thing: laces, fuses, plugs, fluorescent light tubes and light bulbs, etc. The lady customer ahead of me bought a light bulb; Nelly took it out of the box and tested it in an electric socket under the counter, before putting it back into the box - how thoughtful is that? I have never bought a fluorescent tube from the high shelf, so I can only guess if Nelly ever tested them... now that would have been service! The lady left and I was now the only customer. I asked Nelly for a quarter of jelly babies, a bag of beef Tudor crisps and a can of Coca Cola. Nelly weighed the sweets, and then came back to the counter with the pop and crisps. Although the shop had a till, Nelly preferred to reckon up from left to right with pencil and paper - an ability that fascinated me. As I counted the money out on the counter, Nelly's husband Joe came into the shop from the back room and started a conversation with me. Both Nelly and her husband were lovely, warm people; I always felt so welcome when I enter their shop, as they

always had time to chat, and Nelly had such an infectious laugh. Mr Patrick was a very talented artist and photographer, and could often be seen, out-and-about, taking photographs of the locality. He told me he had a large collection of photographs. He talked about his artwork, and offered to show me his private art collection, but, alas, there were so many places to be and so much to do. I left the shop in a very happy mood. I ate the crisps and drank the pop as I slowly pushed the scooter.

"After passing Quality Row and the Banks O' the Tyne public house, which stood next to Carrahar's Field, I stopped on the path outside the Colliery Club.

"Ahead, towards Blackett Street, was the Staithes: a conveyor belt that carried coal over the Road, and down to the awaiting ships - opened 28 July 1936 by the Duchess of York; next to that stood the Durastic. I could also see the roof of the Royal Hotel - known as The White Lead, because of the dust that fell onto it from a local smelting works: Foster, Blackett and James.

"I turned right into High Lane Row, heading uphill. On my left was Roy Austick: electrical and civil engineers, who occupied part of the Simpson's buildings; then there was Simpson's Hostel; there were some foreign gentlemen standing outside in deep conversation. On my right, still on High Lane Row, I passed Witton Road, then Auckland Road, then the Primitive Methodist Chapel; next was School Street. I stopped at the corner and glanced towards the United Methodist Chapel on the corner of Auckland Road. Then, still travelling uphill, I came immediately to the Colliery Board School, and then passed it. I made my way to the thin path under the railway bridge just as a train thundered overhead. An old man wearing a flat cap came down towards me pushing a box barrow, so I hugged the white safety rail with my back allowing him to squeeze passed. When the path was clear, I made my way out from under the bridge; the byway had now changed name to Black Road.

"On my left - over the old stone wall, on the other side of the road - was St. Oswald's Vicarage; and St. Oswald's Church - both entered via the same driveway on St. Oswald's Road: a long cul-de-sac, ahead, next left after the church. Still on the other side of the road, but on this side of the vicarage wall were the tin garages and wooden pigeon crees. On this side of the road, on the path, was a cut, leading to Railway Street; then, further up the path was St. Oswald's Infants' School. I passed the boys' entrance gates. Then, a little further up, I could see Mr Main the lollipop man, standing on the corner of the school at Ralph Street - where the Girls' entrance was - talking to Sammy, in his wheelchair. I stepped off my scooter - afraid he might tell me off for riding on the path. Across Ralph Street, on the right, was the CWS building, the 'Co-operative Wholesale Society', with a butcher's shop at the end, a draper's, a grocer's, a baker's, a greengrocer's and then a hall on the first floor. Further along was what we called 'Fireman's Hill' - a wide hill about 35 feet high, with allotment gardens and chicken coops at the top.

THE REUNION

At the bottom of the hill, on the corner of Hedgeley Road - next right after Ralph Street - was the garage, where the fire station once stood - formerly the pit manager's house.

"Mr Emmerson, the head master, came out of the school with a double line of children behind him, so I scooted over the road, into St. Oswald's Road. I passed the Church; then Nightingale's shop on my right; and then passed the old streets: Peel Terrace and Peel Gardens, etc. When I reached as far as the allotment gardens, on my left, I stopped and looked back; the headmaster and the children had gone - probably to watch a live safety demonstration at the Colliery Board School. I turned around and headed quickly on towards the old metal bridge.

"Standing beside the metal pedestrian bridge, with its loose, thin, metal plate steps - which traversed the railway lines - I watched as some men 'shunters', came out of an old brick-built railway box at the side of the track. They opened the brakes on a few stationary wagons with the aid of hooks on long poles, and, still coupled together, fly-shunted them - that is, gave them a shove and let them run downhill. Once in motion the men walked alongside them, uncoupling and braking them as the inertia took hold and carried them to a siding off the main South Shields to Newcastle line.

"The railway lines travelled from left to right as I faced them. Just over the other side of the lines, and parallel to them, was Oak Street. Leading downhill, away from Oak Street - at right angles to it - was Beech Street and then Birch Street - both leading down to Hill Street. Inside this oblong of streets, that is Beech and Birch, and Oak and Hill, was the Jarrow Central School, and the Jarrow and Hebburn Cooperative Society buildings.

"Looking down Beech Street, I could see the spire of Christ Church on the horizon and hear the Angelus bell peal; and though the air was clear and warm, now and again I could detect the faint, acrid odour from Lennig's - the Rohm & Haas plastics factory at Jarrow. I turned the scooter around, and instead of going back up St. Oswald's Road, I veered left slightly, and pushed my way up, over the old pit heap, towards Hedgeley Road; sulphur and coal dust from the old pit industry, stuck to the wheels. Way over to my left, I noticed that Freddie Culline's fair had arrived on the land behind the Clock Hotel, and the Employment Exchange - a bit early in the year I thought. There was a lot of noise as the men put together the rides and stalls.

"When I reached the corner of Till Street, I could see the structural remains of the old, abandoned 'B' Pit mineshaft, at the back of the houses on Black Road. I went over to investigate. I picked up a stone from nearby and dropped it into the narrow shaft. I listened intently; it took a while

174

before it hit the bottom; when it did, I was so excited that I did it again. After a bit more fun, I headed up the path until I came out onto the T-junction of Black Road to my left and right; and Hedgeley Road, which ran straight away from me for about three quarters of a mile, all the way up to Station Road. Fireman's Hill was situated in the field across the road to my right, and below it, an Alsatian dog barked at the gates of the garage.

"I turned left along Black Road until I came to Victoria Road East. Ahead of me was Jervis Street. To my left, in the direction of Jarrow, was the Clock Hotel, the Employment Exchange, the petrol garage and then the Bowes line level crossing. On the opposite side of the road to the Clock Hotel, facing Jarrow, was Short's sweet shop, Ashman's butchers and then Frobisher Street - with the barber shop and Pratt's shop on one side, and the betting shop and Jessie's chip shop on the other. Further down Victoria Road East, was the laundrette and then the corner shop at the end of Northbourne Road, Jarrow, near the level crossing. Across from me was the bookies shop; then, heading up Victoria Road East in the direction of the Newtown, was Fishwick's fruit shop. Much further up, on the left was Hall's Garage - near the Ambulance Station, on Usher Road. Then on the right, near Byron Avenue, was Clegwell School. I crossed Black Road, scooted up to the crossing, walked over, and made my way down passed Fishwick's to Short's sweet shop. Outside on the wall was a bubblegum machine. I took two pennies from my pocket, pushed them into the machine, and then turned the round handle at the right side - once, then again. A packet of Beechnut chewing gum was dispensed into the little, metal, recess below; it was so much fun that I bought some more just so I could do it again.

"With my mouth full of beechnut, I made my way back up to Fishwick's, then left into Eton Square; the cut there splits either left into Jervis Street, facing the Welcome Hall on Gladstone Street, or right into Oxford Crescent, and out onto Red House Road. I turned right. Ahead of me, surrounded by a wire fence, was Baker Perkins Sports Ground; the factory further down to the left, was where my mother and other ladies made ammunition during the war. Beyond that was the Tube Works, and over the railway lines was Jarrow Park. Looking ahead again, beyond the Sports Field, was the Slag Heap: a mountain of black slag, which towered over the surrounding houses; for many years, the hot slag had been carried by train from Jarrow Steel Works and dumped there, forming the heap. I turned right, up Red House Road, and left into Cambridge Avenue, which I followed all the way round to 'the cut': a pathway leading through the houses to Bede's Well, the Dip and the Slag Heap. I passed through the cut and stopped on the road which travelled the whole length of the back of the houses, all the way from Campbell Park Road to the rear of Baker Perkins.

"Across this road was a narrow path, which led down to the 'dip': a beautiful, small valley; at the bottom of which was a clear stream: the Bede Burn, full of freshwater crayfish, sticklebacks and newts, etc. The burn came down from the Burn Heads, through the lakes, through the culvert under the Campbell Park Road, through the dip as a tributary to the River Don at Jarrow, passed St. Paul's church, into the River Tyne and then out to sea.

"Bede's Well stands some distance from the burn, and it is presumed that as a young boy, St. Bede lived at Monkton Village, and passed the well on his way to St. Paul's church, Jarrow - thus giving fame to the well. Therefore, it would seem logical for Bede, at such a tender age; so as not to lose his way; and to be in easy reach of drinking water; to follow this natural map down to the church.

"I followed the path down to the well: a square hole in the ground with a stream running through it. It was surrounded by a small, square wall, four bricks high, with railings fixed all around on top, secured with a padlocked gate. The well is famous for its health-giving properties; and in times passed, many children were escorted there together on Sunday afternoons, and dipped in the well to be healed. I threw a silver coin into the well for good luck. In times passed, people would throw silver coins into wells, as silver is known to have healing properties.

"Following the path I came to the bottom of the slag heap; tar lay all about, as if it had oozed down like lava from the summit. The watchman's cabin - known locally as the *watchy's cabin* - was empty, as old Hector only worked nightshifts. Some men were working. A man was sitting in a dusty dumper truck, waiting for another man to move an oil drum from the path, while noisy conveyor belts carried substance overhead. At the top of the slag heap was a little cave, known locally as the owl's eye, or the owl's wing; as it looked like a wing with an eye peering over the top. It was a very difficult place to climb to, and manoeuvre into, as one had to do it from above; so the older boys would dare each other to the challenge; not many did it, but those that did were my heroes. I followed the little walkway over the stream, around to the rear of the slag heap. The rear of Windermere Crescent was to my right, just off Campbell Park Road, and Monkton Village was ahead. I followed the path until I came out at Monkton Lane in Monkton Village. I turned right and followed the path, passed the Lord Nelson Inn and then round the bend by Monkton Hall Hospital. I then turned right at the cut, through to Campbell Park Road, over which lay Elmfield Road. To my left was Luke's Lane Bridge, which spans the Newcastle to Sunderland railway; and beyond it, to the right, I could see a large, white cloud of steam emanating from the Coke Ovens.

"I turned right and pushed my way down Campbell Park Road as far as Finchale Road junction, and stopped to view the beautiful flowers in the garden, on the corner over the road: red roses, white roses, Nemesia, red hot pokers and many more. The wonderful and alluring smells filled the air. I love the simple things; and there are many which can bring instant happiness: buying Matchbox cars, and jubblies that freeze your mouth blue, from the top shops on Finchale Road; watching a puppy at play; having a friendly little bird appear beside us while tending the garden; a baby's smile; maybe remembering them is akin to positive sentimentality rather than a sorrowful nostalgic yearning.

"My thoughts were distracted as a lorry came by and obscured my view; so I headed off all the way back down Campbell Park Road, to the dip, near Cambridge Avenue shops; and then crossed the road to the lakes. I stopped at an opening in the fence. There was a path before me, leading through the lakes up to Hebburn Park. The lakes, which once belonged to the Ellison family of the nearby Ellison Hall, had once been home to many birds, pond life and other wildlife, but had been drained a few years previously. The original Hebburn Hall was a small, fortified keep - or pele tower - home to the local lord and his family. During times of siege, water was badly needed; to assure a fresh and plentiful supply, an underground passage was built from the tower house, following the perimeter of the ancient quarry; down through where the park gates are at present and down the path towards Bede's Well. A few brave and trusted servants, or retainers, would crawl the entire length of the tunnel, to procure the precious water. Some speculate that the tunnel came from Jarrow monastery to the pele tower as an escape route for the monks. That is not feasible, as it would be too far to crawl on ones knees; besides, in the 13th century - long after the Viking raids - the Jarrow monks were now well capable of protecting their rare books, endowments and other treasures, behind their studded doors and thick-walled monastery; also, and more importantly, they had Papal protection.

"To my right, at the far end of the field, I could see the roofs of the bathhouse and the ancient lodge house, standing in Leslie's Sports field. Apart from the pele tower - now part of St. John's church - the lodge house was the oldest building in Hebburn. It would be feasible to suggest that this 'oldest building' on the quarry - likely built by the quarrymen as a dwelling - was there long before Hebburn Hall, and had once assisted weary travellers on the ancient carriage and foot roads to the equally ancient Jarrow, Monkton and South Shields.

"In front of it stood a cycle track, leading from Quarry Road, to Campbell Park Road. This track was once part of the old, original Shields Road - the main road from Newcastle to South Shields - which travelled down from Newcastle, on what is presently known as Victoria Road West, around the back of Ellison Hall, down the present cycle path, through where Witty Avenue now stands, down Red House Road and down into South Shields.

"I pushed off again and headed up towards the large metal gates, hanging from large brick-built posts at the park, some distance before me. I could hear children playing. When I passed through the gates I was immediately

overcome by a feeling of calmness and beauty. The varied trees and plant beds all about were in full bloom; the beautiful green field to my left looked as lovely and inviting as a lawned garden; many people sat about there having picnics. I lay down on the grass and rested a while, looking up at the fluffy white clouds, making pictures in my mind. Later, I sat up and made a daisy chain, and hung it around my neck.

"The playing area to my right was in full swing. There were parents and grandparents - young and old - playing with their excited children and grandchildren; some were being pushed on the baby swings, some on the big swings; some on the rocking horse and some on the witch's hat. I was hot and thirsty, so pushed my way to the water fountain, on the triangular piece of land near to the baby swings; I leaned over, pressed the button and took a cool, refreshing drink... ahhhhh! Then I wiped my wet mouth with the back of my hand. After that, I followed the dene hedge, round to the Boer War memorial on the top of the hillock, which had a canon just below it. From the dene below, I could hear a brass band playing. Looking down the path, to my right were the greenhouses full of colour, then the Carr Ellison Memorial; and further down, inside the beautifully designed high metal gates, was the park house, on Cannon Street. The toilets were beside me, so I thought it wise to nip in. When I came out, Larry, a council worker, was sweeping up leaves and putting them into the yellow dustcart beside him; he caught my eye and then called me over. He showed me his large sweeping brush, and asked me if I knew what the extra hole was for in the head. I told him that I had no idea, so he told me that it was for putting a candle in for nightshift.

"My scooter was lying against the hedge; I stepped onto it, about to set off, when I noticed the park keeper coming out of his house, so I stepped down, quickly, in case he reprimanded me for riding around the park. I bade Larry farewell, and walked my scooter quickly back to the Boer War memorial; then around the hillock, up passed Ellison Hall Infirmary, passed the cenotaph and out into St. John's Avenue, across from Hebburn cemetery; where the brave men of the HMS Kelly lie. At a respectful distance from the cemetery, I stepped onto my scooter again, and whizzed down St. John's Avenue, over Canning Street and down to Victoria Road West. I was young and fit, and rode from place to place so quickly it was like magic.

"I carefully crossed Victoria Road West, then ahead down Thistle Street, across Tennant Street, continued down Thistle Street and came out at the Glen Street Methodist Chapel. I then passed the Council Yard, turned left at Station Road and down over the bridge, back to the Quay.

THE REUNION

"It was now teatime, and I was standing back on the top of the Argyle Street/Ellison Street, junction, outside Cuthbert's Church, looking left towards the Colliery. A very loud buzzer sounded. A short while later I could hear a great stampede behind me. I turned to look down the bank; hundreds of workmen were bustling each other as they ran towards me up Ellison Street, like ants from the shipyard and out onto Argyle Street. They gesticulated with their newspapers as they shouted their farewells to workmates, before heading for home - what an incredible site it was! Then they were gone, just as quickly as they came... silence.

"Somehow, in the blink of an eye, it was Sunday morning, and I was still standing outside St. Cuthbert's church. Sundays always seemed to be sunny; everything stopped... no shipyard noise, no buses - hardly any traffic on the roads really. There was a stillness - a quietness as old as time. It might seem strange, but the flowers, the roads and even the houses seemed to relax in the mid-morning, summer heat. I made my way up to Coquet Street, and watched very old, kindly looking ladies - probably in their 90s - dressed in their beautiful outfits; slowly walking by on their way out of St. Aloysius Church. They wore immaculate dark suits, black shoes, and lovely hats covered with net - and some with feathers and brooches. The lovely old gentlemen behind, wore their Sunday best, too: plain suits, ties and highly polished shoes.

"Later, after the church had empty and everyone had gone, a lady carrying a baby in a christening gown, walked towards me, flanked by two attendants: a lady and gentleman of about the same age. I was hoping the baby was a girl, as it is a tradition while carrying the child to church to be christened, to give the Christening Piece from the Christening Tea, to the first male one meets if the child is a girl, or to the first female one meets if the child is a boy. The lady was very happy to see me, and for good luck, gave me the parcel, which I accepted gratefully and respectfully. I put my hand into my pocket, pulled out a silver sixpence and put it into the child's hand for good luck. The lady, very much content, thanked me and then carried the child into the church, followed by the godparents. I opened the parcel; there was a piece of cake, two biscuits and a half crown. I put the money in my pocket, and tried to steady my scooter with one hand as I walked down Ropery Lane, towards the Wooden Bridge, whilst eating the cake and biscuits with the other; ah, what sweet nourishment. My pockets must have known that I only yearned for a sample of the sweets that I had previously bought, for, in most cases, after tasting only one of each, they vanished from my pockets; my cravings satisfied.

"Old John passed me, wheeling his ice cream cart and blowing his whistle to attract customers. I caught a glimpse of Thomas and William in the distance, wearing their cadet uniforms, on their way down to the sea cadets."

When Davy finished his narrative, he spoke to Geordie.

"I don't think I've ever been as happy as I am now, Geordie; I have learned more from you in our short time together than I could ever learn from any history books - it's been a wondrous experience."

****

Alas, all good things must come to an end; soon it was time for Geordie and the captain to leave Hebburn.

Standing outside the gate of Barnard Crescent, Geordie thanked Davy and his wife. "What a wonderful time we've had."

"Yes, what an adventure it's been," added the captain, putting his camera into the boot of the cab. "I especially liked your Durham Cathedral, resting place for the reverent Saints Cuthbert and Bede; and your Beamish Museum, with its quaint little olde shops and old fashioned fully working tramcars."

"Thank you." Davy nodded as he shielded his eyes from the low morning sun.

Geordie clutched his picture of Dents Hole with feeling.

"The beach gave me mixed emotions. But its tranquil beauty made me realise that I need some time alone."

"I understand." Davy smiled warmly. "Just be sure to come back and see us some time." So saying, he gave Geordie, a farewell hug.

"I will; I'll come back when you need me most." Geordie then hugged Davy's wife.

The captain then walked over and shook hands with the couple. "It's been swell knowing you guys. I hope we meet up again, soon. Please say farewell to the family for me."

"Thank you," they replied, cheerfully, "we will."

As Geordie and the captain climbed into the car, Davy looked once again at the face that had launched a thousand thoughts within him. As the car moved off, the horn beeped and the passengers waved. A moment later they were gone. The cheerful pretence fell from Davy's face, like a mask, revealing a grief-stricken countenance.

"He brought a new meaning to my life." Tears rolled down his cheeks. "I held him... and now he's gone. I've never felt like this since the day we buried Dad."

THE REUNION

"Come on in, pet." Davy's wife gently held his hand. "I'll make you a nice cup of tea."

Davy sighed as he followed her inside, slowly closing the door behind him.

Meanwhile, Geordie and the captain sat talking in the cab, as they headed off to Ovingham.

"Rose has agreed to meet us at Harrow."

"Oh, that's nice, Captain."

"Yes, and she promised to have a meal ready and waiting for us at 7 o'clock this evening."

"How considerate;" Geordie patted the captains hand; "she'll make someone a very good wife."

The captain smiled, contentedly.

When they reached the house in Ovingham, Septimus greeted them at the door. "Thank you for the phone call, gentlemen; dinner awaits you in the hall."

"Thank you," replied the captain, earnestly; "I admire your hospitality."

After their midday lunch, Geordie, Septimus and the captain took a stroll around the gardens.

"The truck will be here to pick up Charlie in five minutes," said Septimus, rolling his hands around each other, and grinning like a schoolboy. "And I've arranged for your luggage to be taken to the limousine."

"Thank you," Geordie answered pleasantly; "you're so agreeable."

"One thing," asked the captain; "why so many time pieces?"

"Time is so precious… we don't want to lose a minute," replied Septimus, instantly checking his watches against the church clock.

Twenty minutes later, Geordie and the captain bade Hugo and Septimus a gracious farewell, paid them substantially for their stay, and then headed off to Harrow.

Three hours later, they decided it best to make a quick stop at Jason's house in Heather, so that they - Charlie and themselves - could stop and stretch their legs.

An hour later; after a light meal and a chat; they were back on the hot steamy road to Harrow. Two-and-a-half hours later, they arrived.

Rose was there to meet them as the car pulled into the drive and came to a halt. She made her way to the car's nearside back door as the captain stepped out.

"Oh Robert, I'm so glad you've arrived. You had me worried."

"I'm sorry," he held her hand as they both walked towards the house; "I should have phoned."

A moment later, Geordie joined them at the front of the house. "Good evening, Rose. It's so nice to see you again."

"Thank you kindly," Rose smiled warmly; "the feeling's mutual."

Meanwhile, back in the sunlit drive, John, the truck driver, took his pocket watch from his waistcoat and held it to his face. He then showed his watch to the limousine driver.

"Half seven; two-and-a-half hours from Heather; it isn't bad going, that!"

The limousine driver nodded in agreement, as the sunlight weaved through his silver hair.

Later, when Charlie had been set free to roam about the gardens, and the luggage had been brought indoors, the small party - the two drivers included - went inside for an appreciated meal. An hour later, the sun still bright, they all ventured out to the nearest village pub. At half ten - after an enjoyable evening - Geordie, the captain and Rose, said goodnight to the drivers in the pub lounge, and then headed off to the cottage, by taxi. A red sun now hung on the horizon, as they walked into the drive. The late evening was light, warm and still, and the perfume from the roses lingered heavily in the air. Indoors, Geordie and the captain discussed their plans for the following day, as Rose so kindly made a nightcap.

"Geordie," the captain looked thoughtfully, "the American shipping company I worked for is taking full responsibility for your safe return to the island. They say that due to your unique circumstances, a specially chartered yacht will be put at our disposal tomorrow afternoon at one, with full confidentiality to the whereabouts of our journey. Geordie, they want me to take command of the enterprise."

"That's first rate, Captain; they're so considerate."

Later, after his nightcap, Geordie looked at the couple sitting on the sofa, and felt it best that he should retire to bed. "If you'll excuse me, I'll say goodnight."

"Goodnight, Geordie!" they replied. In a moment, Geordie was gone. The captain went to the kitchen and returned with two crystal glasses and vintage champagne: *Dom Pérignon Rosé 1995*. He then put on some soft music and appropriately dimmed the lights. As he sat once again on the sofa, he moved up closer to Rose and spoke to her in soft and gentle tones; the unmistakable aroma of perfume surrounding him with warmth.

"Rose," he lovingly handed her a glass of champagne; "I have something very important to ask you." Rose sighed softly through her luscious red lips, as the soft, reflected light twinkled in her beautiful, sensual eyes.

THE REUNION

"Tomorrow, I must leave this place, with no valid reason to return. You have come to mean a great deal to me. Since the first day that I met you, I've been overwhelmed by your elegance and charm. I've become accustomed to your looks; the way your hair blows gently in the summer breeze; the way you smile, and the way you walk. I miss you when you're not near me; I miss you so much it hurts. If I go away, never to return, my heart will surely break. My heart 'has' a valid reason to return... Rose, I love you... will you marry me?"

Rose sat silent for a moment, put down her glass, and spoke up, gently, and emotionally. "Robert, I have loved you from the very start; I love you with my very heart... yes, I will marry you!"

Without another word, they placed their arms around each other and kissed.

Rose slid off her black, fashionable shoes, as her favourite music played softly and romantically in the background. It seemed quite a while before someone decided to speak.

"I love you Rose," said the captain, passionately, as he handed her a small felt-covered box. "Please open it."

Rose did so, revealing a magnificent gold engagement ring encrusted with diamonds. "Oh, thank you, Robert. I'm so excited." She placed the ring on her finger and held her outstretched hand to the light, moving it from side to side, watching the colours as they sparkled from every facet of the stones.

"It's so beautiful, Robert," she added, glancing from the stone to the captain. "I love you ever so much."

"I think we should marry in England as soon as I return."

"I agree." Rose smiled.

"I should tell you, Rose, I am not a wealthy man, but I have a large house in the States, and enough money to get us by."

"Robert, dear," Rose hugged him, "I'd be happy to live with you in a shack."

"Thank you, my love."

The next morning, at breakfast, Geordie was informed of the engagement.

"Congratulations! I was wondering when this would come about."

The captain didn't question how Geordie knew - he just accepted his word faithfully. For Geordie seemed incapable of error, or the telling of untruths.

CHAPTER XII

THE JOURNEY BACK TO THE ISLAND

An hour after breakfast - with Charlie on the truck, and the luggage packed in the boot of the cab - Geordie and the captain were ready to leave. After an emotional farewell in the drive, Rose cried for a while, then dried her tears and braved a smile, allowing Geordie and the captain to set off for Portsmouth.

They arrived early, at the port. After watching Charlie and the luggage safely winched aboard, Geordie and the captain stood on the dockside a while, saying their appreciative farewells to the two local drivers. They paid the bachelors over generously for any inconveniences they may have incurred, especially their time away from friends and relations.

"It was an overwhelming and adventurous experience," said John, as he received his cheque; "but it's nice to be back on home soil once again." Martin, the limousine driver agreed.

As Geordie and the captain boarded the large yacht, the drivers bade them safe journey. A short while later, they waved farewell, as the yacht moved slowly out of the harbour, and headed on its way to the distant Pacific Ocean.

Once out of port the powerful sail-less vessel picked up speed and cut smoothly through the water. At the bridge, Captain Wiseman handed over temporary command of the vessel to the first mate and then went over to the main deck to join Geordie. The weather was glorious.

Geordie tilted back his head, noted the sun's position in the clear blue sky, and then looked at his watch. "It's the summer solstice, Captain."

The captain strained back his head, shaded his eyes with his left arm, and looked up at the sun, which was almost exactly overhead. He then shaded the wristwatch on his right arm with his left hand and squinted at the date. "Ah, the twenty first of June; why of course it is. It's a good day to get engaged don't you think?"

"Most certainly, Captain."

The journey was smooth and trouble free. The yacht was at sea for four days, before landing at the Panama Canal in Central America. This fifty mile long canal took thirty five years to build, from 1879 to 1914. After crossing through it, they were off again, on their journey to Geordie's island.

Back at the bridge, the Captain turned to Geordie, "You know, Geordie, it's nice to be back in command of a ship - it's where I belong. One day, I'll buy my own yacht and travel the world with Rose."

"I can guarantee that, Captain."

Three days after crossing through the Panama Canal, they dropped anchor a mile from their destination.

"Well, Geordie," the captain viewed the beautiful green island, with its alluring golden sands, "there's no place like home."

"There's no place like this home;" Geordie closed his eyes and breathed in the invigorating air; "we're part of each other; it's a part of me, and I'm a part of it."

Soon, a boat was lowered onto the water, along with a specially designed craft for Charlie. Geordie, the captain and the bosun climbed into the boat, while a crewman took the wheel of Charlie's craft. When they had all landed, the bosun and the crewman were overcome with the feeling of love and well-being that emitted from the beautiful island, and permeated their very souls.

They all headed for the clearing, taking Charlie with them. After an hour there, they decided to take a scout around the island, and found it was just as they had left it. It seemed that nature had preserved itself. Back in the clearing, Geordie and the captain sat on the steps of Geordie's bungalow, having a private talk, as the bosun and the crewman stood marvelling at the enormous round table.

"Geordie, we could stay a few more days, if you'd like the company."

"Thank you, Captain, you're a very kind man, but it's time that I was alone."

"I understand. Oh, Geordie, I almost forgot," he added; "with the royalties, and one thing and another, you've accrued about two hundred thousand pounds; what will I do with it?"

Geordie pondered for a second. "Please give it to Davy Rigger - he'll know what to do with it."

"It will be my pleasure."

Geordie looked at the captain in a fatherly way, and placed his hand gently on his arm. "Before you go, Captain, there is something I must show you." He took the captain indoors and led him into his cool, dimly-lit bedroom, the louver shutter being closed. He then showed him a large wooden sea chest, out of which, he took a small, beautifully decorated box - about a foot square. He placed this upon the old table that stood beneath the window. "I have never had a son; but if I had, I would have been proud if that son could have been you. Robert, this is my engagement present to you and Rose." So saying, he opened wide the lid of the box. The darkened room suddenly lit up. The box was filled with sparkling jewels and gems: diamonds, emeralds, opals and rubies. Geordie slightly pushed open the window shutter, allowing a bright shaft of sunlight to flood in. It passed through the jewels, forming rainbows of colours on the ceiling and walls.

"They're beautiful, Geordie. They must be worth millions!"

"Four million pounds sterling; I valued them from memory whilst in England. Apparently, they can only be compared to jewellery of rare Indian beauty - of the first water in fact."

"But how could we take such a gift?" The captain stood mesmerised by the splendour of the jewels. "It would leave you with nothing."

"That isn't so." Geordie ran his fingers through the jewels. "To me, they're nothing but pretty glass beads. This is what makes me happy." He pushed wide the louvre shutter and swept his arms out over the picturesque view. "Here I have everything. I'm rich simply by just being here; rich in love and happiness. I have no desire for gold or jewels, and have no concern in Uncle Thomas's claim that there's a mountainful over yonder."

The captain received the gift with great pleasure and appreciation.

"Thank you, Geordie - it's more wealth than I could have dreamed of. With this, Rose and I will be able to buy our own yacht, and visit you any time you wish."

"I would be very pleased if you would visit me again soon... to celebrate my next birthday.

"It's a deal, Geordie!"

Soon, it was time for the captain and his crew to leave. As the crewman and the bosun readied the vessels, Geordie and the captain said farewell.

"Thank you once again for the precious gift;" the captain hugged Geordie; "Rose will love it. We'll both see you again soon."

"I look forward to that. Goodbye Captain."

"Goodbye Geordie."

The small vessels headed out to the yacht, and boarded it. Then the yacht itself set sail, becoming smaller and smaller on the horizon until eventually it sailed out of view.

Bon voyage.